Nicole stuck the

"Excuse me?" A glimmer of hope zipped through her.

"Next month, I'll come to give you that review," Brad said.

Later, she would blame it on stress.

Nicole strutted over to where Brad stood. She pulled him down toward her. Still clutching his starched white shirt, she raised on tiptoe and planted a firm kiss on Brad's mouth.

The act didn't have any meaning, at first. Anger still sizzled through her petite frame, and she wanted to rip someone's head off because she had been blindsided. The intent was to lash out, scream, vent.

One look at Brad with his wonderfully sculpted lips, and instead she wanted to kiss him. Another shocker for the night was the faint tremor of delight shooting sparks throughout her body. Instead of a few seconds of brazen behavior, she lingered. Swooned was more like it.

His lips opened and she followed suit, giving him entry for the deliciously lazy swirl of his tongue. With a soft sigh, she sagged within his massive arms.

He pulled away first and the small space between them allowed the cold night air to quickly douse the flames of desire. "Should I take that as a yes that it's okay to come and review your B-and-B?"

Nicole didn't respond at first and turned to head over to her car. The truth was that she couldn't trust herself to talk.

BOOK YOUR PLACE ON OUR WEBSITE AND MAKE THE ARABESQUE ROMANCE CONNECTION!

We've created a customized website just for our very special Arabesque readers, where you can get the inside scoop on everything that's going on with Arabesque romance novels.

When you come online, you'll have the exciting opportunity to:

- View covers of upcoming books

- Learn about our future publishing schedule (listed by publication month and author)

- Find out when your favorite authors will be visiting a city near you

- Search for and order backlist books

- Check out author bios and background information

- Send e-mail to your favorite authors

- Join us in weekly chats with authors, readers and other guests

- Get writing guidelines

- AND MUCH MORE!

Visit our website at
http://www.arabesquebooks.com

FINDERS KEEPERS

Michelle Monkou

BET Publications, LLC
http://www.bet.com
http://www.arabesquebooks.com

ARABESQUE BOOKS are published by

BET Publications, LLC
c/o BET BOOKS
One BET Plaza
1900 W Place NE
Washington, DC 20018-1211

All Kensington Titles, Imprints, and Distributed Lines are available at special quantity discounts for bulk purchases for sales promotion, premiums, fund-raising, and educational or institutional use. Special book excerpts or customized print-ings can also be created to fit specific needs. For details, write or phone the office of the Kensington special sales manager: Kensington Publishing Corp., 850 Third Avenue, New York, NY 10022, attn: Special Sales Department, Phone: 1-800-221-2647.

First Printing: June 2003
10 9 8 7 6 5 4 3 2 1

Printed in the United States of America

This book is dedicated to my husband, Bryan Samuels.
I love you.

ACKNOWLEDGMENTS

It is always great when you have a close supportive network of sister authors: Candice Poarch, Celeste Norfleet, and Angela Winters.

For my special pals who always keep me laughing (Olivia Gillis, Maria Liwanag, Eugenia Bettis)—thank you.

Thanks for another one, Chandra Taylor and Karen Thomas.

One

The taxi's wheels hummed against asphalt keeping time with the painful throb in Brad Calverton's head. He pinched the bridge of his nose, concentrating on preventing the onset of a migraine. The three-hour time difference since leaving the West Coast accompanied by a medium-sized serving of soupy chicken potpie on the plane contributed to the waves of nausea that rocked his insides. Right now he craved a stiff shot of caffeine, a good night's sleep on a firm mattress, and a monthlong case of amnesia.

With some effort, he raised his head, wincing in the process. He could barely open an eye to glance at his watch. Four o'clock. His flight had been due to arrive two hours ago. At least no one but his secretary knew to where he'd run off, although every reader of *Today's News and Gossip* knew why he would want to hide.

The driver braked suddenly, snapping Brad's head forward. A frown, which had already marked his brow, instantly deepened. "Think we can get there in one piece before sunset?"

The driver muttered under his breath and shot him an irritated glare through the rearview mirror.

Brad didn't care. Impatience ate big chunks at his nerves. His grandmother used to call these familiar bouts his gray funk and he was knee-deep in one. Every muscle in his back knotted into a bunch along his spine. Shifting his long legs along the backseat did more harm than good. The first thing he wanted when he arrived at the bed-and-breakfast was a

massage. He pulled out the brochure from his inner pocket
and read the blurb about a deep-muscle massage. He wasn't
sure what that entailed, but the thought of someone kneading
out his tension lifted his exhaustion just a little.

His gaze shifted out past the window. Looking up, he considered the dark clouds. It might be late October, but the
weather seemed more like a typical summer day with thick
humidity. The dark gray mass unrolled its heavy cover across
the sky. A premature twilight quickly enshrouded the area,
filtering through the trees. Thunder rumbled and his acidic
stomach answered. "Damn! What else can go wrong?" he
muttered under his breath.

The road visible about a mile ahead resembled a two-lane
parking lot of brake lights. He blew out an exasperated sigh.
Part of his tension stemmed from his deep-seated aversion to
visiting Maryland. Too many memories and too much un-
finished business faced him. It was only because he was in
such a desperate state that he agreed to his friend's tip about
visiting the B&B and possibly bringing his dream to fruition.

The taxi turned onto the ramp toward Annapolis from the
tree-lined parkway linking Baltimore to Washington, DC.
Brad glanced appreciatively at the change of scenery from the
narrow tunnel of trees, which seemed to partner with the
crushing weight of his dark memories.

Business complexes came into view and spacious elegant
homes were partially hidden among the sparse greenery. At
least the driver zipped through the local roads bypassing the
long lines at the major intersection within the city limits of
Maryland's capital.

Minutes later the taxi turned onto a country road that cut
through acres of farmland on either side. When Brad was
about to ask any driver's least favorite question, "Are we there
yet?" the taxi stopped in front of a blue colonial. Its darker
blue shutters added a stateliness that inspired an admiring
smile. A large wooden sign swung in the increasing wind gust
at the curbside. MONTGOMERY'S BED-AND-BREAKFAST EST. 2001.

Rosebushes covered the arched entrance of the gate that led to black double doors with brass trimmings and matching knocker. A white picket fence barely waist-high followed the perimeter of the property cordoning off farmland beyond what he could see. "A real charmer," Brad praised, nodding appreciatively at the view.

The neat, colorful garden on the property was in direct contrast to the bustle of rush-hour traffic that he'd only just left a few minutes ago. The idyllic setting offered a retreat from the hectic pace of daily life. Already a sense of serenity overcame him and he longed for a place where his ego could heal out of the way of the paparazzi's telephoto lenses. He walked through the archway, enjoying the feeling that he had just entered a touch of paradise.

He compared what he saw with the brochure featuring the property prominently on its cover. The still image of the bed-and-breakfast didn't do the live version enough justice. One of the new additions not in the brochure caught his attention. A trellis was built against the side of the house, which featured more rosebushes woven into the lattice structure. Under the four windows facing him were small shrubs neatly manicured and placed under each window across the width of the house.

From his inner jacket pocket, he retrieved a minicassette tape recorder. Slowly he turned around getting a good visual of the property and landscaping attributes of the front yard. He lifted the tape recorder to his mouth. *"More than I expected. Property is in perfect location and condition. Will make excellent retreat. Appointment set with local social services department. Just need to figure out selling price and date of availability."* He pressed STOP and placed the recorder back into his pocket. He hoped the old lady who owned the property didn't linger over his offer if the urge hit him to begin negotiations.

He looked up to admire the second floor. A fat raindrop hit him squarely on his forehead before his first step toward the B&B. The pregnant clouds burst and unloaded their water with force before he could make it up the cobbled path. His clothes stuck uncomfortably to his body in a matter of seconds. He held his briefcase close to his chest in a brave attempt to keep it dry. There was no help for his overnight bag, much less his expensive loafers that squished noisily in quickly formed puddles.

He grimaced.

His mood plunged. He did not want to believe that his drenching spelled impending disaster. But after his public humiliation when his supermodel girlfriend was splashed across tabloid pages hand-in-hand, kissing, smiling, and snuggled next to her photographer on a European beach, he was a little short on positive thinking. A scowl descended on his face.

The front door swung open and a young woman appeared wearing a welcoming smile. Her dress, light and colorful, wrapped around her legs like a second skin from the sudden gust of wind. She didn't seem to mind the blast of rain in her face.

"Welcome to Montgomery's Bed-and-Breakfast. This is your lucky day, I have one available room. We're all wet, aren't we?" she greeted, with a singsong lilt.

As he got closer, he saw the light twinkle in her eyes. He envied her lightheartedness. "Your empathy is a bit lost on me since you're quite dry." In quick, long strides he was at the doorway, dripping in front of his greeter. At close range, her light brown eyes pulled at him. Quite suddenly he thought how appropriately her short, wispy curls framed her face, accentuating her small chin. But, he still wanted to be in his foul mood.

The woman's smile wavered and then regained its brightness. "My apologies. Here, let me take your bag. We . . . I will have you in your room in no time, and a filling, home-cooked meal will be served in the dining room later."

Brad managed to keep his usual automatic sarcasm to himself and merely shrugged. When she stepped back, he wiped his feet and followed her into the foyer. Thankfully he was out of the rain, but now chilled and uncomfortable with his foul mood and sick stomach.

Nicole closed the door behind her rain-soaked guest. She extended a hand toward her office. "I'm Nicole Montgomery, the owner. Welcome to Glen Knolls, Maryland. Traffic must have been terrible. Please, if you would, you can follow me to my office so that I can take care of the particulars. It'll only take a minute, and then you can get out of those wet clothes."

He handed her his credit card before she asked. She hoped the temperamental credit card machine worked. Brad Calverton, as the name read on the card, stood stiffly in front of her.

There were stares and then there were stares. His intense scrutiny burned through her, broadcasting his ornery disposition loud and clear. "Mr. Calverton," she began, "oh, dear. I'm looking here in my journal and you were listed to arrive today, but I'm showing a cancellation from you."

Great. Just great. Even the surprise knockout B&B owner had it in for him. "That's incorrect. I didn't cancel and I know my secretary wouldn't have, either. As a matter of fact, I personally made this reservation a week ago." He glared back at her. "On someone's recommendation."

Nicole gave what she hoped was a cheerful smile, wondering if he could hear the bottom in her stomach drop. Clearly he now questioned the truth of the recommendation.

"Not to worry. I do have a room available. Lucky you, it has the oversize tub and fireplace." She laughed lightly. "I guess the fireplace isn't exactly necessary right now. But from the look of things, the oversize tub might be the right size for you. And by the way, it's the honeymoon suite."

She kept the smile on her face, determined to let it remain there until he returned one or at least responded even with a stern eyebrow. Eternity could have passed by and he merely stared right through her. She surrendered. "Well, um . . . how long will you be staying?"

A beat passed between them.

"Two nights."

"No problem." Nicole slid the card through the machine and saw the error message almost instantly. Now would not be a good time to tell him the system was down. She'd have to call the toll-free customer service number. A call guaranteed to take at least five minutes. "Looks like I'll have to call it in. I won't keep you, though." She wrote down the number for processing later. "Here's your card." Nicole paused. "Do you need help with your bag? I usually have a college kid help around the house, but he's taking a heavy load this semester."

The quiet foyer burst to life as several guests ran in from the rain. Their exertion and almost childish excitement at the afternoon storm swirled around unnoticed by her latest guest.

"I can manage. But I would like to schedule an appointment for a massage." He rolled his head around. "I could really do with one." He grinned, a bit sheepish. "Maybe it'll put me in a better mood."

"The masseuse is unavailable this month." She dragged on each word, offering a rueful smile. "Would you believe she pulled her back? I'd be happy to give you some recommendations for local spas." She bit her lip. Strike two. Her day had been peachy until her unhappy giant of a guest landed at her doorstep.

Brad's expectant smile withered. "I'm going to my room. Do you at least have something for a pounding headache?" He rose, turned his back on her, and headed for the staircase before she answered. Wet shoes squeaked on the yellow pine floor with each angry stride.

"No problem. I'll bring it right up with a glass of water. Your room is the first door on the left." She waited until he was midway up the staircase, before following him. The small distance restored some of her confidence. "Will you be eating dinner here? Breakfast is part of your package, but occasionally I feature Gertie's home cooking. She's Glen Knolls's pride and joy when we have our annual bake sale."

He didn't answer until he stood at the top of the stairs. "If you can manage, I'll be eating here tonight."

Before she replied, he unlocked his door, entered, and shut the door without a backward glance.

Nicole shook her head and blew out a sigh. "I'll manage, even if it kills me," she muttered.

Her four bedrooms were now occupied. Some of the other guests specifically came to enjoy the Chesapeake Bay and the waterfront shops before the weather changed. Others visited for the quiet and solitude. She took her role as hostess seriously and she aimed to make Mr. Calverton's stay comfortable and memorable.

More accurately, it was her mission.

A few guests had already become repeat customers since she opened over a year ago. Success inevitably required loyal customers and a good reputation and she treasured each visitor who came her way. It was more than having happy customers. This venture—her own B&B—provided a balm to the dark fears she harbored.

She'd discovered her passion later than the average well-adjusted person. Thirty-two years old and faced with a stunning career as a young executive in the insurance industry, she'd blown it. She'd played hardball in a man's world. Convinced that her success could only be achieved by hiding any weaknesses or imperfections, she'd earned several unflattering names. The high standards she held for herself meant that she demanded equally high standards from others in her work and personal life.

Despite her aim for perfection, one tiny lump in her breast last year changed her life. In that instant, she thought about her mother's older sisters who had died from breast cancer. She had worked so hard to hide her vulnerabilities. Success didn't suffer weakness, and this dreaded disease had crippled her confidence. With her career and love life in shambles, she had been angry and scared when the doctor shared the diagnosis with her.

The word *cancer* and all its power chased her to retreat. She'd undergone two surgeries and six months of radiation and chemotherapy on autopilot. After the treatments, she needed a haven. In the mountains, she found a peaceful sanctuary and recuperated at a B&B.

In that short time, she decided on a different path for her life, resulting in her own B&B and a full house. A feeling of accomplishment overcame her as she hustled to get the evening meal served. There was no denying that she had been given a second chance and maybe, just maybe, her B&B could have the same miraculous effect on a guest the way her very own experience had unfolded.

After telling Gertie about the additional guest, Nicole went to her room and retrieved the red and white bottle of tablets. She took a quick glance at her reflection in the mirror of the medicine cabinet. Her short curls looked slightly disheveled, but she brushed a few stray curls with her fingers, pleased with the effect. Her other features spelled disaster. Her lips barely had any color left from her habitual biting of her lower lip.

She sighed. A beauty queen she wasn't, and never claimed to be. But since she had taken on her new role as bed-and-breakfast owner, her starched professional image had been slowly etched away, leaving in its stead a plain woman in off-the-rack dresses, devoid of makeup, accessories, and high-priced hairdos.

"I'm not going up there until I get myself together," she told her reflection while fiddling with her hair. It wouldn't have been a big deal, except for the way he had examined her earlier from head to toe. If he'd smiled after taking her all in, she would have been flattered. Instead, his look had examined, judged, and dismissed her with an annoying arrogance.

She didn't want to appear to be too made-up, though. The sienna-brown lip color with a glossy finish suited the natural shade of her lips and earthy skin tone. Tugging her blouse straight, she was ready to deal with Mr. Calverton, the not-so-bad-looking Mr. Calverton.

Her knock wasn't immediately answered. Nicole wondered if she had caught him at a bad time. Hearing his approaching footsteps, she perfected her pose with the serving tray carrying the bottle of tablets and water glass balanced on one hand.

"Ah. At least one wish has been granted." He stood in the doorway in a plush gray bathrobe. A towel lay around his shoulders and intermittent trails of water rolled from his hair.

While she admired him, he tossed back three tablets and gulped down the water. Strong muscular neck. Nice.

"That should hit the spot in a few minutes." He set down the glass. "Thank you. You just might have saved my life. Let me know when I can return the favor." He winked and offered a quick smile.

Nicole bit her lip. Now wasn't the time for the jitters, not while holding the tray. But she was out of practice with experiencing such strong attraction. "Glad to hear," she finally managed. Her eyes fastened onto the black hairs tightly coiled on his chest where the robe gaped. Nicole admitted that looking at his chest was better than drowning in the dark brown eyes that either cut her with sarcasm or regarded her with wry amusement.

"Was there anything else, Mrs. Montgomery?"

"Sorry." Her face burned. She didn't mean to be so adolescent, gawking at his chest and entertaining thoughts of what he looked like naked. "No, there's nothing else. Dinner will be at seven o'clock. I hope that's not too late?" She compromised between the eyes and chest, settling for his chin and its dimpled indentation.

He nodded.

Duty fulfilled, there was no longer a reason for her to remain at his door. "By the way, it's *Miss* Montgomery."

"I'll see you at seven, *Miss* Montgomery." He raked a hand over his hair, then closed his robe in a tight overlap. "I'm

Brad Calverton. Sorry you had to meet my evil twin earlier. It's been a long day." A broader smile spread over his features.

Nice teeth.

He stuck his hand out to her. Nicole shook it, marveling that hers seemed to disappear into his massive paw. He reminded her of a bear, potentially warm and cuddly. But for the most part, cranky and baleful.

"Not to worry, Mr. Calverton. Rest up. Gertie'll have a delicious meal for you to enjoy in another hour." Nicole walked away, although she sensed that he remained at the door watching her. Self-consciously she hoped nothing was out of place and fought the urge to make adjustments. What if he noticed that her hips were well padded? Or that her legs were as skinny as a bird's? Out of the blue, she wanted to flirt and without contemplating the consequences, she gave in to the urge. Very deliberately she relaxed her hips and walked with a pronounced sway.

Carrying a sneaky smile, she remained calm until she went downstairs and disappeared around the corner. She collapsed against the wall dividing the sitting room and dining room. What was the matter with her? Being flirtatious and brazen wasn't her style. Besides, Brad Calverton wasn't her first male guest. He wasn't even the first male guest that she thought was attractive. There was no denying, however, that this man who had come grumpily through her door had made an impression on her. Maybe it was the way he looked at her when she spoke.

Another time, another place, she might have stepped up to the challenge, she thought, but that was a bold lie. For the most part, men didn't seem to make it past the first or second date.

When that part of her life fizzled, she threw herself into her work. As a senior counsel, she was usually the first to arrive and the last to leave, working monstrous hours. Her path led up the corporate ladder and it became her focus to blow the glass ceiling wide open. She was on her way until a male colleague sabotaged a major project, resulting in her having to

be closely supervised and made to jump through countless irritating hoops.

Nicole looked up in the direction of Brad's room. Nice to
look at and admire. As long as she kept it that way, she didn't
have to deal with any male ego games and eventual betrayal.

With that plan in mind, she headed off to tackle the next
project—dinner. Used to her new role, she entered the
kitchen, donned an apron, and started chopping onions, while
Gertie stirred and mumbled over several steaming pots.

Conversation around the dinner table flew back and forth,
with major doses of intermittent laughter. Nicole didn't have
time to share in the different conversations, as she went from
the kitchen to the dining room with hot covered dishes.

Back in the kitchen, she picked up a large serving dish of
fluffy, white rice. "Gertie, looks like a full house tonight. I
guess that surprise rainstorm didn't help matters." Nicole
couldn't deny feeling pleased about her no-vacancy status.

All the guests present and accounted for, including Brad,
awaited dinner. The bits of lively conversation around the
table meant that everyone was in a good mood.

"Miss Montgomery." Gertie motioned her over with her head
when Nicole returned to the kitchen. "Soup's ready. You know
Miss Violet looks forward to her bowl to start her meal."

Nicole agreed and took the laden tray into the dining room.
The scene could have been from a commercial advertising a
lively Thanksgiving dinner with extended family.

Miss Violet, a matriarch through and through, sat at the
head of the table sporting her new Afro. Fashionable and
equally vibrant, the natural style suited her prominent features, which she claimed were from her Native American
ancestry on her mother's side. Tonight, she wore an African-
print dress that sat loosely on her frame. Her hands flashed
like a conductor as she chatted. Wooden carved bracelets

clacked together and her delicate drop earrings danced from her earlobes.

"You know, Nicole, you continue to amaze me," Violet said as Nicole set down her soup. "I come to this place every two months and each time, you've added a piece of furniture, a painting, and now the ruffled curtains." She pointed at the rose drapes with gray sheers. "Did you make them?"

Nicole laughed, a bit embarrassed from Violet's open admiration. "No way. But I fell in love with the ruffles on the edges." Nicole had made a conscious decision to decorate in classic country charm. Oversize paintings from local artists of various fruit and vegetable combinations decorated the walls. The watercolors picked up the slate gray and deep rose theme in the room, along with a green border above the chair railing. Her latest purchase of a cherry-wood china closet was the final touch.

Nicole hurried off to get more food.

"At last, your soup has arrived." Nicole distributed the starter meal. "Two salads coming right up, Mr. Calverton, Sadie."

"Please, Brad will do."

She nodded and blushed, her face growing quite warm.

His lips twitched with a half smile.

"Oh, geez," she exclaimed once she was safely back in the kitchen.

"What's up?" Gertie asked. "That look you've got seems wicked. Miss Violet at it again?"

Nicole shook her head. Her heartbeat tripping over itself had to slow soon. Better yet, it had to keep this nonsense to a minimum. It didn't help that Brad followed her with curious assessment whenever her eyes drifted to his face. Nor did it help when he stared at her face while she poured his iced tea.

"I'm only acting like an adolescent."

"Who with?" Gertie stopped stirring. "The tall brown-skinned hunk?"

Nicole stuck the l—
"Excuse me?" A glimmer of hope zipped through her.

"It's that obvious, huh?"

Gertie shrugged and turned back to her pots. Nicole didn't miss the tug of her lips as she bit back a smile.

After a deep breath, Nicole kept her gaze fastened on the task at hand: one grilled chicken for Miss Violet; two steak dinners for the Jeffersons; and grilled chicken with pesto pasta for Brad, Traci, and Harry.

". . . so that must have been exciting."

Traci's annoying voice pierced Nicole's concentration. The bottle-blond was very pretty even beneath the thick layer of makeup.

"Gee, Brad, sounds like you have an exciting life. Seeing all those fancy places." Traci turned a petulant pout to her companion, Harry. "Why don't you take me to all those places?" She leaned over to Brad, winking her heavily lined eye. "Brad, if you're ever looking for company let me know."

The plate slipped out of Nicole's hands as she approached the table. It fell with a loud thud. "I'm so sorry."

Brad picked up a lettuce leaf that bounced off the plate and handed it to her. His eyes never left Traci's exuberant face.

Nicole couldn't take her eyes off Brad.

"My traveling would bore you," he replied with a hint of laughter in his voice.

"Bobby and I go everywhere together. Don't we, honey?"

Nicole looked over to the newlyweds and found herself wistfully watching Sadie pick up her husband's hand and kiss it lovingly.

"That's right, sweetie. Together forever."

Nicole resumed distributing the meal. When she stepped behind Traci's plate, she fought the urge to upend the remnants of the young woman's soup onto her lap. One look at Harry's embarrassed face made Nicole feel sorry for the middle-aged man who had gotten more than he bargained for in a sex kitten like Traci.

The low-cut blouse couldn't have fit any tighter, outlining her ample breasts. Darn it if she didn't have the gray eyes and fine features that catapulted women like her onto magazines' prettiest women lists. Nicole's own plain brown eyes couldn't go without contact lens or her thick glasses, which she saved for evenings alone or around her immediate family.

"Brad, how have you managed to skip marital bliss?" Violet asked.

Brad responded with a hearty laugh. He inclined his head toward Bobby and Sadie. "I'd say that most of the time those two words don't belong together. And if more people wouldn't succumb to the pressures of family, friends, and even society, there wouldn't be as many divorces."

Miss Violet chuckled. The only person in the room to do so.

"So, in other words, you'd rather travel the safe route than follow your heart."

Nicole stopped pouring coffee. It wasn't really what he said, because it was quite logical without the emotional frills. Instead she saw a hard edge in his squint and sudden tightening of his jaw that spoke volumes.

"My Harry did that," Traci chirped. "He married his first wife because her father forced Harry, who worked for him, to marry his ugly daughter. She couldn't attract a man to save her soul." Traci blundered on with her trademark unsophisticated manner, "But he left her, and here we are. Right, Harry?"

Harry's face turned beet red. He visibly squirmed in his chair. Any redder and he would have blended into the color of his shirt.

Nicole immediately went to his aid. "Harry, I forgot to tell you, Gertie made your favorite tonight—bread pudding. I know you like it served a certain way, but I couldn't remember." She dropped her tone a notch. "Gertie is waiting for your instructions if you would like to pop your head in for a second."

He looked up, then, a grateful glimmer in his eyes. With a soft "Excuse me," he left the table.

Traci returned her attention to the meal, oblivious to the confusion she caused.

"Getting back to this matter of matrimony, wouldn't you trust your heart, Brad?" Violet resumed the direction of the conversation.

Nicole had removed the dishes, filled and refilled coffee as the conversation chartered this exciting course. So when Violet motioned for her to take Harry's seat, she didn't object.

"I want you to hear this, Nicole. You young people worry me with this cold approach to falling in love." Violet shook her head, causing her earrings to dance.

"I didn't say I didn't believe in love," Brad answered.

"But marriage is a no-no."

"Yes."

"Why is that?"

He shrugged, but offered no further explanation, his expression carefully shuttered.

"I can honestly say that Bobby is my soul mate. Six months ago we met and fell in love in the blink of an eye." Sadie sighed. "Then we made the commitment to be with each other as husband and wife." She played with Bobby's earlobe and he beamed under her attention. His face resembled a puppy's, soft and round, with a permanent small smile.

"Nicole, do you believe in soul mates?"

Nicole stiffened. Everyone's attention shifted to her.

"I believe in soul mates," Traci chirped. She bit the tip of the fork and smiled flirtatiously at Brad. "My soul mate will be a super-duper tall man. About six feet or so. Skin, dark and smooth like an African bronze statue." She leaned forward and propped her chin. "And his eyes will be the color of midnight, promising exciting discoveries behind his long thick eyelashes."

Nicole gasped at Traci's blunt maneuvers. Although the woman's description of Brad was dead-on, she didn't fancy hearing it from her candy-red, pouty mouth.

"Shush, child," Violet chided. "Before you make a fool of yourself, go and see how your Harry is doing."

"But, I'm not finished telling you about my soul mate."

Brad cleared his throat. "I'm more interested in hearing whether Nicole believes in soul mates." He turned his full attention to her.

There, he did it again. Smiled at her. Nicole thought about answering truthfully. She could see that her answer mattered to him, but she couldn't quite determine why. Nicole considered the topic of soul mates. With the three heartbreaks she had suffered in her thirty-two years, it was obvious that she couldn't identify hers before she committed with her heart. "I believe soul mates exist, but there has to be the right timing and chemistry for that extra-special benefit to a relationship."

"Difficult, but not impossible," he translated. "I agree."

Nicole breathed a sigh of relief. She was surprised that his opinion mattered to her. She glanced over at the clock on the mantel. "Ooh," she exclaimed. "My apologies for holding up the last course—dessert." Nicole hurried into the kitchen.

Despite Traci's blunder, Nicole had enjoyed the dinner table conversation. As a matter of fact, the congeniality among her guests gave a charge to her self-confidence. It helped her define her purpose to be instrumental in bringing happiness to people.

She finished serving her guests and excused herself to help Gertie in the kitchen. Harry never emerged again and Traci had admitted defeat with Brad, but only after much effort. Finally disgusted with him, Traci rolled her eyes at him and left the room, swishing her ample hips with gusto. Nicole looked over at Brad to see if there was any sign of regret. He was talking with Bob and had missed the grand finale.

Good.

"Okay, Gertie, I think we're done here. I'll finish up the preparation for the morning. You scoot along." As she wiped down counters, covered and refrigerated leftovers, she could hear her guests depart from the table.

"Thanks, Miss M."

Once dinner was over, most of her guests would either return to their rooms for the night or go walking around the town. Since the rain continued, all were probably in for the night tonight. Nicole continued cutting up fruit for breakfast the next day, laying cantaloupe and melon wedges and grapes on a tray. Once she was finished, she turned out the lights in each room, leaving a small lamp that cast a soft yellow light in the foyer for those who suffered bouts of insomnia and were in need of a quiet spot.

As the houseguests settled down and a soft quietness descended, weariness burrowed into the fibers of her muscles. Its presence visited daily, mainly at the end of each day. Nicole only wished she could muster her reserve energy, but even that needle hovered near empty. The remedy that provided temporary relief would have to do—a foot soak accompanied by a bowl of cherry vanilla ice cream.

Nicole changed into a more comfortable cotton blouse and jean shorts. She opted to put a hold on the foot soak, but still wanted her ice cream. The rain had cooled things down a bit, but the humidity was still high. She walked through the sitting room to enter the screened-in porch on the side of the house. No one had taken refuge here, for which she was glad. With her handsome new guest constantly on her mind and causing all sorts of physical reactions, she wanted to be alone to sift through her chaotic feelings.

She sat in the far corner and put her aching feet on the opposite chair. With the bowl of ice cream on her lap, she spooned small servings into her mouth. The cool creamy treat with sweet pieces of cherry tasted heavenly. She closed her eyes to relax while listening to the rain hit the trees. The clean fresh scent and heady, repetitive beat of the rain shower stirred comforting childhood memories. Under the relaxing spell of the weather, she tuned into the throaty calls of the frogs and chirping crickets. She sighed, a lingering, sleepy smile on her lips.

***

Brad looked at the time—almost midnight. He finished recording more details about how he could convert the rooms with minimum cost. Luckily there wouldn't be much makeover necessary. Maybe he would have to adjust for more masculine decorations for the new tenants: teenage boys rebelling at anything standing in their way to self-destruction. The retreat for troubled teens had slowly worked its way into his heart, first as a kernel of an idea, now to near fruition.

At first, he had rejected the project. He'd only admit to himself that it was because he didn't think he had it in him to make it a success. But the seed had been planted and no matter how he tried to kill it, the idea continued to grow in his mind.

If the B&B sold in the next thirty days, he could have the retreat up and running by the summer of next year. Although he wasn't going to personally handle buying the property, he wondered how fast Nicole was willing to get things rolling along. Maybe she was still up. Even if she didn't want to discuss business, he'd get to satisfy his secret wish to see her again.

He quietly made his way down the stairs, pausing over the creaky floorboards. A soft light bathed the first floor. Standing in the foyer, he could see into the parlor on the left and the sitting room and dining room on the right. He could tell from the darkness behind the staircase that no one was in the kitchen. From the look of things, no one was downstairs, including his pixie-faced hostess.

He bit back the disappointment of not seeing her, so he chose to take this quiet time to explore further. From room to room he noticed a decorative theme. Nicole clearly liked the Afro-centric ceramic statuettes that produced stilled reproductions of black culture. He entered the formal living room in the parlor to admire a set of pieces that captured a gospel choir singing under the ministrations of the conductor, a preacher and his congregation, and a woman in the throes of

feeling the spirit. Several other scenes with the black statuettes were displayed on side tables.

Brad continued exploring, moving into the dining room.
The sideboard displayed a crocheted trimming with two
bowls of fresh fruit. He grabbed an apple and bit into its
crisp flesh. He looked through the open doorway leading
into the kitchen. Any remnants of the earlier dinner had
been removed. Silver pots and pans hung in place from the
overhead hooks. The huge restaurant-sized refrigerator
hummed. The dishwasher clicked into another cycle. From
where he stood, he saw the door marked PRIVATE ENTRANCE.

He hesitated for a few seconds, before boldly striding over
and knocking on the door. He hoped Nicole was a night owl,
but after a few seconds he gave up since there was no response from behind the door.

Walking back to the stairs, he glanced toward the sitting
room and noticed the porch for the first time. Still holding out
hope that Nicole might be out there, he walked through the
room, deciding almost immediately that this room was his favorite. The furniture faced the fireplace in a tight horseshoe
for warmth and conversation. Off to the sides of the room,
two large bookcases with titles covering various celebrity
biographies, black literary figures, and popular fiction stood
from floor to ceiling.

He stepped onto the porch and looked around. As he turned
toward his right, he saw Nicole in the corner, looking at him.

"Oops, sorry. Didn't think anyone was here. I'll go back
in." He didn't budge.

Nicole moved her feet from the chair. "No, don't do that.
I like to come out and wind down. As you can see, the porch
is big enough for two." She motioned to the chair for him
to join her.

The soft light provided sufficient brightness for him to dis-
cern the odd shapes of furniture. He peered at her, looking for
evidence that despite her invitation, she really didn't want
company. Even with shadows partially hiding the edges of her

face, he saw the tiredness etched around her eyes. "Hey, you know what? I think it's bedtime for you."

"Do I look that bad?"

"Bad? No. Tired? A big yes." Looking at her and seeing her eyes dreamily watching him, he felt like a big heel for giving her such a hard time earlier.

"Tiredness is my middle name." She waved her hand with an air of dismissal.

"And I'm sure I didn't help matters when I arrived."

She steepled her fingers under her chin. "As long as you leave more uplifted, all is forgiven. Can you handle that?"

"Your command is my wish." He was actually flirting.

A streak of lightning lit a forked path. They looked up at the jagged effect, which lit the sky in a vibrant burst of white light against the dark sky.

"Looks like we might float out of here," he remarked.

"We need the rain. There was some talk of water shortage."

"I'd heard the same for New York. Maryland has always been hot, hazy, and humid. I remember some hot summer days."

Nicole shot him a questioning look. "You're a native of Maryland?"

He kept his face slightly turned away from her. Possible answers warred within him, but it didn't make sense to lie. As long as he could keep any further questions on his life in Maryland at bay, there wouldn't be a problem. "Yes, I am. But don't look for me to be the spokesman for the tourist board. It's been a while and I've adopted New York as my home."

"I've been here all my life, although my parents now live in Florida. Used to work in DC, but that's ancient history. What drove you to New York?"

He placed both hands behind his head and stretched. "Oh, man, that subject is too deep for a night like this. Let's change the subject, onto brighter things. How is business?" Thank goodness it seemed that Nicole took the cue and didn't press, although her curiosity practically oozed out of her.

She shrugged. "Business is fine. I had my fears in the beginning, not that the butterflies are gone completely. You know how it is starting something new. With some things, I learn as I go, but overall I depend on Gertie and a few of the college kids to keep me on top of things." She giggled. "Gosh, I'm just spilling my guts to you."

He leaned forward, closing the distance between his face and hers. "Any regrets?" Beautiful round eyes. Button nose. But the lips, he really liked their bow shape.

"Honestly, I do feel overwhelmed at times. I second-guess myself and wonder why I ever thought this was a good idea." She paused, pursing her lips. She smacked her thighs. "But, I can't let it defeat me. It's hard to express what this bed-and-breakfast has to come to mean in my life. In some higher sense it's making me a whole person. I've heard the statistics about new businesses failing and how competitive the hotel industry is, but I'm not going down without a fight. I love this place and as long as I feel that connection, then I'll work night and day to keep it running." Her eyes shone and the pure expression of joy made him question the information he received. When she talked about the B&B, a deep-seated pride crept into her voice.

"Looks like you've done a good job of things."

"Yeah, right. Everything seemed to be going down the tubes earlier today, remember?"

He chuckled as she wrinkled her nose. "You can blame it on me. I had that negative aura thing going on. But you maintained a cool head, so you get my vote for hostess of the year." He laughed.

"In my previous life I had to handle worse than you dished up. As the saying goes, 'The customer is always right' . . . even if he's a bear." She offered him a wide smile.

He realized it was the first time he saw her smile—really smile—not the instant kind that sprang up whenever she talked to a guest or answered the phone. He wondered if she shared it with anyone special. Young woman, financially self-sufficient, intelligent . . . heck, there had to be someone who claimed her heart. Well, whoever it was, he was a lucky man, and it was time for Brad to exit before going down a path that he had no business going. "Think my bed is calling me."

"Yeah, it's late. Tomorrow is another day."

On the verge of drifting into a deep sleep, Brad reluctantly came awake to a constant drip. He reached a hand out to turn on the lamp near his head. He squinted. It took a few seconds before he could bear the light. Just a few feet away from his head was a small puddle on the floor. Sure enough, water leaked in a steady rhythm from the ceiling. Tracking the path of the water, he saw the dip in the ceiling where the water collected before landing on the hardwood floors. He groaned into his pillow. "Man, oh, man. What else?"

A quick glance around the room revealed nothing that could be used to capture the water from the leaking roof. He'd have to get Nicole. Downstairs, he noticed the light was still on in the porch area. He could see her through the windows sitting where he'd left her. This time, she was fast asleep with head bowed. Stepping out to the porch, he walked around her sleeping figure.

"Nicole," he called softly. She didn't respond. She must have gone to her room, changed, and returned to the porch. The dressing gown had fallen open at her knees, revealing her legs and matching peach slippers. "Nicole," he called a bit louder. She shifted and a book she had been reading fell to one side of the chair. Brad leaned over and pushed the cover closed so he could read the title. *How To Run a Bed-and-Breakfast—Successfully.* He hoped she had reached the chapter on how to fix a leak. This time, he shook her shoulder, "Nicole, wake up."

She opened her eyes and stared at him. The blankness gave way to recognition, then confusion. "What's going on?" She tried to get up, but fell back.

"Here, let me help you." He placed his arm around her back. "No emergency," he reassured her.

"Geez, I must have been in a deep sleep. I meant to read a little." As if seeing him for the first time, she asked, "What's not an emergency?"

"A leak in my room."

"Strike three."

He frowned. "Huh?"

"Oh, nothing," she replied, shaking her head. "I'll be right there. I'm not sure if I can do anything tonight. But first thing in the morning, I'll have someone on that roof."

"Okay, I'll be waiting." He returned to his room to see a bigger puddle on the floor. From the bathroom, he took towels and laid them down. No sense in letting the water leak downstairs, adding to Nicole's problems.

He heard her enter the room. Dressed in faded jeans and a T-shirt, she had brought a deep bucket and a mop. Although he was the guest and she, the proprietor, he didn't feel comfortable standing there doing nothing, while she mopped up the remaining water. "What do you need me to do?"

"Not much. I'm worried that you won't be able to sleep with the water dripping into the bucket all night." She bit her lip. A habit that normally would annoy him, on Nicole it gave her an innocent appeal. "I've a pull-out sofa in the living room in my apartment. You're welcome to stay there for the night."

"Thanks for the offer, but I think I can live through some dripping. Anyway, I've changed my plans. I'm leaving tomorrow."

"Oh."

Disappointment flooded her face and Brad could have kicked himself for telling her in the middle of the latest disaster. "A meeting I can't reschedule is the problem," he offered. "I'm sure I'll be back."

She didn't reply. Instead, she mopped and cleaned up the area without looking at him. Once everything was in place, she offered a soft "Good night" and left.

***

Early the next morning, Nicole was in her office facilitating her guests' departure. Bob and Sadie were leaving, and she didn't forget that Brad would be leaving, too. The sound of laughter and conversation from the stairway made her look up. Bob and Sadie came down first with Brad following, laughing heartily at something that was said upstairs. She looked past the newlyweds and fastened on Brad dressed in a polo shirt and khakis. As he came down the stairs, he looked over at her, locking her gaze with his.

Nicole got the Jeffersons' paperwork together and handed it to Bob for his signature. "Hope you enjoyed your stay."

"Absolutely wonderful," Sadie gushed. "We plan to come back for our anniversary. I do hope that Gertie will be cooking those fabulous meals." She giggled and patted her stomach. "I must have gained at least five pounds."

Nicole beamed. She needed that little morale booster, especially before dealing with Brad. "I loved having you here and please do come back." She gave them her brightest smile before turning to Brad.

"Were you able to get some sleep?" Her gaze remained fastened on the paperwork on the desk.

"No."

Her pen stilled. "It was the bucket, wasn't it?" She stared at him, mortified to think that he had arrived and would leave with a bad feeling about her B&B.

"I couldn't sleep because I kept thinking about you."

He had to be kidding. Yet, his face was serious. "Me?" she finally squeaked. Her face burned in her shock. She had slept all right, but her dreams consisted of his chiseled face with that sexy dimpled chin.

He shifted, looking sheepish. "I figured you thought I was leaving because of the leak. That's not it at all. I've really got another meeting that popped up."

Considering how he reacted when things weren't going his

way, she still had her doubts. However, the fact that he bothered to reassure her made a deeper impact. Her mood lightened. "Sorry to hear that you have to cut your vacation short. I figured you for a busy person." At least he cared enough to apologize to her; a nice ending to a disastrous stay.

She followed him to the door, making small talk. A taxi had already been called and now waited for him. As it pulled off, he gave a small wave before settling back into the cab. There was no reason for the deep disappointment that settled upon her, yet it did. *Pull yourself together,* she admonished herself. It had been some time since her last relationship. Maybe that would explain the infatuation for a mere guest.

"Is he gone?" Traci came running out from the dining room. "Darn, I wanted his autograph."

Nicole's irritation gave way to curiosity. "Autograph? Whose?"

"Brad's, of course."

Bob and Sadie, who were still waiting for the airport van, walked over. "Didn't you know?" Bob asked, his eyebrow cocked.

"I thought you knew," Sadie chimed in. "Well, I figured you'd know. Geez, honey, she didn't have a clue."

Nicole looked at the three faces staring back at her. "Okay, would someone tell me what's going on?"

"That was Brad Calverton. *The* Brad Calverton, famous reviewer of B-and-Bs. His column is syndicated throughout the U.S. in all the major newspapers. Sometimes he appears on the Travel Channel."

"If you get a good review from him, then you're set. Kinda like Oprah," Traci offered. "But a bad review and you'd better get the For Sale sign for the front."

"But I'm sure he could only give you a good review, Nicole," Bob said, glaring at Traci.

"I'd like to do a review on him." Traci wiggled her hips and smiled.

The second taxi pulled up.

"Let's go, Bob. See you, Nicole." Sadie looked disgustedly over at Traci, and shook her head.

Nicole's brain hadn't stopped buzzing since she heard Brad was a reviewer; a reviewer who visited her B&B, who had reservations screwups, no massage, and a leaky roof. After he finished ripping her new passion into tiny shreds, she hoped she would break even on the sale.

Two

Nicole appreciated the sudden quiet that always occurred between each wave of guests' arrivals and departures. A few days of running in high gear, being perky, and dishing out hospitality even when she didn't feel like it overwhelmed her at times. The calmness that followed afforded her a chance to restore her energy. Today, she appreciated it even more. With a full house, there was much paperwork to be completed and supplies to be replenished. Only then could she plan to curl up with a good book. It was the perfect incentive to get her going.

Only Violet remained after the holiday weekend. The elderly woman had gone to mill around in the many small craft shops in the Glen Knolls historic district. Her extended visits to the B&B had elevated her to a friend whom Nicole looked forward to seeing a few times a year. Retired and living off her three deceased husbands' estates, Violet traveled extensively, savoring diverse experiences that contributed to a youthful exuberance that Nicole envied.

What she really envied, or rather yearned to experience, was Bob and Sadie's relationship. It forced her to think of what it would be like to be wrapped up in the raptures of love. Now, as the thought filtered through, it still felt like an ill-fitted garment, an itchy wool sweater on a summer day. She squirmed trying to get comfortable with the idea of falling in love, allowing herself to surrender and losing control of her emotions.

Would it be so terrible to look forward to chocolates and

flowers on Valentine's Day or a love letter slid under her pillow? It would be a new frontier for which she had no experience. Now, the yearning had emerged, softly nudging her, building up in intensity, and needling her when she least expected it.

Its timely creation was forever etched in her memory. It shared the day and timing when the doctor told her the results after the radiation therapy. Two long weeks she waited by the phone, biting her nails and agonizing about what the outcome could be. A time when she sat on her living room floor and pored over photograph albums, reliving the joys in her life. It was all so fleeting. She had taken so much for granted. When he'd delivered the final news in an even tone, all she could think was that she had been given a second chance. A great relief had washed over her and she had cried.

With certainty, she knew she didn't want to be alone. Although her apartment, sparsely furnished with functional items, provided shelter, she couldn't call it home. It doubled as her cave where she hid each evening, afraid to enjoy life, wondering if she deserved to do so. To adore and be adored. She sighed, breaking the reverie, no time for the mushy stuff right now.

"Gertie, I'm going to be buried under paperwork for a couple of hours. Holler if you need me."

"No problem, Miss M. Did you want me to go to the supermarket? We're out of a few things. Besides, I've got the car today. Woody got his out of the shop yesterday."

"Thanks. Good news about the car. Hope it didn't cost a fortune."

"Hmm. You know how they charge you an arm and a leg for every little thing. I'll leave in a bit. I'll let you know."

Normally a trip to the supermarket served two purposes: the function of replacing necessities and a therapeutic way for Nicole to come down from a hectic schedule of being everything to everyone for a few days. Without a trip to replenish the pantry, she would have to work through the aftershock that her B&B would be badly reviewed. Based on the hectic day and night she spent with Brad Calverton, he had no choice but to demolish what little reputation she'd managed to build.

Another time, she would have appreciated such a visit, would have been proud. A renowned reviewer selecting her establishment was significant. But the reality had a way of slapping back any feelings of accomplishment. She paced back and forth, wringing her hands at the dismal thoughts that staked their claim. Replaying each disaster made her hit her head in frustration.

It wasn't fair. Why couldn't he have come a week earlier when she'd hired a local storyteller to share a colorful rendition of the town's history; or a month ago when a soap opera star visited; or when the local newspaper had written an article on her third-month anniversary? With the snap of his fingers, Brad could change it. Nicole fought the urge to scream from pent-up frustration and at feeling controlled by the uncontrollable.

A knock on the door interrupted her. "Come in."

"Just me." Gertie popped her head in. "I'm off."

Nicole sighed and followed Gertie into the kitchen. She didn't have the luxury of dedicating an entire day to disparaging Brad or his mission of betrayal, although she wouldn't pass up the opportunity to give him a piece of her mind.

"Jerk! Fathead! Pretty boy! Snake!" Anger ignited and flared. This B&B was hers and hers alone. Like hell would she let him tear apart what she'd spent time and energy to build. She didn't know what she had to do to repair the damage, but she wasn't giving up.

The doorbell buzzed. Nicole glanced at her watch. No one was due to arrive, unless it was a delivery. Maybe Violet had returned. "One sec," she shouted.

The door opened and Nicole suppressed a groan. In her present state of mind, however, she wasn't altogether sure if she kept the groan to herself. If the groan did manage to escape, it was well deserved. Audra Washington, the thorn in her side since she'd bought the B&B, couldn't have picked a worse time to make her customary visit.

"Hi, Nicole," Audra offered breezily. She waved a heavily jeweled hand, glittering with diamonds for accentuation. In an unexpected gesture, she pulled Nicole into an embrace. "How are you doing, sweetie?"

"Fine," Nicole replied between clenched teeth. Her eyes rolled in disgust. The hug reminded her of a typical scene in a mob movie when the intended victim was kissed on both cheeks before meeting his unfortunate demise. It would seem that her last act would be to inhale Audra's cloying perfume until she died of suffocation.

"What can I do for you, Audra?" Nicole took a step back once Audra had released her. "I'm very busy."

Audra walked toward the sitting room, looked around, and returned to her place in front of Nicole. "Shame, shame, lying to your friend. Place looks kinda dead to me." She pouted red glossy lips. "Now, don't look at me like that. Can't help being blunt. Besides, no need to hide anything from me. I told you that I'm your friend . . . your mentor." She clapped her hands together and smiled. "Friend to friend, doesn't look very busy to me," she finished.

"Um . . . well . . ." Nicole began slowly. Her thoughts collided with each other, reeling at Audra's audacity. She cleared her throat. "Thank you for extending your friendship to me. Maybe another time we can have a visit and chat, but right now I've got several things to do." A small smile was all she could offer.

"My, I do think that you are giving me the royal heave-ho. Lucky for you, I have an appointment to get to." She donned her shades, which masked ice chips for eyes. "I'm having an open house in a few days for local business owners. Here's an official invite," she said, shoving a small card into her hand. "Would love to see you there, babe. Good opportunity to network. Never know when you may need a little cash."

Pulling her shades down her nose, she looked over the

rims. "By the way, how are the margins looking? Curtains need replacing. Look homemade to me. Floor could do with a shine. Some guests wouldn't hurt, either. Do come, I may have a business proposition for you. Don't let opportunity pass you by, sweetie."

Nicole took the invitation, glancing down at the gold lettering. As soon as Audra left it would end up in the trash. She wanted nothing from this woman whose style resembled a barracuda's. Business proposition, indeed.

"Well, I'll be going." Audra walked to the door, but before heading out of the house, she turned. "If you need help selecting a suitable outfit, give me a call. It's a classy affair." Her eyes flitted over Nicole and she followed with an immediate response of a wrinkled nose. "Ciao."

"What a class act," Nicole muttered once the door closed.

The doorbell rang seconds later. She stiffened, marshaling her strength to deal with Audra's grand finale of stomping her insecurities into the ground. Luck visited her and she overcompensated with a huge welcoming smile. "Oh, good to see you, Charlie. The rain did me in this time. The hole is in the first bedroom, right up the stairs."

Charles Gatewood had been her handyman since she opened. He was an essential component to her small team. Maintaining proper standards and keeping up with the building and business codes demanded prompt attention.

"We'll take a look-see, then give you a prognosis."

"Thanks. I'll be around, just yell if you need me." She raised her eyebrows. "No bad news, okay?" Great. It was her luck that Audra had to have passed him on her way out, which meant that it would be thrown at her during Audra's next visit.

Nicole headed back to her apartment, determined to concentrate on business. Only then did she realize that she still had the invitation in her hand. Audra Washington—real estate agent whizz. Her reputation in the community set her on a pedestal, as she received various awards and recognition. Deep connections had been forged with the mayor and local congressmen, which she flaunted at every opportunity. Maybe making Audra her friend was a good idea for purely business reasons.

As a friend for personal reasons, it would never work. Nicole didn't have many friends, but the few she did have didn't manipulate or patronize her. Most of all, she trusted them. There was an unsavory element about Audra that left her cold. If Audra extended a hand in friendship, you had better keep an eye on Audra's other hand for the unexpected blow.

"Miss Montgomery, have you been toiling over that paperwork since I left?" Gertie passed back and forth in front of her apartment door while she put away the items she'd bought. "You've skipped breakfast. Lunch will be right up."

Nicole smiled at her mothering, only then realizing how long she'd been at work. "You really shouldn't spoil me. I can do it."

Gertie walked up to her and stood in front of her desk with her hand on her hip. "Lunch will be up in five minutes and you are eating, young lady. First, you were looking all down in the dumps this morning. Then I come back to find you staring down at those papers as if you're waiting for them to talk back to you. In the meantime I don't plan to sit by and watch you starve to death."

She clucked her tongue and went back toward the kitchen, raising her voice. "You're nothing but skin and bones. A girl in my day had meat on her bones: strong shoulders, ample bosom, wide hips, and strong legs."

"Sounds like that girl should be balancing two milk pails on her shoulders, too. That's not me. Although I'm not sure what is."

"You're a lady, through and through. I see those blisters on your hands. Plus you lost weight, worrying yourself about everything. Your face doesn't have a wrinkle on it. Fresh as a babe, but you're working like a real trooper. That's why I like working for you. That's why I like you."

A warm flush spread over Nicole's face. Gertie wasn't given to many emotional displays. Her kind words touched her.

"You're too kind. It certainly has been a learning experience being on my own. Looking at my hands and sore feet, I look the part of a run-down hag."

"Hard on yourself, ain't you? One thing I can take care of for sure is that stomach. I'm going to help you along with soup, a grilled cheese sandwich, and the last piece of the bread pudding."

Nicole's traitorous stomach growled. Whether or not she wanted to take the time out to eat, her appetite needed to be satiated. The porch beckoned and she followed the urging to work in the screened-in room.

Fifteen minutes later, Gertie appeared with a lunch tray. Nicole saw her grilled cheese sandwich, warm and gooey, just waiting for her attention. Targeting the crust first, she nibbled around the edges.

"Saving the middle for last?"

"Miss Violet, how nice to see you. You're back early."

Violet came across the garden and entered the porch.

"Had to visit a travel agency about my return flight to Florida. Trying to get an upgrade and handling it over the phone was trying my nerves." Violet eased into a chair opposite Nicole's. "Eating like a bird? No wonder you've got such a slim figure. Don't have to worry about this." She patted her thighs.

Nicole giggled. "The longer it takes me to eat, the longer it takes me to get back to work."

The inner door opened and Charlie appeared. "Have some bad news for you."

Suddenly, the piece of bread in her mouth became difficult to chew. Nicole braced herself for the doomsday message. "Go on," she urged, letting him know that he could speak in front of Violet.

"Apparently the roof hadn't been changed for a long time. It's still the asbestos type, which just means that disposing will be more difficult. I'd suggest that you do the entire roof."

"Cost?" she asked, stomach churning.

He scratched his head, adding numbers in his head. "Run you about three thousand, give or take."

The piece of bread went down her throat in a gulp. She imagined that it would be more "give" than "take." Realizing that Charlie awaited her reply she nodded. What else could she say?

"I've put a makeshift cover over the hole until I can fix it, proper like."

"What's your schedule? I've got a couple coming in to-morrow."

"The earliest will be this weekend, maybe Saturday."

Four days. She needed to check the weather forecast. Better yet, a fortune-teller could cut right to the meat of things and tell if she would still have a bed-and-breakfast a year from now. "Thanks, Charlie. You need a deposit, right?"

"Yep, but hold off until I check around. I may be able to cut a few deals."

She appreciated his frequent discounts and shifting his load to accommodate her. Insurance was another option, but at what cost?

"Don't let it get to you," Violet offered.

"I feel as if my energy has been sucked away."

"That's natural."

Nicole drew her knees against her chest and rested her chin. "I'm trying to hang on with every part of my being, Miss V. But it's getting harder and harder." She fought back tears, biting down on her lip to force back the emotion. A weight seemed to settle in the middle of her shoulder blades. Too afraid to ask what could happen next, instead she dwelled on the unexpected expense.

"Pack up and go back to what you're used to."

Nicole's head shot up. "How can you suggest such a thing?" she demanded, pinning Violet with a glare.

The woman looked back at her with no expression.

"Give up. Just give up, just like that," Nicole repeated.

"It's obvious this B-and-B is beating you. Think about the

corporate life you described to me. Expense accounts and corporate credit cards at your beck and call. Winin' and dinin' Congress members around Washington, DC. You're young, beautiful, and intelligent, yet you're wasting all that struggling with a venture that has you guessing whether you're going to make it from month to month." Violet leaned forward and touched the side of Nicole's face. "Quit."

Nicole pushed away her hand and stood. Her eyes shot sparks down on Violet's head. "No one is going to write me off, until I want to be written off. I lived a great lifestyle a couple of years ago and can go back to it with the snap of my fingers. But let me tell you"—she wagged her finger at Violet, who sat back in the chair arms folded—"that life held nothing for me. Nothing in here." She pointed to her chest. "This B-and-B has given me a sense of purpose and, as I build and repair things around here, it becomes a part of who I am. I saw this neglected shell of a house that sheltered a generation of families, now forgotten and on sale. I can relate to that and, call it crazy, but these walls speak to me. I can find myself. I can rebuild and repair myself. It's going to take a lot more than an arrogant bed-and-breakfast reviewer, a stupid leak in the ceiling, and that she-devil sniffing around to bring me to my knees. So, if you'll excuse me, I have work to be done."

"Well, that deserves a standing ovation." Violet stood and clapped. "That's the spirit I see in your eyes when you aren't feeling sorry for yourself. Keep that fire and it'll chase the blues away."

With a deep breath, Nicole's anxiety lifted. She smiled, then laughed openly at being drawn into fiercely defending her misgivings. "Thanks, Miss V. I needed that."

Two months later Nicole drove down Main Street in her minivan with newfound confidence. The warm weather boosted her attitude. Sixties in December. Snow was a long way off the radar screen, despite the numerous Santa and reindeer decorations and fake icicles decorating the boutique storefronts. She pulled into an empty parking spot in front of the local used bookstore.

The door jingled a small bell, announcing her entry. Nicole walked down the aisles, casting a cursory glance through the stacks. Her mission was highly ambitious, but she looked forward to the challenge.

Nicole took a book and randomly flipped through the pages, intermittently looking at the colored photographs of a variety of garden styles and accompanying instructions. She read a few paragraphs and felt comfortable with the terminology and required equipment, although her mind automatically calculated the approximate cost for the entire project.

She left the bookstore with her new purchase tucked close to her chest. One more stop at the advertising agency and then she'd be on her way home. The current brochures had been done on her home computer and copied at the local copying center. They were passable, but she wanted a more glossy, upscale look to entice visitors.

She arrived a few minutes before her appointment and made herself comfortable in the reception area. The plush furnishings and piped-in music screamed money at her. After a few minutes of squirming in the chair, forcing herself to stay put and follow through with the appointment, she grabbed the day's newspapers sitting atop a pile of magazines.

Nothing special caught her attention on the first few pages. Her eyes honed in on any articles about Congress. Her old stomping grounds still got a rise out of her and she skimmed the news reports on its upcoming recess schedule. Time for the congressmen to head back to their home states and attend community events.

She continued flipping through and stopped at a page featuring travel information. A sigh escaped. No trips to the Caribbean in her foreseeable future, no matter how tantalizing the deal. Her B&B created a large sucking sound as it slowly depleted her savings. Frugality was the rule of the day and possibly also the upcoming year.

She had almost turned the page when she spied a familiar name—Brad Calverton. Immediately she zeroed in on the column, a syndicated piece, that discussed the ten no-nos for a B&B host. She read the list, cringing as she saw bullet points that appeared to be talking about her and her B&B. His grand finale dropped a stone in her stomach. He called it sharing his two cents, but Nicole still squirmed under his brutal opinion that any host who could identify with two or more points should do the world a favor and close up shop.

Nicole refolded the newspaper.

"Miss Montgomery? Mr. Edwards can see you now."

Nicole looked up into the receptionist's face, full of confidence and good cheer. She wondered how it would look if she ran out of the office at full speed.

She pasted on a shaky smile and followed the efficient woman. One step at a time. Brochures, then home, then think about closing up shop as a favor to the world.

Audra punched the END button on the cell phone. Pleased that her appointment hadn't canceled, she pressed down on the accelerator and her BMW Z3 shot down the thirty-five-mile-per-hour road at fifty, a shiny midnight blue bullet. Top down, she reveled in the feel of the wind whipping through her hair, feeling powerful.

It was too early to celebrate a victory, but her careful orchestration had set things into motion. She manipulated each piece on the gameboard of her dream. Despite setbacks, she remained patient, waiting for the right time. So close as she was to achieving what she wanted for so many years, her heart beat excitedly at the possibilities.

The last obstacle, Nicole Montgomery, was about to be bulldozed aside. She hoped that her nemesis showed up to the reception. It would be the perfect setting to unveil her intentions. Nicole, out of choices, would have to grab at anything that appeared able to help her. Audra did feel sorry for her, just a bit, not enough to change her plans, though, because the young woman wasn't her target. It all had to do with timing, and Nicole was in the wrong place.

She pulled into the company's parking lot and turned into her reserved space. Once inside, she walked directly to her office. No time to spare hobnobbing with anyone. Employees went out of their way to greet her and have her notice them. Their fawning attitudes amused her, especially since as a partner, she held their future in her hands. Naked ambition burned in some of their eyes, and she saw herself in them when she had first started working in the corporate world.

Wearing a new Chanel suit, she was the picture of expensive conservatism. The cream-colored suit, accentuated with splashes of red on the pockets and trademark gold-plated Chanel buttons, had been professionally altered to highlight her legs. As a matter of fact, all her hemlines were altered above the knee.

"Any messages?"

Her assistant handed her several pink slips.

Audra rifled through the small pile. "Any emergencies?"

"No, ma'am. Mr. Peterson said to give him a call when you came in."

"Did he give any clue as to what he wanted?"

"Said it was about the reception."

She walked over to her office. "Bring me a cup of coffee, will you?" she requested and closed her door.

Quickly, she rifled through the messages, rearranging them in order of importance. She called her partner and discussed logistics of the reception. After hanging up, she leaned back in the high-backed leather chair and looked out her window, which overlooked the naval academy. She'd received good news. The state delegate would be in attendance. For some of the long-term goals of the business, it would help to have influential backers.

After her assistant brought her coffee, she raised the mug in a one-sided toast to the latest recruits running around the campus. "Here's to our mutual success."

Her intercom buzzed. "Your eleven o'clock appointment is here."

She leaned over. "Send him in." A rare nervousness swept through her.

She turned and waited, holding her breath.

The door opened.

"Hello, Brad."

Three

Nicole had a few more errands to run before heading for home. Her mind stayed in a whirl, tossing around several marketing ideas that formed out of what the public relations agent shared with her. She braked at a red light. The few minutes of inactivity provided an opportunity to ponder her situation. Nicole tapped her ragged fingernails against the steering wheel, staring unseeingly ahead.

Every turn she made seemed to have a line of obstacles that she had to outmaneuver. She wasn't a quitter and didn't want to entertain the idea that she'd made a mistake and maybe for once, she had taken on a project that was too much to handle. It was too late to do anything about it. Her eight-month-old B&B had worked its way into her heart.

A car honked behind her, its driver showing his impatience. The light had turned green. She hit the accelerator with a decisive tap, and a sense of satisfaction overcame her as a plan of action formed. At the next intersection, she made a right and headed toward the parkway.

Half an hour later, Nicole pulled into the Small Business Administration field office parking lot. As she passed the glass windows before reaching the revolving door to the building, she studied her reflection. Her wind-tossed hair stuck out in a few places and she patted her flipped-up hairdo. Pushing through the door, she sighed knowing that there wasn't much she could do with her casual outfit. It hadn't been in her plan for the day to head to the SBA office.

"Hi there, may I help you?"

Nicole offered a friendly smile to the receptionist, a college-aged girl with a head full of microbraids. "I don't have an appointment, but wanted to talk to someone about my business and whatever financial help I can obtain."

The receptionist handed her a clipboard. "Fill this out and someone will meet with you shortly."

Once she'd handed in the information, Nicole was escorted to an office and introduced. She tried to gauge the SBA representative's mood.

"Mr. Walker, I'm going to get straight to the point. I'm interested in my options to obtain financial help."

"Have you received any money through the SBA since you started the business?" The SBA representative stood while she sat, making her feel like an insect.

"No, I used my own money because it was quicker that way. Well, most of it."

"Tell me about your business."

Nicole shared her business plans, including the new marketing objective that she'd recently formed with the help of the public relations rep.

Finally he sat behind his desk. "Pretty impressive." Mr. Walker put on his glasses and jotted down notes. His balding scalp had a high sheen caught by the fluorescent lighting in the office.

"As you probably know our funding has been cut back." He raised his hand to stem her protest. "But, where there's a will . . ."

Nicole tried to hide the bitter drop of disappointment wallowing in the pit of her stomach. She still had her pension fund and some money-market accounts.

"What brings in the money?"

Nicole looked Mr. Walker in the eye to see if he was patronizing her. "People."

"Exactly. This means that you have to increase your occupancy rate. I'd suggest that you have discount specials, beef up advertising, and work on getting favorable reviews in the local papers. Later, you can focus on the national scene. I also notice that you're not registered with an agency to handle reservations and advertising."

Nicole rubbed her forehead. "Some of those things take money, including being registered. There's a hefty fee that may be worth it eventually. However, at the moment, I take care of my own reservations."

"Okay, before you can get funding from the SBA, you'll have to show that you applied for a loan and were turned down."

"You're kidding me."

"No. That's policy. Check the SBA Web site."

Nicole thanked Mr. Walker, ending the interview. Her thoughts Ping-Ponged back and forth, weighing her success at getting a loan. She'd probably have to jump through so many hoops and lay her life bare with only a high-interest loan as her reward. And as for the third item about getting a good review, well, that might have to wait.

Darn it! She couldn't think of a single soul at the community newspaper to give her the opportunity to feature her B&B, much less review it. Maybe a free weekend offer to one of the reporters and pulling out all the stops couldn't hurt.

Suddenly, she felt exhausted. The bank would have to wait.

Brad lay on the couch in his office, with his long legs propped on the sofa's arm. He interlocked his fingers on his chest and stared at the ceiling as his assistant filled him in on the details of his next project.

"Brad, are you listening to me?"

"Yes, Freddie. I'm going to Hawaii over the Christmas holidays," he repeated in a droll voice.

"Don't try to fool me with your indifference. Lots of people would give away their firstborn for a free vacation to Hawaii."

Brad closed his eyes without defending his position. The

theme of the latest project simply reminded him that this Christmas would be spent alone. Shaunice, his supermodel ex, didn't even have the decency to tie up the loose ends; instead he got to read about his abandoned state in a gossip magazine. When he'd called her to confirm, her assistant provided him with a curt explanation: "Shaunice will no longer be in need of your company."

Brad rubbed his head to rid himself of the memories. "Romantic getaways. Just my luck."

Freddie looked away and busied herself. "Well, it was scheduled more than a year ago."

"Oh, I'm not blaming you. I know. It's just not a great time in my life to be reviewing romantic B-and-Bs. In order for me to do it any justice, I'm going to have to put myself into the role of a man in love. Ha!"

"Maybe it would help to think of someone, a movie star, a model . . . er . . . any woman who'll trigger some kind of romantic thought within you. Think about why it would be a wonderful place for you and that special someone. Also, think about how you would come back and tell me, so that all I would want to do was go to this paradise with the man I love."

"Problem solved. Gee, Freddie, that was so easy."

Freddie tossed a paper clip at him. "Stop being a smart-ass. Get your butt on the plane by tomorrow for your next project in Nantucket. You'll also have to do an interview with the local television station. Begone now, I've got lots of work to do." She waved her manicured fingers at him.

Brad sighed and righted himself on the couch. "Cracking that whip, I see. I'm beginning to think you like playing the boss lady. Okay, I'll go off and play like a good boy."

Freddie saluted him and he went out of his home office.

Brad walked out of the building onto Park Avenue, blending into the heavy foot traffic. He headed north toward the gym, hoping that his volunteer coaching would boost his spirits. The blustery wind might divert the best intentions, but he'd brave the crisp air as long as he could stand. Freddie's advice had ignited a memory, soft and pleasant with a touch of sweetness. Nicole Montgomery reminded him of romance. He wrapped his coat tightly around him, lowering his shoulders to block the wind and any traitorous thoughts about Nicole. He had no doubt that she'd make someone happy one day, if she wasn't already linked.

But—and there was always that caveat—if he *was* looking for a special woman to share his life, Nicole had several points. He liked the easy smile that covered her face, setting anyone at ease. When she spoke, her voice rang clear with a slight lilt that he found uniquely endearing. And then there were her feet. He never fancied himself a "foot man," but he'd sat with her on the porch and she had her tired feet propped on the chair. Each painted toe, wonderfully unscathed by a tight shoe, and her beautiful arches had him fighting the urge to gently place her feet in his lap as he stroked away the tired ache.

He paused at a busy intersection waiting to cross. He looked up at the display of a digital clock above a national bank. "Hell," he groaned. He waved his hand to hail a cab. His daydreaming would make him late for his class. He hopped into a waiting cab and headed for the Stokley Carmichael Recreation Center.

"Hey, Coach Calverton, whaddup?"

Brad slapped high fives as he walked into the recreation center. "Hey, guys. Sorry I'm late. Run your laps and meet me in center court in five minutes." He watched them jog warm-up laps around the center. His next assignment would take him away from them for about a week. He hoped a specific few would stay out of trouble while he wasn't around to be on their backs.

For the next forty-five minutes, he refereed their basketball game. "Okay, guys, gather round. I'm heading out of town for a few weeks. I won't be around, but I'll be checking in on everyone."

"Aw, man," Big Ed complained. "There's nothing for me to

do." The six-foot, solidly built teen flicked the sweat off his brow.

"Any of you have plans for Christmas?" Brad asked.

"What Christmas? Ain't any different from any other day. Some church ladies will come over with a few presents and then we'll have to look decent for them," another teen added.

Brad laughed. "I know how it is, man. But at least you'll get a good home-cooked meal."

"Yup. Turkey, potatoes, bread, macaroni and cheese. Mmmm-mmmm. Good," Big Ed remarked, rubbing his stomach.

When Brad boarded the jet, destination Hawaii, he knew he'd miss his boys. From personal experience, the Christmas holidays were the toughest to get by, especially having to deal with the sentimental commercials with grandparents reuniting with their grandchildren or a happy husband giving an expensive, sparkling piece of jewelry to his always-smiling wife. The ads hit him deeply because he couldn't even summon up a substitute family at his disposal.

His only relative, Grandma Ada, was long gone. He'd lived with her from three through ten years of age. He could remember nothing of his mother, and his grandmother never spoke of his father. All his love, loyalty, and caring were meant for only one person: Grandma Ada. Even at his thirty-five years, tears could form at the mere thought of what he used to have.

When the jet landed, Brad shook himself out of his doldrums. Many would love to be in Hawaii with free accommodations. But he'd managed to dampen the potential of a light and cheerful vacation.

Mr. and Mrs. Ikeda, his host and hostess, met him at the airport. He knew this was only because of his expected recommendation and the guaranteed exposure, but it was still a nice touch that he appreciated. Dressed in colorful, flower-printed, matching shirts, they draped him with the traditional lei and warm aloha greeting.

Half an hour later, they arrived at the B&B. Brad had grumbled about having to travel so far afield to do a review, but he couldn't help being instantly soothed by the rippling sound of the Pacific Ocean rolling softly into the beach. As he looked out into the inky blackness, listening to the night-filled sounds of insects, he welcomed the warm breeze against his face. Maybe this paradise could soothe the demons that caused such painful memories because of his grandmother's death on the day before Christmas Eve.

"Hey, ladies." Nicole kissed each of her girlfriends' cheeks. "Anything new since last month?" She slipped into the booth and picked up the oversize menu. Their monthly lunch meetings gave her an outlet from the demands of the B&B and kept her in touch with her girlfriends since college days.

"Shirley, here, has a new beau. She's glowing like a girl on her first date because he's taking her home at Christmas to meet his family in Connecticut."

Shirley giggled. "Oh, stop it, Toni."

It pleased Nicole to see Shirley getting out since her messy divorce from her childhood sweetheart.

"Have you all ordered?"

The waitress stood at their booth waiting for their orders.

In no time the foursome placed their orders.

Toni pulled out her lipstick and retouched her lips.

"Why exactly do you put on lipstick before eating? You've been doing that since college and I can't figure it out." Nicole turned a perplexed frown toward Toni, who sat next to her.

"It's because I have beautiful, full lips that require my constant attention." Toni air-kissed her image in the compact mirror. She looked over at Donna and Shirley. "Yes, I'm vain. Most of us are. The difference is that I'm not afraid to admit it." She snapped her compact closed with a satisfied smirk and batted her hazel eyes at them.

"Yeah, whatever," said Donna, nibbling on her nails. She wore no makeup and her hair was pulled back into its customary ponytail.

"In your case, Donna, it's not vanity. You haven't evolved to appreciate femininity, embracing that tomboyish lifestyle that is cute during high school, but played out in college, and quite inappropriate at this stage in life."

"Hmmm. I wonder, dear cousin, if that's why I have a man and you are still trying to get one?"

"Ooooh!" Nicole and Shirley hooted at the verbal sparring. It was all cool since they were as close as sisters.

"Okay, I'm not about to sit here for an hour and listen to both of you," said Nicole. "Oh, good, here's the food."

For the next few minutes, silence reigned as they began to eat.

"How's business, Nicole?" Donna asked, pushing her half-finished plate away from her. "Still excited about it?"

Nicole bit into her cheeseburger and took her time chewing, then swallowing. "It's trying my nerves, that's for sure. The latest is that I was being spied on by a hotshot reviewer."

"That's a good thing, right?" asked Shirley.

Nicole slammed down her cheeseburger and wiped off her fingers covered with barbecue sauce. "No, it's not. Have you heard of Brad Calverton?"

"Nope." Donna shook her head, her chin-length bob brushing each cheek.

"I have," Toni answered. "I once saw him on a TV talk show. I don't remember what he said, but man, oh, man, did he look good!" She turned her attention to Nicole. "He was at your B-and-B, why didn't you call me?"

"First of all, I didn't know who he was and by the time I found out, it was too late." Thinking about the experience tempered Nicole's appetite. She threw her napkin onto the cheeseburger and fries.

"Too late for what?" Donna frowned.

"Everything that could go wrong went wrong. I know that I'm going to get a bad review for thousands of people to read. He doesn't hold back any punches. I read one of his reviews." Nicole held the glass of iced tea against her forehead.

"Oh." Their collective sympathy didn't lift Nicole's spirit.

She put down the glass and traced a random pattern around it. "I'm going to need more money to get things fixed and do some marketing. But that's easier said than done."

"You know, Nicole," Toni began in a soft voice, "you can always go back to your old job."

"What kind of advice is that?" Shirley asked, frowning at Toni. "This is what Nicole wants to do."

"And that doesn't make any sense to me. I'll never understand why you left that plush job," Toni pushed.

"Look, I'm not getting into that now." Suddenly the booth seemed stifling for Nicole. She wasn't about to sit on trial with her friends as judge and jury.

"Get off her back. She had good reasons. You did, didn't you?" Donna defended, but was unable to hide the doubt in her voice.

Nicole sighed. She drank the remainder of her iced tea, buying time as she pondered the questions. "For the upteenth time, it was the right time for a major change in my life. Now I want to focus on me and having a family."

"Family? Are you taking about the pitter-patter of little feet?" Toni asked.

"Baby and husband."

Toni sat back. "I feel like we skipped a few chapters because I'm not following this at all. You up and decided one day that it was time to have a man and a baby."

"More precisely, a husband and the father of my child."

"Whatever! At least your mother would be pleased about that part," Toni said.

They all laughed, easing the tension that had heated up so quickly.

"Yes, she would be happy that her daughter is following in her footsteps," Nicole agreed.

"Getting back to this reviewer person, why do you think he'll give you a bad review?" Shirley patted Nicole's hand.

"Because he couldn't get a massage and his room had a leak."

"Wow. He had to sleep with a leak?" Shirley asked.

"I did offer my apartment."

"You're lying." Toni leaned forward, grinning widely.

"It was the best thing that I could think of to make up for the problem."

"And nothing happened?" Toni asked, biting her lip to stifle another smile.

"No, nothing happened. I'm not a nympho," Nicole declared in a huff.

"Like you," Donna added, arching an eyebrow at Toni.

"A healthy sexual appetite is normal. But I guess a Deepfreeze like you couldn't comprehend," Toni glared back at her cousin.

"Me and my Deepfreeze are quite happy," Donna shot back.

"I guess so. You'll probably need another pack of batteries for the holidays," Toni replied.

Shirley, always the peacemaker, held up a time-out signal. "Speaking of holidays, is anyone finished with their Christmas shopping? I'm leaving on Tuesday to go home for the holidays."

Toni took the cue. "Donna is spending Christmas with my family. We're driving to the eastern shore on Thursday. How about you, Nicole?"

"I'll be here. I've got a couple coming in for the Christmas break."

"What! You're not going home?" Shirley asked.

"No. I'm a big girl. I don't have to run home for every holiday and every event."

"What's going on with you, Nicole? You were always a

workaholic, but lately it's been different. You don't go home much. Plus we don't see you, except for monthly lunches. You just don't want to be bothered with us sometimes," Donna said.

"I haven't missed one of our lunches," Nicole defended.

"No, you haven't. But that's all you make it to," Donna added.

"Leave her be. Sorry for jumping down your throat. You don't have to answer to us, Nicole." Shirley squeezed her friend's hand.

"I'm not trying to distance myself from you, guys. I've just had a lot to deal with in the past few months. I promise I'll come to the next event."

"Good. Are we all back for New Year's Eve?" Shirley asked.

They all nodded.

"Party at my house. Bring your own bottle of champagne or wine, a list of resolutions, and a change of clothes, because you'll be too drunk to drive home," Shirley offered.

"I'll be the first one there," Nicole volunteered.

"Now I know you're lying." Toni poked at Nicole's shoulder.

The four women gathered in the restaurant parking lot to say their good-byes. Instead of talking about where they would meet for the next month, each woman volunteered a food item that she was willing to make. Nicole opted to make an angel food cake with strawberry topping. By volunteering to bring an item, she was more likely to attend the girls' night out.

Christmas came and went without much hubbub. Nicole couldn't remember such an unappealing holiday season such as this. Her guests came and stayed for two nights, enjoying their Christmas in a very reflective, solitary way. Nicole respected their privacy and remained in her apartment for most of the time. Her mother didn't let her off the hook so easily and Nicole had several minutes of being scolded by her over the phone.

Once the elderly couple left, Nicole cleaned up the bedroom. A strange restlessness settled over her as she walked through on a final inspection of the B&B. Despite the furnishings and decorations, her B&B felt empty—not like a cozy, warm bed of activity that depended on the presence of people. She went into her apartment and flopped onto an overstuffed sofa.

She pulled her feet under her and hugged the pillow. Loneliness wound its way through her. Family, friends, and business she possessed. Yet, a void sat in the pit of her soul.

New Year's Eve rolled in on a cold blustery day. Nicole looked out the window, gauging whether a snow shower would come that day. By midday she knew that she wasn't going to follow through with meeting her friends. The howling wind echoed the starkness of her life. She did what she did well—retreat and close herself off from anyone. She sighed, knowing that her friends would not take her no-show lightly. She decided to make the angel food cake anyway, out of some weird sense of obligation. Maybe she'd take it to Shirley with her apologies, tomorrow.

By seven o'clock that evening, she'd taken her shower, put on a new flannel nightdress, painted her toes and fingers, and literally watched them dry. Soft jazz played in the background while the TV played with the MUTE button activated. If she was awake close to midnight, she'd do the countdown with whatever celebrity whom she happened to see on the TV.

The doorbell rang. Nicole jumped up, trying to figure out where she was and what was going on. She'd drifted off to sleep an hour earlier with only a soft light on at one end of the room. The jazz CD had long since stopped. The bell rang again.

"Who the heck is it?" She looked at the clock. She'd slept longer than she'd thought.

She slipped on her robe and hurriedly made her way to

the door. Thank heavens her neighbors weren't close to her, because the noise of the ringing doorbell was deafening.

She turned on the porch light and looked through the window. "Oh, crap!" She paused with her head leaning against the door before turning the lock.

"Come on, Nicole. We're not leaving, so you might as well open this door." A round of knocking and pounding ensued.

Nicole shook her head and opened the remaining lock. "What do you all want?"

Toni pushed her way passed Nicole. "What's your problem?" She stood at about five feet tall, but riled up, she was a powerhouse of anger.

Donna turned on all the lights, walking through from room to room. "It was freaking cold out there. What took you so long?"

Nicole sighed. There was no way she was getting out of this. She closed the door and headed toward the kitchen without saying a word to her three friends.

"We need plates, silverware, and glasses. Wineglasses, preferably," Shirley shouted.

Nicole leaned against the counter and folded her arms. She watched as her friends opened and closed cupboards, retrieving the needed items. "You know, I said that I couldn't make it. I wanted to be alone this evening."

"Since we know you better than you know yourself, we knew that you would back out as soon as the acceptance left your lips. So we came up with plan B. Here, take this glass of wine and follow us." Donna pushed the delicate glass into Nicole's hand. "I think we're all set for our midnight feast. Let's go into the little den room you've got over here. Toni, have you already started the fire?"

Toni shouted her affirmative from the den.

"Great." Donna rubbed her hands together.

"I'm not changing out of my nightdress," Nicole snarled.

"Neither are we," Donna said with a smug smile. Each

woman took off her coat, sporting sleepwear. "Drink your wine and chill."

Shirley hooked her arm into Nicole's. "I want to know why you canceled out on us. Something is going on with you and you're not telling us. We made a pact in college, remember? None of us would hold back anything, good or bad, from each other," Shirley said.

"We're not in college anymore. I don't force my way into your business, so why are doing so with me?" Nicole extricated her arm, her temper rising.

"You're not going to get us on the defensive. This is not a court trial. We're your friends and, at times, we're like sisters. We care about you. We love you and we know that you're keeping something from us," Donna scolded.

"Are you pregnant?" Toni frowned, trying to read the situation.

"No." Nicole slammed down the wineglass on an end table and stood. "Look, what do you want from me? You can't get into my head. I was having a rough day and decided to take it easy tonight."

"Rough with what? There're no people." Toni opened her hands to encompass the room.

"You're going to throw it in my face that I have no people here on New Year's Eve? My B-and-B is one big joke to you. 'Let's go watch Nicole fail.'"

"You're being unfair, but you're entitled to wig out because Lord knows, you're wound up tighter than a drum. When you're done thinking that the world is against you, come back down to reality and join us. Pass me the chicken, please." Donna opened the container of fried chicken and served herself.

Nicole suddenly felt silly. Her friends were eating and drinking as if she weren't in the room. The food smelled delicious and she saw golden corn muffins being passed along with fried chicken and potato salad. She wanted to have her tantrum, but Donna always knew how to defuse her. Her stomach growled, opting to go with the opposing team.

"Oh, move over so I can eat. Shirley, don't hog all the potato salad." Nicole snuggled her way between Donna and Shirley.

They ate and chatted about their respective Christmas holidays. Nicole munched on a piece of chicken breast, savoring the seasoned meat. She saluted Shirley for her contribution to the meal.

"Where's the angel food cake?" Toni asked. "I know you, and you would've made it anyway."

Nicole laughed and went to the kitchen to retrieve her cake. She might not have that special someone to share her cake or this evening with, but she had some darn good friends whom she'd taken for granted. She walked out with her cake extended as a peace offering. "Hey, guys, I'm sorry that I'm such a witch."

"Not quite the word I would have used, but since you're no longer in self-denial, I'll accept your apology." Donna took the cake.

"You've wondered why I wanted the B-and-B so badly and I know you've pretended to understand, but I can guarantee that you have no idea." Nicole paused to gain the courage to tell the secret that she'd kept even from her family. A slow heat crept up her neck as she steeled against her usual coping methods of retreat and hide. She gulped a mouthful of wine. "Nine months ago, Shirley called us for our usual buddy check to do the monthly breast exam, remember?"

"Did you find anything?" Shirley asked softly, a worried frown descending over her face.

Nicole nodded. "I found a lump in my right breast." She placed her hand on the spot and closed her eyes tightly for a couple of seconds.

"Oh, Nicole," Shirley called out and came over to put her arm around Nicole's shoulders, giving her a quick hug.

Nicole brushed her cheek against the comforting hand. "I

was so damned scared. I cried and I couldn't believe that this could happen to me. I went to the doctor and he confirmed the lump. Then, I had to have it removed. The hardest part came with the waiting for the diagnosis. To keep sane, during that time, I packed an overnight bag and drove until I got tired. I came upon a wonderful B-and-B in the Shenandoah Valley in Virginia." Nicole cringed as the lie passed her lips. She wasn't ready to bare it all.

"Why didn't you call us? We would have come with you," Donna said.

"I'm sure you would have, but I needed to be alone. Nothing like this had ever happened to me. I did everything right—graduated on the dean's list from high school, magna cum laude from college, got my master's. This had to be some cruel trick. At the B-and-B I came to terms with it, I think. I'll be honest. I did view it as a betrayal by my body, and because my life wouldn't be the same, I had to rethink priorities. How could I go back to working those long hours for a billion-dollar industry that couldn't care less about me? If I never came back, it would be an inconvenience, but the impact wouldn't even cause a ripple. And all the things that I wanted to do that I'd put off because I didn't have the time or it wasn't a priority, suddenly became urgent reminders of what I may never be able to do. By the time I left that B-and-B, I wanted to be able to recreate a similar place where people could celebrate, reminiscence, or contemplate life and its gifts. It also provided a lifestyle that was much slower, allowing me to stop and smell the roses." Nicole offered her glass to Shirley for a refill. She'd confessed and the floor hadn't opened up to swallow her.

After a second of silence while each person contemplated what had been said, Donna cleared her throat. "What did the doctor eventually say?"

"It was benign." Nicole noted how the tenseness left their faces. They accepted her as a strong woman.

Shirley hooted and clapped.

"Things worked out for me, but I couldn't forget how low I'd felt. I decided to go ahead with my plan."

The clock's loud tick punctuated the pregnant pause.

"But this isn't you, Nicole. I think I get what you're trying to do, but running a B-and-B isn't you." Toni looked around her.

"She's right." Shirley nodded.

"Don't get us wrong, it's just that you were good at what you did. You were a natural. How many twenty-nine-year-olds could say that they were a vice president of a lobbying firm pulling in a six-digit salary? You traveled. You've met U.S. presidents who knew your name without having someone whisper it ahead of time in their ears. Hell, you went to school for this . . . and all that money. Now, you're finding yourself?" Toni rolled her eyes dramatically. "You're right here." Toni pointed at Nicole.

Nicole studied each face. Donna with her heart-shaped face and full features. Her big, brown eyes reflecting confusion. Shirley, slightly overweight, sat back in the sofa looking concerned, but quiet. Finally, Toni stood across from her with lips pursed, waiting for further explanation.

Nicole smiled sadly at them. "I'm not asking for understanding. I'm just explaining."

"Okay, I can buy that. I'll need to sleep on this," Donna said.

"Otherwise, how are you doing? No more health problems?" Shirley asked.

"No. I've been given a clean bill of health."

"I'm not going to tiptoe around your feelings. You can go and soul-search all you want, but don't ever keep something like that from me or us again," Toni threatened.

"Through thick or thin." Nicole said the familiar pledge and held her hand out. *Tell them the truth.* Quite easily she could relive how ill she had felt after chemo, the weight loss, the nightmare of losing her hair. But, she couldn't tell them for some inexplicable reason. Maybe some day.

She took a deep breath and shook off the past. Her friends

expected her to be their rock and she wasn't about to disappoint them.

Each woman put her hand on top of the last hand. "Through thick or thin," they shouted unanimously.

Shirley looked up at the clock. "Oh, my gosh, we're about to miss the countdown. Think about your resolutions, everyone," she said.

"Eight—seven—six—five—four—three—two—one."

"Happy New Year!"

They hugged and kissed each other, sipping the remainder of the wine. "Another year. *Whoo-hoo,*" Donna chortled, her voice slurring under the influence.

"Another log, Toni." Shirley poked at the fire.

"Sure, call me Cinderella. So, anyone sharing their resolutions?" Toni asked.

"Mine hasn't changed. Losing weight." Shirley patted her ample rear and slid her hands down her thighs, wincing from the experience.

"That's about three years in a row for that one," Toni teased.

Donna shook her head, opting to remain quiet about her resolution.

All eyes turned to Nicole.

Nicole openly laughed at her friends' expectant faces. "You all look like kids waiting for gifts. Why is my resolution so important?"

"Out of all of us," Donna started, "you've had a major year of adversity. I figure you've got to have a juicy resolution. Is it an exotic island to visit? Are you going to enjoy a daredevil stunt?"

Nicole shrugged. "Nothing quite like that."

"Knowing you, though, you'd want to go climb a mountain." Shirley laughed. "Well, I don't do mountains."

"Nope." Nicole looked down at her hands. "Well, it's just that . . ." She paused to take a deep breath. "I want . . . a . . . special someone."

"A man?" Toni choked.

Nicole narrowed her gaze toward Toni. "A man. A husband. A family." She dared any of them to laugh at her.

"Wow. You've blown me away on that one. All those blind dates I've tried to hook up with you. All those men whom you chewed and spat out. I can't friggin' believe it." Toni plopped ungracefully into a nearby chair and put her head on Donna's shoulder.

"Have anyone in mind?" Shirley asked.

"Oh, shut up, Toni." Donna pushed her cousin's head off her shoulder.

"What about him?" Shirley motioned with her head.

Nicole looked over in the direction and saw the same newspapers she was looking at earlier.

Warming to this new subject of discussion, Shirley leaned forward. "Did you see this? I remember you talking about him and I saw the article. What about him? He's a professional, he's cute, and should be financially independent."

"I don't think so," Nicole said slowly.

"Why not? Don't tell me you want some lame man that you've got to take care of to make you feel whole," Toni quipped.

"Of course not. It just won't be him—Brad Calverton."

"I guess you're right. It wouldn't work." Shirley folded her arms.

"And why not?" Nicole shot back. She wasn't sure why her friend's acknowledgment plucked a nerve.

Shirley shrugged. She read a portion of the article, her lips moving silently. Then she folded it. "I can't see the two of you on the same beat. But what do I know? Haven't even met him."

Nicole didn't respond. She'd met him. He was quite lovely, but she'd blown any possibility of meeting him again, for business or pleasure.

"I think Nicole, here, has gone soft on us. She's allowed a

lump to take hold of her guts and make it into mush. Our girl is abdicating the throne of Queen Bee," Toni mocked.

"Not so fast. What exactly are you trying to say?" Nicole said through gritted teeth.

"That you don't have the guts to get a man, your man, this year," Toni challenged. "Starting with the cutie reviewer."

"What if he's a sadistic SOB?" Nicole complained.

"Then I will revoke my dare," Toni said.

"And what will you do if I win the dare?"

"Don't worry about what I will do. I don't plan to lose."

"Actually I missed exactly what the dare was." Nicole frowned.

"A simple one: I dare you to kick the old Nicole back into gear and put this Pollyanna babe to rest. Go get your reviewer to come in here and give you another review, and if the mood moves you, then you can turn on the charm."

"That's ridiculous and a bit coldhearted," Nicole retorted.

"I agree. The poor man wouldn't know what hit him if Nicole set her sights on him." Donna clapped enthusiastically with a big grin on her face.

Maybe it was the wine, maybe it was having spent Christmas alone, or maybe it was her three girlfriends conspiring about her, but Nicole took a definitive step.

She stood and nodded, patting her chest. "I, Nicole Montgomery, will have the great reviewer, Brad Calverton, back at my B-and-B for a fantastic review."

"And . . ." Toni motioned for her to continue.

"And, nothing. I would rather go out and select my own mate, thank you very much, than have the lot of you choosing anyone for me." Nicole drew the line. Getting rejected for the review would be a terrible setback. Getting rejected as a woman would be humiliating.

"Wimp!" Toni accused.

Four

Brad sat on the deck, with his back toward the pool and the crystaline ocean in front of him. A bowl of cut papaya chunks was placed within easy reach as he jotted down a few more notes. He'd visited Pearl Harbor and the USS *Missouri* memorial offering a silent prayer to all those who lost their lives during that horrific period. Today he looked forward to spending a lazy day, soaking up the tropical air, and filling his appetite with fresh fruit. Tonight promised to be a bit more stressful, since he was flying out on the last plane, which was due to arrive in Baltimore at around seven o'clock in the morning.

"Mr. Calverton, there you are." Mrs. Ikeda approached, dressed in a flowing, bright yellow pant suit. Brad admired how neat she looked, even her hair shaped her head like a helmet, every strand in place. "Off to do my Tai Chi. Join me, won't you?"

He shielded his eyes as he looked up at her. "Thanks for the offer, but I'm not cut out for Tai Chi." He'd never tried Tai Chi and didn't care for the mental picture of him towering behind the petite Mrs. Ikeda performing curious poses in slow motion.

"Oh, everyone is cut out for Tai Chi." She tilted her head to one side and stared at him, causing him to squirm. "You need it. You need to get the energy flowing through you, especially since you write." She folded her arms. "You're all wound up, Mr. Calverton. I can see it in your eyes, your movements, and

I bet even your emotions are wound up." She touched him softly on the shoulder. "Well, if you change your mind, you know where I am." She hesitated for a few seconds and when he didn't move, she offered a small smile and left.

"Damn. The woman reads me like an open book." He rubbed his hands over his face, as if to rid any outward evidence.

He turned his attention back to his notes. He managed to write a few sentences, but then the rest of the page remained empty. In the margin was a sole word—*Nicole*. Now where the heck did that come from?

He snapped the journal shut. It had been a good move on his part to shorten his stay at the B&B. Getting attracted to another woman so soon after a nasty breakup was asking for trouble. Nicole, with her saucy eyes and her pert mouth, could be bad for him. She had too much class to be treated as a temporary girlfriend while he got over the hurt.

Five minutes later he gave in to the unusual impulse to put aside his inhibitions and accept Mrs. Ikeda's invitation. He had too much on his mind. Nicole and her smiling face conflicted with his vow to remain unattached and uninvolved; the excitement of finding the perfect property for a retreat for boys at risk; and his pending deadlines for a cable show and his syndicated review columns left him quite exhausted.

So what if he knew nothing about Tai Chi? For the next hour, he could immerse himself in an activity that held no expectations for him. Dressed in shorts, a T-shirt, and tennis shoes, he headed toward the white sandy beach. The private strip led to a distinct path between the lush green carpet of foliage, intermingled with brightly colored flowers and the soft lapping of the azure waters. He must take another dip in the ocean before returning to the frigid temperatures of the East.

Mrs. Ikeda had already begun her routine and offered him a warm smile. Like a graceful bird, she lightly glided into each movement, shaping her arms and hands into various positions. An aura of peace surrounded her and he couldn't help envying that state of being one with mind, body, and spirit.

He'd enjoy it with the backdrop of a paradise, but there was no guarantee that once he returned to his hectic life, he'd have time to scratch his head, much less spend an hour or so performing ancient Eastern arts.

Once he overcame the initial embarrassment of feeling like a geek, he allowed himself to relax and pay attention. Behind Mrs. Ikeda, he, in turn, eased into each position and slowly mimicked her motions leading into the next position. He couldn't tell whether it was his tropical surroundings, the ancient Eastern art, or his present reflective attitude that caused him gradually to overcome the holiday blues.

"Mr. Calverton, I'm glad you joined me. If you have a moment, let's walk along the beach, as sort of a cooldown."

Brad nodded. He wasn't in a major hurry to do anything.

"Here, I usually carry some fruit for my walk." She offered him a mango. "Squeeze it with your hand, like this." He copied her technique, massaging the ripe fruit.

"Okay, now bite the tip off." She spat the small piece of skin aside and then sucked the thick juice directly from the fruit.

"Delicious," he remarked, after wiping some juice off his chin.

"Have you enjoyed your stay?"

"Yes, I have. One day I must return."

"I agree, but I hope that you will return with a special someone. But you look like a solitary soul so this may be a difficult mission for you."

"Being single isn't a bad thing."

"No, it's not." She peeled the skin off the side of the mango.

Brad copied her removal of the mango skin and bit into the fleshy texture, marveling at its sweetness.

"I don't believe that you are alone because you want to be alone. What has caused you so much pain?" She stopped unexpectedly and he had walked a few more steps before realizing that she was not beside him. "Forgive my inquisitive nature. My husband would be horrified at my boldness, but I tend to follow the emotions or words that constantly fight to get out. At the moment, I'm quite consumed by the mysterious air that surrounds such a celebrity."

Brad laughed. "I'm hardly a celebrity. I do, however, like my privacy." He allowed his unspoken request to linger.

"As well you should." Mrs. Ikeda offered a slight bow.

"I guess it's time for us to head back." Brad looked at his watch.

Mrs. Ikeda nodded and turned to head back to the B&B. "I hope Hawaii will be a second home for you—a place for you to reconnect with yourself."

Brad didn't answer. He couldn't. There was nothing to say without revealing too much of himself. No one since his grandmother was unable to unlock his heart for examination. The social workers had tried, the few foster parents he encountered had tried, even his ex-girlfriend had tried in her immature sort of way with ultimatums. He'd mastered the art of concealment and although Mrs. Ikeda gave it a good shot, he planned to leave Hawaii intact, just the way he'd arrived.

Thankfully, she didn't push as they walked along the beach. The sounds of the incoming tide and their footsteps crunching on the sandy beach made his mind drift. He inhaled deeply, trying to record the heady scents of the flowers and the freshness of the rain forest. Too bad all this couldn't be bottled up to rid himself of dark memories. He grew tired of reliving the time after his grandmother's death, when social services came to take him away to a foster home. In between his stay with various foster families, he lived at the home for boys where he'd contemplated running away and, at his darkest hours, even entertained thoughts of suicide.

Despite the heavy baggage, he managed to make something of himself. Never looking back, he shook off his past like a ragged coat. Lately, though, memories nudged at him and he didn't like it one bit. The flashbacks made him think about his grandmother and the promise that she'd extracted from him. She had gripped his small hand in her bony one, making his bones crack. She'd commanded that no matter what, he must keep in touch with their neighbors, the Williamses. The family had taken him that night and tried their best to make him feel comfortable. When the social worker came to pick him up two days later, he'd lashed out in blind fury at all of them, including the Williamses, feeling that they had betrayed him. He hung his head in shame at not ever telling them thank you.

"Thank you, Mr. Calverton."

"Excuse me?" Brad shook off the doldrums.

"I'm glad you took me up on my offer."

"I surprised myself."

"That's good. We all need to realize that we have so much more potential than what we normally see in our everyday lives. And you, Mr. Calverton, have so much creative energy that still remains to be unleashed." She stepped toward him and touched his chest where his heart beat. "Don't be afraid or you'll miss life's priceless gifts."

Brad clenched his jaw to keep from crumbling under his hostess's kindness. Little did she know that she had cracked open a hidden, inner sanctum that demanded his attention. If nothing else came of this trip, there was one thing he had to do. Regardless of the pain and anger, he had to visit the Williamses. He had to return to his neighborhood and the past.

When his plane landed, Brad said a quick prayer of thanks. His body felt tight and he couldn't wait to get out of the plane and its claustrophobic nature. Zombielike, he retrieved his luggage and headed toward the exit to hail a taxi.

"Hey, big boy."

Brad turned toward the familiar voice. "Audra?"

"Don't look so confused. I'm surprising you!" She tiptoed and kissed his lips.

Brad took a step back, his brain screaming *Whoa*. "You've definitely surprised me. What's up?"

"Figured that we could chat about our new venture." She linked her arm through his and pressed her breast against his arm. "And, you are welcome to stay at my place."

Brad looked into Audra's eyes and saw the blaring, intense desire. He guessed that he should feel flattered, but instead, felt nothing. He pulled his arm free. "I'll take you up on the ride, but I'm really tired and look forward to being alone." He didn't mean for his tone to sound so flat, but he couldn't conjure any emotion on her behalf. Frankly, there was a harsh edge to her that he didn't much care for, but given her gritty background, he understood it.

"Fine." The teasing smile disappeared. Her eyes glittered angrily like dark gems. "I'm parked in the short-term area."

Brad spotted the signs of Audra's anger as she led the way to the car. She stomped a few steps ahead, with no attempt to make conversation. He sighed, but didn't regret his action; although he did fear that he'd have to pay for rejecting her.

After Audra paid the parking attendant, she shot him a glance. "Nicole Montgomery will be at the reception tomorrow night."

"Okay."

"I think you should bring up the subject of her selling the property."

"During the reception? I figured that I should broach the subject on her turf, especially after I've gotten confirmation about the financial backing."

"Don't wimp out on me, Brad." Audra glared at him before returning her attention to the road. "I want this deal settled and over with, as quickly as possible. The financial backers will be at the reception, also."

"What's the hurry?" Brad's temper was on a slow burn. He didn't like being pushed around and he sensed that Audra had some other deal percolating under the surface.

"No hurry. I'm just looking out for your best interests before that woman lets the place fall into a dump. Then it wouldn't be worth anything."

"Aren't you exaggerating?"

Audra pulled into the circular driveway in front of his hotel. She stamped on the brake, causing the tires to squeal. "I'm doing you a favor. Remember that."

Brad stared in front of him to remain in control. His temper burned. "Why am I having trouble believing that you are doing this for my benefit? I'll see you tomorrow evening. Let's not make it any sooner."

Along with tired muscles and an ill temper, Brad's head pounded as he walked toward his hotel room. He ordered room service, impatiently awaiting the fresh, brewed coffee. In the meantime, he stripped off his clothes and headed into the shower. Maybe the water would soothe his anger.

Nicole rolled out of bed, feeling very optimistic. Toni's taunt about bringing out her old self got her motivated. After a quick shower and a bowl of oatmeal, she got on the Internet to find information on Brad Calverton. An hour later, she had his contact information. She didn't expect to be able to speak to him directly, but whatever information she could glean would be some progress.

She dialed the number and paced while the phone rang. A young woman answered. Nicole hadn't prepared anything specific, but it was too late. "Hi there, I'm Nicole Montgomery. May I speak with Mr. Calverton?"

"He's unavailable. This is his personal secretary, Freddie Tuner. How may I help you?"

"Well, Mr. Calverton had recently stayed at my B-and-B and I wanted to discuss a business matter with him."

"Oh, I remember now. Actually, he's in your neck of the woods. He talked quite favorably about you. He's at the Blackburn Hotel Suites in Annapolis. I know that he'd love to hear from you."

Nicole hung up, pleased with herself. Not only did she find out that Brad was in the area, but she'd gotten his hotel information. Plus, she couldn't hide the flip-flop she experienced when she heard that he'd talked favorably about her.

Dressed in a dark red pant suit with a crisp white shirt, Nicole left her B&B and headed for Annapolis. She'd have to rely on her skills as a lobbyist to accomplish what she had in mind. In the hotel's parking lot, she added another touch of lipstick and smoothed down her eyebrows. She walked purposefully into the lobby, noting the upscale quality of the furniture and décor. As the elevator doors closed, she allowed herself to lean against the chrome wall. Her heart kept a frenetic pace and she held her stomach to try and regulate her breathing. What the heck was she planning to do, anyway? The chime of the doors opening on her floor brought her back to attention. She turned down the hallway, following the sign on the wall. Her steps slowed as she approached the beige-colored door. The doubts built up, pushing forward into her consciousness.

Nicole closed her eyes and knocked on the door.

"One sec."

She plastered a smile on her face, in case he peered through the peephole. With one hand on her stomach to calm the quivering, she bit her lip in anticipation.

The door opened. "Miss Montgomery, come on in."

"I apologize for showing up at such an early hour."

"It's okay. I was expecting you."

Nicole looked shocked.

"Freddie."

Nicole nodded, feeling stupid. Of course, his secretary would tell him that she'd called.

"So what can I do for you, Miss Montgomery?"

Nicole saw and felt the assessing rove of Brad's eyes. She'd braved more intense situations than this dealing with politicians and CEOs. The important thing was to hide any signs of weakness. "I'm here to discuss a matter that has me concerned."

His eyebrow shot up, but he didn't respond.

"The other day when you arrived. I didn't realize you were a reviewer. When I later found out, I was . . . um, a bit surprised." She let out a dry laugh.

Brad didn't smile back, but merely stood with his hands stuffed into his pockets. "Would you like some coffee? Please have a seat."

Nicole wondered if he'd listened to what she'd just said. But she nodded for the cup of coffee, anything to buy her some more time. As she accepted the cup, his fingers brushed her hand and her eyes shot up to his to see if he noticed the electric tingle that sped through her.

The phone rang and they both turned toward the noisy machine.

The minute he answered, he turned his back toward her and dropped his voice to a harsh whisper. She couldn't help listening, since the room was only so big. Whoever was on the other end had to know that they had made him furious. The continuous replies of "No" got harsher every time. "Shaunice, it's over." He slammed down the phone and turned to her.

"Sorry about that. Now what can I do for you, Miss Montgomery?"

Nicole noted the scowl, the thin line of his pinched lips, and eyes that bored through her. She took a deep breath and went for it. "I want a second chance. I know that your first visit to my B-and-B wasn't the best experience. But my business is still new and one of your bad reviews could bury me." She took a pause to see how her confession was being taken. Although his eyes still carried an angry frown with eyebrows drawn down, his shoulders visibly relaxed. "Would you come back to my B-and-B?"

"No." The phone rang and he turned toward it, but made no move to answer.

"I can't take no for an answer." Nicole walked toward Brad.

She waited for him to take his attention from the phone and refocus on her.

"You don't have a choice. I'm incredibly busy."

"So you're just going to bury me without a second thought? Must be nice sitting in your ivory tower, casting judgment on others." She let the sarcasm drip from her voice.

"Why did you come to my B-and-B in the first place? Twelve months in the business and you decide to make me an example, right?" She jabbed at his chest with her finger, too furious to care. "Well, let me tell you something, I'm not going to be intimidated by you or what you think you can do with one of your stupid reviews. You haven't seen anything yet, Mr. Brad Calverton."

He grabbed her hand and pulled her against his lean frame. "I hope not." With the other hand, he smoothed her hair from her face. "You're a spitfire, aren't you? Even dressed appropriately in that shade of red." He stopped talking and merely looked at her. As the seconds ticked by, his frown lifted and his expression softened.

Nicole's rage suddenly wavered and dissipated under the spell. The man must have magical powers, because her knees threatened to buckle at any moment. Up close, she admired his eyes, dark and intense, framed with thick eyebrows. Her gaze flicked over his nose and moved downward to his lips and chin. Then back to his lips. Her breathing came short and she blinked, hoping to break the spell. When she opened her eyes again, she could swear that his face was a hairsbreadth closer. Her lips parted to make a comeback, but Brad spoke again first.

"I didn't refuse your offer out of need for a power trip, Miss Montgomery. It's just not in my schedule. Let me put your mind at ease. I had no intention of reviewing your precious B-and-B. I showed up on your doorstep out of personal motivation; actually it was Freddie's and another . . . er, friend's."

Nicole pushed away from Brad, mainly to get the smell of

his delicious cologne out of her nose. "You don't have to make it seem like it's beneath you to review my property."

"Don't get yourself into another snit. I've had a long morning. I'm tired and irritable. This was not the best time to approach me, even in your kick-ass red suit." He rubbed his hand through his hair and a yawn erupted. "I flew back on a red-eye from Hawaii and I've got some business to take care of, so if you don't mind . . ." He leaned over, held her arm, and kissed her on her cheek. "It's been a pleasure, Miss Montgomery," he whispered in her ear and then placed another delicate kiss on her cheek.

He propelled her toward the door and if Nicole wasn't sure that she would look ridiculous, she would have hung on to a piece of furniture and demanded that she be allowed to stay for a few more minutes. Instead, she pulled away her arm and straightened her outfit before reaching for the doorknob. "Good-bye, Mr. Calverton."

Back in the elevator, she allowed herself to think about the kisses on her cheek. She'd wanted to turn her face, so that one would fall on her lips. What a hoochie she would have been. It had been too long since she had a relationship, and obviously her body craved the physical pleasure that wasn't close to being fulfilled. And no reprieve appeared to be in sight.

Audra sat in her car across from the hotel's entrance. She'd gotten halfway home before she'd talked herself into not giving up so easily. When she returned, she'd lucked out with a prime parking spot and backed her small car into the spot. Her intentions weren't clear even to her, but she wasn't done with Brad, as yet. Some men didn't know what they wanted, until a strong woman showed them what they could have.

"My, my, what do we have here?" Her hands gripped her steering wheel, as a slow burn of jealousy washed over her. It was obvious that it wasn't a coincidence that Nicole showed up at the same hotel that Brad was in. She opted not to have a showdown with Nicole. The right time would present itself. As Nicole got in her car and drove past, Audra reluctantly thought about how attractive Nicole looked. She wished she knew how long she had been in the hotel, because she'd have a better sense of what could have happened—or not happened—between Brad and Nicole.

"Damn it." Audra slammed her door shut and headed into the hotel. Brad hadn't given her his room number, but he had certain routines and she knew enough of them to make him predictable. Taking a guess, she walked up to a door and knocked.

"Look, Nicole—Audra? What do you want?"

"Sorry, it's just little ol' me. May I come in for a sec?"

"Sure, must be in my stars to be harassed this morning."

"Then, I won't waste your time by getting straight to the point." Audra sashayed past him and sat on the king-size bed, crossing her legs provocatively. In a brazen move, she pulled her skirt up a little, showing the length of her thigh. "I want to know if you're interested in having a hot and very physical relationship with me."

Brad didn't move toward the spot she patted with her hands. "Audra, you're an attractive woman. But, we have too much in common with the past for us to have any future. We're both trying to get some distance from it all."

"I don't want your baby, Brad, just your body," she stated in a deep husky tone.

"Thanks for the compliment—I think—but it might be overrated."

"Not from where I stand. Try it, you might like it."

"Sampling isn't my style. I like to window-shop before making the purchase."

Audra sighed and bit back the bitter taste of disappointment. It was laced with anger, but being angry didn't work well with Brad. "Don't aim too high, Brad. You might get disappointed when the sting of rejection bites you. I don't have lofty expectations. What you see is what you get." She pulled the skirt toward her knees and uncrossed her legs.

Brad shook his head. "Thanks, but no thanks." He glanced at his watch, his expression shuttered.

She knew immediately that she'd lost him. The direct approach hadn't worked. She picked up her pocketbook and walked to the door with her head high. "If you change your mind, you know where I am."

Brad didn't respond, his face carefully blank.

Once his door clicked shut, Brad let out a sigh of relief. First his ex-girlfriend had called him, begging for a second chance. He couldn't really get into it with Nicole paying him a surprise visit. But it wasn't so difficult in telling his ex that he wasn't interested.

Then Nicole's surprise request blew him away. All this time she'd thought he was reviewing her. He didn't mean to sound so cold about reviewing her or not, but Shaunice had really stirred up his feelings. When he'd bent to kiss Nicole on the cheek, he inhaled the soft scent of her body, wondering what she would've done if he'd crushed her body in a tight embrace and kissed the hell out of her.

He'd have loved to explore the possibility in his mind, but then Audra showed up at his door. She was like a sister to him, a wayward one, but nevertheless, he couldn't ever contemplate anything but friendship, or something close to it, with her. With their backgrounds intertwined with pain and few joyous occasions, he conceded that she spoke the truth. He was trying to run from his past. But just because she spoke the truth didn't mean that it would change anything.

Five

Nicole had just finished cleaning up the suite when the new arrivals knocked on her door. She ran down the stairs and opened the door, ready to welcome her guests. A family of four stood in her doorway.

"Welcome. Come on in."

In a matter of minutes, she'd checked them in and showed them to their rooms, the parents in one and the teenage girls in the smallest room. She chuckled after overhearing the girls argue about what side of the room they wanted. Thank goodness her apartment was on the first floor on the other side of the house.

She was expecting one more reservation. If she was lucky, she could finish hanging the new lace curtains that she'd bought for the fourth bedroom before they showed up. But no sooner had she gathered up the older curtains than she heard a knock on the door. "It's show time," she muttered.

Two women stood at her door. They looked like they had been hiking or, at the very least, on a walking tour. Clad in worn jeans and boots, they had a bag pack stuffed and bulging.

"Do you have any rooms available?"

"Sure—only one, though." Nicole stepped back to let them enter. The woman with long locks smiled and entered first, surveying the surroundings. The other one, who looked younger, had her hair pulled back in a ponytail. She walked with a slight limp.

The woman with the locks extended her hand. "Sandy Johnson. This is my cousin Tia Johnson."

"Nicole Montgomery." She handled the paperwork and then gave them two keys for their room.

"I can't wait to take a shower," Tia exclaimed. "Sandy had me hiking through some swampy area. Almost broke my damn ankle following her nimble butt over a stream with all these rocks."

"Can you handle the stairs?" Nicole asked.

"Pay her no mind," said Sandy. "If we could get some ice in a little plastic bag, we'll do just fine. This is the last time I take you anywhere."

"Promise?" Tia shot back.

Nicole slowed her pace so Tia could take her time maneuvering up the stairs. She felt bad that their room was at the end of the hallway, but it was the only one left.

An hour later, her other reservation showed up in the form of a young couple who had eloped. They came into the house giggling in each other's arms. Nicole smiled indulgently, marveling at anyone being giddy over someone else. In between the kisses and the "I love yous," she processed their deposit and showed them to their room.

This is what she liked about having a B&B. One day, she might not have any guests and then in another second, she had a full house. She'd better see about lunch because the city council reception was later in the afternoon. She'd come to appreciate Audra's invitation and had to make sure that she was prepared.

After the lunch had been served, she was wiped out. The family of four had left to go to the Baltimore Harbor, letting her know that they wouldn't be back for dinner. Meanwhile the two ladies had settled in the den with a couple of books and a bowl of chips. They said that they would probably head into town to eat at one of the country-style restaurants, and the honeymooners had headed into town for a candlelight supper. Nicole was grateful that she didn't have to prepare anything.

Standing in front of her closet, she wondered what on earth to wear to the reception.

"Try the navy blue skirt set."

Nicole whirled around, yelping in the process. "Toni, damn it! Can't you knock?"

"I did, but you were too wrapped up with your clothes. What's going on?"

"I'm trying to figure out what to wear for the reception. I don't want to stick out with an outfit that's over the top, but I don't want to underdress either."

"Who's at this reception?"

"Local politicians, businessmen. Audra." She rolled her eyes.

"Yuck. In that case, you have to look like a knockout. I change my mind. Skip the blue skirt suit and wear the olive-green pant suit with the honey-colored silk blouse." Toni pushed the clothes aside and looked down at the rows of shoes.

"I'll wear these." Nicole held up a pair of taupe pumps with a three-inch heel.

"Perfect." Toni walked up behind Nicole and played with her hair. "How are you styling this?"

"I'll curl the front and have it come down my forehead and gel the sides back."

"I approve. I want to do the makeup, though."

Nicole frowned. "I'm not sure. I'm not trying to look like a bimbo."

"Trust me."

Nicole snorted. She flopped down on her bed and leaned back against the headboard. "What brings you over? Aren't you working today?"

"I attended a training seminar. It was over early. Besides, I wanted to see if you made any headway with the dare."

"No. I tried, but he rejected my request for a second visit."

"Hmm. Must be in the way you asked him. Let me think on it."

"Let it go, Toni. He's not planning to review my lowly B-and-B."

"Okay, but what about getting with him on a personal basis?"

"I don't think so." Nicole glared, indignant, at Toni. She would not humiliate herself further dealing with Brad Calverton.

"I thought you wanted a family and all that stuff." Toni waved her hand in the air.

"I do, but what makes you think that Calverton is the only one to make this happen for me? You think either too much of him or too little of me."

Toni slid off the bed and walked over to the vanity where she'd set down her pocketbook. She retrieved a folded paper and returned to her perch on the bed. "Here, look at this. It's an article about your guy. The photo does him justice. He's a cutie. I can see why you get tongue-tied around him."

Nicole grabbed the paper from her friend's outstretched hand. She glanced over the article. "This is from a gossip magazine."

"So?"

"They lie."

"Maybe, but there's a kernel of truth in them. Just read the thing."

Nicole read the article, wondering how much was true. It discussed how Brad had been dumped by a supermodel. The woman's photo was grainy, but Nicole could see that she was a beauty with a long slender body and clothing that highlighted her narrow hips and voluptuous chest. The article went on to discuss Brad's rise to fame and the lack of information about his past. She turned her attention to his photo, which was remarkably clearer, but portrayed him as a furious man, yelling at the photographer. The date of the supposed breakup coincided with his visit to her B&B.

His admission that Freddie had made the arrangements suddenly made sense. No wonder he'd been in a bad mood.

Then she'd accused him of using his power to crush her. She closed her eyes, wishing she could apologize.

"Hey, are you sad for him and the doll baby?"

"It's not that. I just never thought about him other than being a reviewer. I went over to his hotel today and yelled at him." She covered her face in her hands.

"He's in town? And you went to him? My, my." Toni grinned, drumming her fingers against her cheek.

"He probably already left." Nicole refolded the paper and handed it back to Toni.

"You keep it. Maybe your reviewer will come back into your life."

Nicole silently hoped for that to happen.

Audra walked down the hall in the Golden Oaks Home. Her heels clicked against the linoleum floor, and she only nodded at the nursing home staff, not trusting her voice to utter a greeting.

"Hi, Daddy, it's Audra."

Her father turned to look at her with his familiar distant gaze. His dementia had gotten worse and the intermittent flashes where he remembered her had grown scarce. She wondered where he was today, what memory he was locked in.

"I'll sit here, Daddy, and we'll have a chat. I've got a great deal pending, if everything goes right."

"These days are hot. Gotta find work. My babies are so doggone hungry. Guess I'll take that job cleaning out the pig-pen."

"Shh, Daddy." Audra cringed. Her father had brought up those days when she, her brother, and her sister sat in the small run-down shack they called home, hungry and waiting for their father to return home. Many days, she'd have to duck the officials who were sent by the school. When her father didn't come home, she took on the responsibility of seeing that her brother and sister made it to school on time and in clean clothes. She remembered advising them to make sure they ate all their lunch and if possible to pack a few items in their clothing for later. She tilted her head back in effort to stem the flow of tears that stung her eyes.

"Don't cry for me, honey. Hell, nobody cries for me. I do all the cryin' because I'm mother and father of them kids. They are the only things keepin' me goin'." Her father smiled at her, his eyes glittering with unshed tears. He took her hand and kissed it. "Audra, you make me proud."

Audra gasped and jumped from her chair to the edge of his bed. "Daddy?" She begged for another sign that he knew that she was there.

"We gotta go to church on Sunday. The pastor will have my hide if I don't take them kids to church. Besides, if I take them, he'll give me food for a couple of days. And Joi needs a new dress, that girl just keep on growin'."

Audra swallowed her disappointment and resumed her seat. She gave her father's chatter half an ear. She hadn't talked to Joi in a while and Greg was in the military, stationed somewhere far away. Eventually they had all ended up in foster homes. Joi and Greg managed to stay together, but she had to fend for herself. They had struggled as a family, and now led very separate lives. She sighed. No need to dwell on it. The present was what mattered and she was on the verge of becoming a very wealthy woman. Audra stood and kissed her father on his head. She'd make her visit in another two weeks, just enough time to get the smell of the disinfectant out of her mind. She walked out the doors and inhaled deeply, then got into her BMW Z3 and sped off without a backward glance.

By the time Nicole arrived at the County Ballroom, the reception was in full swing. A spiffily dressed band played big band music, cash bars were set up on opposite sides of the room, and in between were extravagant displays of various meats, cheeses, fruit, and bite-sized pastries.

Raising a nervous hand to her hair, Nicole fidgeted, wishing that she was home trying her hand at crocheting. The olive-green pant suit hit the mark and she could relax at the thought that she fit in with the average clothing style in the room.

A waiter walked by with glasses of white wine. It was her favorite, and maybe it would take the edge of her nerves. Her watch showed that she had only five minutes left before the program began and various awards and speeches would be made.

"Ah, Nicole, good to see you."

Nicole turned toward the saccharine-sweet voice. "Hi, Audra." She couldn't think of anything else to add to her greeting.

Audra leaned forward and air-kissed her cheek. "Sorry I've been too busy to stop by and visit lately. How are things going?"

"Fine. I've been busy, too." She gripped her glass of wine close, hoping that Audra wouldn't surprise her with another display of affection.

"Really? I would think that you wouldn't get many visitors this time of the year."

"Hadn't really noticed with the families that have come and gone in the past few weeks. As a matter of fact, I have a full house now."

Audra cupped her elbow and pulled her toward the middle of the room. "I want you to meet a few businessmen."

"Uh . . . okay." Nicole couldn't pull her elbow back so she gave in to the pressure of meeting these mysterious businessmen.

"Todd Druthers, hello there. I'd like you to meet Nicole Montgomery, the woman that owns the little B-and-B in town."

"Nice to meet you, Miss Montgomery. I look forward to talking with you."

Nicole smiled. But inside she was terrified at what Audra was up to. From the looks of Druthers, he was all business, so it wasn't a matter of Audra hooking her up romantically.

"Nicole doesn't like to talk about her B-and-B that much. Can't say I blame her, though. Todd, are the others here?"

Todd scanned the room and nodded when he recognized someone across the room. "Yes, Bill and Gene are both here."

Audra leaned into Nicole. "I'll explain later. Just follow my lead," she whispered. Then she motioned to the other men to come. "I've reserved a private room for us. Please follow me."

Somehow the impending business meeting didn't make Nicole feel comfortable. Last in line, she followed and wondered what the whispering and sideways glances meant. Well, she'd find out soon enough, no doubt.

Audra led them into a room that was obviously a conference room with a flip chart and marker board. The chairs and table were arranged in a hollow square. Audra took the prominent spot, sitting at the front in the middle. Given her height and personality, she looked as if she was holding court. Nicole remained closest to the door, acknowledging the nibbling bites of panic.

"Audra, I'm not sure I know what this is all about. Why are we in a meeting?" Nicole gave a shaky smile to the men. She felt like a rabbit caught in the middle of a pack of wolves. The she-wolf had her hands clasped, propping her chin.

"My dear friend," Audra began.

The reference sounded so false that Nicole's eyebrow shot up.

"I am doing you a wonderful favor. Bill, Gene, and Todd have taken time out of their busy schedules to provide you with the opportunity of a lifetime."

"Who are these men?" Nicole didn't bother to soften the demand in her question.

"These men are trendsetters in their profession." Audra motioned with her hand in an expansive gesture.

"That's nice, but what does their trendsetting have to do

with me?" Nicole didn't ignore the alarms ringing in her head. Her hands shook slightly and she wished that she had never agreed to come to this reception.

"Please, Miss Montgomery, maybe I can explain," Todd offered. He nodded toward Audra, who took the hint and remained silent. "My partners and I are interested in purchasing your B-and-B."

"But it's not for sale," Nicole protested in a shrill voice.

"We know. But with the plans for redevelopment, we feel that we'll be offering you more than you would probably get otherwise."

Nicole looked at each face to see if this was some sort of cruel joke. All eyes were trained on her and she looked away first. There was no way this meeting could go on any further. She needed time to think, time to let it sink in. She could lose her B&B. She stood on legs that trembled slightly. "I didn't call this meeting, but I'm going to end it here. I'm not going to pretend. You've shocked me. However, it's too premature on your part to expect me to sign my business over to you. Good evening, Audra. Good evening, gentlemen." Nicole walked away from the table, ignoring Audra's call to her. She walked out of the room and headed toward the exit. She was in no mood for a reception.

More people had arrived since she'd been in the impromptu meeting. She squeezed through the pockets of people animatedly talking and drinking. Her aim was to get as far away from all of this as possible. She pushed through the revolving doors, welcoming the fresh air on her face as she stood on the bricked sidewalk.

"Miss Montgomery."

Nicole jumped and turned toward the familiar voice. "Mr. Calverton." She continued to walk toward the car park area. She didn't care if it appeared rude.

"Is everything okay? You look upset."

For goodness' sake, the man was following her to the car park. Nicole sped up her pace. She wanted to be alone and she wasn't sure how long she could maintain her composure and not follow the urge to have a tantrum.

He reached out and grabbed her by her arm. "What's the matter? It might help to tell a stranger. Well, I know that I'm not quite a stranger—"

"Please, Mr. Calverton. Yes, I'm upset, but I'm really not in the mood to be chatty. I have to leave and I'm already sounding rude." Nicole looked down at his arm and then up at his face, hoping he would get the hint.

He didn't loosen his grip, but scanned her face and then stared deeply into her eyes. "I've never been known to leave a damsel in distress." There was no trace of humor that she could detect.

Nicole wanted to rail at him and pour out the anger that burned in her chest. Yet there still existed some pride about her rejected plea earlier. Although his eyes held such kindness that had the power to draw her in and the heat of his touch made her wish for things that she had no business craving, she mentally shoved that far away. She pulled her arm from him. "There's only one problem with your announcement," she said matter-of-factly. "I'm not in distress."

"You're being stubborn. My perceptions are never wrong."

Without warning, he touched her forehead and rubbed his thumb against her skin, a feathery movement. "Let's see if I can at least wipe away that ferocious scowl."

Well, that did it. Nicole's breathing increased; she even felt light-headed. Such a physical reaction to a man who could easily ruin her business.

"There, that's better."

Of course her frown disappeared. Now she probably looked as if she were in a trance. She hung on to the thought about his review, to keep herself grounded. Determined, she walked toward her car without looking back.

"I'll be there for Valentine's weekend," he stated from where he stood.

Nicole stuck the key in the car door before turning to him. "Excuse me?" A glimmer of hope zipped through her.

"Next month, I'll come to give you that review."

Later, she would blame it on stress.

Nicole strutted over to where Brad stood. She pulled him down toward her. Still clutching his starched white shirt, she raised on tiptoe and planted a firm kiss on Brad's mouth.

The act didn't have any meaning, at first. Anger still sizzled through her petite frame, and she wanted to rip someone's head off because she had been blindsided. The intent was to lash out, scream, vent.

One look at Brad with his wonderfully sculpted lips, and instead she wanted to kiss him. Another shocker for the night was the faint tremor of delight shooting sparks throughout her body. Instead of a few seconds of brazen behavior, she lingered. Swooned was more like it.

His lips opened and she followed suit, giving him entry for the deliciously lazy swirl of his tongue. With a soft sigh, she sagged within his massive arms.

He pulled away first and the small space between them allowed the cold night air to quickly douse the flames of desire. "Should I take that as a yes that it's okay to come and review your B-and-B?"

Nicole didn't respond at first and turned to head over to her car. The truth was that she couldn't trust herself to talk at the moment. Her legs felt weak, her stomach did flip-flops, and she was very embarrassed.

She got in her car and started the engine. Only then did she look up . . . and she dissolved all over again at the sexy grin Brad threw her way. "You've got a deal, Mr. Calverton. I'll look forward to seeing you."

Her mind raced with this new turn of events. It might be a little too late, but if she was going to fight against any redevelopment plans, she might need all the ammunition she could get. A famous reviewer could do the trick.

She sped off without waiting for his reply, without

questioning why he'd changed his mind. She simply wanted
to go to her sanctuary, to her home, to her B&B.

She pulled into her driveway, surprised to see another car
in her spot. Maybe another guest had arrived; the white sedan
didn't look familiar. She walked into the living room, looking around for the new face. It was quiet on the first floor,
although she could hear the muffled voices of her guests upstairs. She headed into the kitchen, still looking for the car's
owner.

Noticing a light under her door, she surmised that the person was now in her apartment. She opened the door
expectantly.

"Hello, dear." Her mother got up from the couch in her
small living room and came toward her.

"Mom? What a surprise!"

"I'm here for a conference. I'm giving a lecture for the
Pharmaceutical Association. It's a three-day deal."

Nicole started to undress while her mother spoke. Her
body and mind screamed for comfort. "Well, it's nice to see
you."

"Hmmm."

"What does that mean?" Nicole poked her head outside her
bedroom.

Her mother walked back to her place on the couch and
picked up a porcelain knickknack from a small end table and
studied it. "'Nice to see you'? Yet you don't visit for the
Christmas holidays, nor for New Year's. All your father and I
get is a quick phone call or two, telling us that you are so incredibly swamped that you can't take time out to get on a
plane, fly for a few hours, and visit us in Florida." Her mother
set down the decorative piece.

"Mom, please don't make a big deal."

"Far be it from me to make a splash."

Nicole tied her robe tightly around her, partly for security.
Her mother sat primly on the edge of the couch, which was, like

all her other furniture, nondescript. Her decorating efforts went into the B&B, not her little home.

"I'm just curious why you've pulled yourself away from us. I worry about you."

Nicole understood that her mother worried. Her mother might as well have had a graduate degree in being organized and hated when Nicole and her father didn't follow her well-laid plans. "There's no need to worry, I'm fine."

"No, you're not." Her mother pulled out her compact and glanced in the mirror to adjust a few sections of her hairstyle. "I know something is a bit askew. I can feel it. When I talked to Toni, she confirmed it."

Nicole reacted sharply. "What did Toni say?"

"It doesn't matter what she said. I'm waiting to hear what the problem is from your own lips." She stood and walked into the kitchen. "Have a seat. I'll make us some tea and we can chat."

Nicole did as she was told, unsure of how much information Toni had shared.

Her mother busied herself, getting the cups and saucers, while the water boiled. She didn't look at Nicole, but concentrated on steeping the tea bag and adding sugar. A few minutes later, she brought the prepared tea and sat opposite her daughter.

Nicole surveyed her mother in her slate-gray suit, panty hose, and comfortable shoes. She was a picture of professional neatness. Ever since Nicole was old enough to be aware of it, she felt like a weak substitute next to her mother. Her accomplishments were nothing compared with the inroads her mother had made as top of her graduating class in pharmacology, as the first female African-American pharmacist for the Redding drugstore chain, and now as a sought-after guest lecturer. Walking in her footsteps kept Nicole tired and stressed.

"I know you have your own life out here, running your

business and all, but in the last year you've avoided coming home."

"I've just been busy. The bed-and-breakfast takes up a lot of my time. But I love keeping busy," she added.

"That part is definitely true, although I never understood the career switch."

"I guess you wouldn't understand because you discovered your passion early on and went after it."

Her mother laughed. Nicole liked seeing her mother laugh, it erased the hard edge that she always seem to have.

"Being a pharmacist isn't my passion, honey. Yes, I'm good at it, but it's not my passion."

Shocked at her mother's admission, Nicole got herself comfortable on the couch, tucking her feet under her. She sensed a night of discovery ahead of her.

"I'm a practical kinda gal. There were certain things I wanted in my life, a certain sense of financial security and lifestyle. I knew I was good in math and science, so I decided to go into medicine."

"What's your passion, then?"

"Dance. Ballet, to be exact." Her mother chuckled and lowered her head.

"I never knew. My gosh, why didn't you go after that dream?"

"Because the odds of my making a living from that were against me. I knew that I'd have to struggle for a long time. Plus, I was good, but not great."

"Do you ever wish you had at least tried?" Despite what her mother said, Nicole sensed that not pursuing dance had made a big impact on her mother.

"Not really. I don't let myself think about it, which is why I'm glad that you went for it and decided to try your hand at running a B-and-B."

"Really!" Nicole exclaimed, her face breaking into a wide grin. "I-I never thought you were happy about it. I thought you would see it as a senseless pursuit."

"Why? I've always supported everything you ever did."

"I know." Nicole squirmed as the truth eased its way out. "Maybe it's because I didn't tell you or Dad why I switched."

Her mother set down her teacup, her attention rapt.

"Something made me put it into action a bit faster than I'd planned."

"The lump that you thought you had?"

Nicole's mouth opened and closed with a gulp. "You knew? Wait—I know. Toni. Big mouth."

"Don't be angry. She's worried about you. I just wish you hadn't chosen to close the door on communicating with me. I used to pride myself in having an open dialogue with my daughter. Somehow I feel as if I failed you by not being there for you."

In the soft lighting, Nicole swore that she could see tears shimmering in her mother's eyes. Her mother who always stayed calm and cool in every emergency. Suddenly, she felt stupid for being so selfish. She leaned forward and hugged her mother tightly. "I'm so sorry, Mom. Too many things in my life weren't going right. I'm so used to succeeding and I know people expect me to be the best at everything. When I felt that lump, I got angry at my body and I couldn't handle it. Nothing or no one had ever failed me like my body did."

"But you're okay. It was all a false alarm."

Nicole pulled back from her mother. She picked at a few balls of lint on the cushion. "Not really." She held her breath and waited.

Her mother remained silent.

"It made me change my life. I couldn't tell Toni or any of the others. I didn't want their pity. I threw myself into all of this. I needed to prove to myself that I could take something from the ground up and make it into a great success. It might seem shallow, but I needed this, Mom."

"Oh, baby. My baby." Tears glistened on her mother's cheeks. "I'm so proud of you." She pulled Nicole into her arms and rocked her.

Nicole felt the emotion build and let the dam burst. Her tears flowed, releasing the guilt that had been trapped. "There's so much I want in my life now."

Her mother handed her a tissue. "I can imagine. But don't let work consume you or be that thing to hide behind and then forget the important things in life, like a family."

"I'm trying not to," Nicole replied.

"Honey, I'm serious about not turning your back on family or friends. I guess it's my turn to share. There's nothing I regret in my life, not your father or you. But I walked away from one relationship to go to another."

Nicole stopped in the middle of blowing her nose to stare at her mother.

"Yes, I was in love with someone else before your father."

"What happened?"

"Nothing dramatic like infidelity. He was a farmer's son with a family business to guarantee his future. He was enough for me until I went to spend the summer in New York with your aunt Tessa. That was a summer to remember." Her mother chuckled. "And, I have no intention of sharing those details with you, young lady." They shared a laugh.

Then her mother grew serious. "I came back home just before school started and didn't even bother to go see Jonathan, right away. The minute that he finally saw me, he sensed the change in me. I was more confident, dressed more hip, and couldn't care less about the county sale for his prized cows."

"So you broke it off."

"Yes. After I graduated that year, I headed back to New York where I'd already met your father. We had gone out on a few dates. That day, I walked right up to him and said, if you go to school and graduate, then we should get married. I had this whole presentation on how I would have a fabulous career and, along with his ambition as a dentist, we would live a comfortable life. In a way it was a marriage of convenience, but over the years, we grew to love each other. Thirty-five years of marriage later, I'm happy and content."

"That sounded like something from back in the day. I hope I have some sizzle and passion with my intended."

"That's why I'm telling you, so you have the right priorities." Her mother yawned. "Sorry, hon, it's been a long day."

"Why don't you stay and leave early in the morning?"

Her mother stood and straightened her clothes. "Thanks, but I still have to tweak my presentation for tomorrow. I'll welcome the solitude of the hotel." She picked up her pocketbook and headed to the door. "So, when will we see you?"

"Memorial weekend. Promise." Nicole raised her hand to swear.

"Okay. I'll plan something special for your homecoming. Bye, sweetheart. Take it easy and keep following your heart." She kissed her on her cheek, patted it, and left.

Nicole leaned against her door and waited for her mother to reverse and head down the road, before turning off her lights. "What a night! Drama at the reception and drama at home." She faced the couch, addressing it with a shake of her head. Right now, she was too exhausted to process any of it. Thankfully, she had a good talk with her mother and it felt good to lighten the load on her conscience. She couldn't forget that Brad had changed his mind; she'd find out later why he decided to give her a second chance. Although she didn't care for whatever underhanded tactics Audra had cooked up, she'd live with two successes out of three today.

Tomorrow after she got a good night's sleep, she'd fight her other battles. She walked into the bedroom and saw the light on the answering machine blinking. She pressed the button and let the messages run through while she brushed her teeth and prepared for bed.

The first message was from Charles Gatewood, the man she'd hired to repaint her picket fence. Next, Audra's voice came through asking Nicole if she was okay, because she thought that she might have misunderstood the meeting's intent. Nicole rolled her eyes and spat toothpaste foam with a vengeance into the sink. The last message played and Nicole paused when Brad stated that he would have his three teenage boys with him when he came.

"What three teenage boys? He couldn't possibly have three kids." She tried to recall previous conversations with him and whether he'd discussed family.

Nicole erased the messages and noted Brad's information in her appointment book. She didn't have any guests who had reserved a room for that weekend. So it would be Brad, her, and the boys—just like a family. She climbed into bed and settled into a comfortable position, with a satisfied smile. Now that she knew when the great Brad Calverton would come to visit her B&B, she'd give him a weekend he'd never forget.

Six

A sunny Monday morning met Nicole already showered and dressed in a soft pastel yellow dress. Its edges were trimmed with ruffles that made her look as if she were ready for an old-fashioned tea party. All she needed now were laced gloves and a wide-brim hat. But Nicole had deliberately selected the dress for the task before her. Her stomach was in knots, so she opted out of having breakfast.

She made a hastily scribbled note for Gertie. When she arrived, Gertie could get started on breakfast for her full house. Nicole checked herself in the hall mirror. She wiped away a lipstick smudge from the corner of her mouth and grabbed her keys.

In a matter of minutes, she parked in front of the city's municipal building. The security checkpoint was a bit daunting, but she made it through without setting off any alarms to shatter her nerves. A directory listing the building occupants and departments was screwed into the wall. Nicole squinted as she looked down the alphabetical listing. Spotting the right name, she headed toward the elevators and pushed the button for the fifth floor.

The elevator beeped, signaling the arrival of the car. The doors opened with a whoosh and Nicole sidled past other people. She walked toward a massive desk in front of the target office positioned like a goalie on a soccer field. A mature woman sat behind the desk, fingers racing across a keyboard. She faced a flat screen computer and didn't stop or glance up until Nicole came to halt before her desk.

"Good morning, ma'am. May I help you?"

"I'd like to see the mayor."

The lady looked over her half glasses. "Do you have an appointment?"

Nicole shifted from one foot to the other. She tried to determine what answer would be to her benefit. "No, but this is very important."

The secretary chuckled and resumed typing. "It always is. What's your name?"

"Nicole Montgomery. I wanted to talk to him about the rezoning plans for Glen Knolls."

"He's got lots of meetings today. I'll buzz him and see if he can see you for a brief minute."

"I'd appreciate that." Nicole walked over to the small waiting area and took a seat. She watched the woman pick up the phone, then turn her back and talk softly.

A few seconds later she swiveled around in her chair. "He has a few minutes before his next appointment."

Nicole smiled, swallowing her nervousness as she entered the mayor's office. She hadn't planned on what to say.

"Hi, Ms. Montgomery? I'm Mayor Wallace." He offered his hand, which she shook with a firm grasp. The warm smile from the older man set her at ease.

"Thank you for seeing me. I won't keep you."

"Not a problem, I'm here to serve." To his secretary, he said, "Ms. Murray, please let me know when Mr. Peterson arrives."

Nicole saw that the office was decorated with various framed awards and citations. It didn't scream "cozy" with the dark brown government furniture. She leaned back in the unforgiving, wooden chair and waited for the mayor to sit.

"Ms. Montgomery, what can I do for you?"

"Well, sir, I attended the city hall reception last night."

"Grand event, wasn't it? I didn't get there until late. Had

another engagement across town. Delicious food." He patted his ample stomach and tried to pull his jacket closed.

Nicole didn't know how to get his attention back to the issue. "As I was saying, Mayor Wallace. I attended the reception—"

"Good food—"

"And in a conversation, I learned that there are plans to re-zone Glen Knolls. You don't know this, but my B-and-B is in the area and a commercial zone will cause me to lose business. I'm wondering what this all means and why there hasn't been a hearing for the community."

"Calm down, calm down." The mayor leaned forward. "I'll admit there has been talk, but that's all. You know how rumors are, more nonsense than substance."

"I got this from a reliable source. There're even some investors and land developers breathing down my back." Bringing it back up ignited Nicole's anger.

"Nothing has come through this office about rezoning. But if it does, I'll be sure to give my constituents a chance to get their voices heard."

He came around the desk and grabbed her up by her arms. Nicole knew when she was being manipulated. She felt the gentle steering toward the door. "I guess our meeting is over."

"I do have a busy schedule, Ms. Montgomery. But I'm glad you brought this straight to the top. See you at the polls."

Nicole couldn't say anything, but followed the firm, per-suading arm. She nodded to Ms. Murray and headed for the elevators.

There had been no goal in mind, other than to confirm the truth. Now she walked away from the municipal building even more confused than ever. The mayor had denied any such plan, but there was that nibbling kernel of doubt that the smooth-talking politician was blowing smoke in her face. She could return home, but she'd just be preoccupied with this issue. There was only one thing left to do.

***

Audra pushed the button on her electronic date planner. The gadget fit comfortably in her hand and she manipulated its screens with a stylus. Her calendar showed that she had to show a house in fifteen minutes.

After telling her assistant to forward her calls, Audra headed out of the real estate office to her car. She was grateful that she wore her overcoat with the dip in temperature, although the day was sunny and clear. With teeth chattering, she briskly sped her way to the car.

"Audra, I need a moment."

Audra froze, then turned in the direction of the familiar voice. She spied Nicole leaning against her car trunk with her arms folded. The thought crossed her mind to ignore Nicole and keep going.

"I wouldn't, if I were you." Nicole sensed that Audra might keep walking.

Audra read the icy undertones and knew she'd have to deal with Nicole. "Okay, let's talk. We'll have to do it in my car because it's too cold out here to have any kind of conversation." She opened her car door without waiting for Nicole's response. The break in eye contact gave her some time to take a deep breath and get it together before she had to listen to Nicole whine.

The passenger door swung open and Nicole looked in the car before getting in.

"So, what's biting you in the butt so early in the morning?" Audra leaned back against the door and stared at Nicole, hoping to intimidate her.

"Last night. What exactly was that all about?"

"I thought it was perfectly clear. The land will be rezoned. You will be bought out whether it's by the government or the developer." Audra recognized the signs of panic flitting around in Nicole's eyes. She pressed on. "The businessmen who spoke to you are making you a better deal than you would ever get with the government." She leaned toward Nicole, still smiling brightly. "If you're worried about your business, you can always build a bigger and better B-and-B a few blocks over."

"I spoke with the mayor this morning."

Audra sucked in her breath, waiting.

"He said that it's all a rumor."

Audra narrowed her gaze on Nicole. Damn. She never thought that Nicole wouldn't roll over. "I wish you hadn't done that. The information is still in the confidential stage. I'm sure the mayor wasn't ready to lay it bare."

"I have my cell phone handy. I'll dial, you can talk to the mayor. I want to hear him say that the land will be rezoned. I want to hear him say that my land will be taken from me. You started something and I'm not going to let you have a single blade of grass on my property until I've done everything to stop you."

Audra kept the smiled pasted on, but she had retreated. Nicole's anger had shown some backbone that Audra hadn't known she had. It was time to regroup. "Calm down. You petite women are as ferocious as pit bulls." She turned the key in the ignition and started the car. "Look, I've got to get going to my next appointment. Let's not let this stand between us, okay?"

Nicole got out of the car. She leaned down, looking in through the door. "I don't know what game you're playing, Audra, but I will have your license if you don't back off."

"Whatever. Close my door." The smile was no longer prominent. Audra glared at Nicole until her door was closed. Then she gunned the accelerator, tires squealing in protest.

She drove down the road ten miles per hour faster than the speed limit, but didn't care. A traffic violation was the last thing on her mind. Nicole had drawn the line for war and had all but declared it. She fitted her ear with the earphone device and pulled out her cell phone. "Call Brad." She waited as the phone automatically dialed the number. It rang until the answering machine clicked on with its customary message. "Hey, Brad, it's Audra. Call me. It's an emergency." She yanked out the earphone, her anger in full force. It was time to take the kid gloves off and teach Nicole a lesson.

Brad entered his apartment, glad to be back home. He'd taken a six A.M. shuttle to New York. A good, strong cup of freshly brewed coffee was what he needed. Before unpacking, he headed into his kitchen and prepared his official eye-opener for the day. His telephone rang and he cringed at the sound. Work was never far. He walked around to the box that identified the call. Audra's cell phone number popped up. A frown played across his forehead. After three rings, his answering machine played. He waited to hear what she wanted after the beep.

He shook his head and walked back into the kitchen. The coffee had finished brewing, so he poured a full mug and inhaled the robust flavor. Audra always had an emergency. Usually he could deal with her histrionics, but not today. He'd eventually return her call.

The mail was stacked on the dining room table. Freddie had the only extra key to his apartment and she cleared his mailbox every few days. He flicked through the mail, setting aside the envelopes that looked official. With a cup of coffee in hand, he walked over to his sofa with the mail tucked under his arm.

Later in the morning, he decided to work on his article about the top romantic spots. The computer screen showed his work in progress with the cursor blinking for his input. He cracked his fingers and stretched them over the keyboard. Though he physically sat in front of the computer to work, his will didn't comply. His cocky announcement that he would revisit Nicole's B&B weighed on his mind.

He picked up the phone and dialed his assistant. In the cold, harsh daylight, he had his doubts about revisiting the B&B. A few days with Nicole would scramble his senses. She'd added fuel to the flame when she'd impulsively kissed him. It had caught him by surprise, but he was determined that the next time, he would be the one in charge.

"Hey, Freddie," he said into the phone.

"Brad, what's up?"

"Got an assignment that I hadn't counted on."

"Uh-oh."

Brad chuckled. The idea of taking on any extra tasks seemed suicidal given the fact that he had so many other assignments looming and placed on hold.

"What have you gotten yourself into now?"

"I have to go back to Montgomery's Bed-and-Breakfast."

"You're kidding me!" Freddie hooted over the line, making Brad feel foolish.

"No, I'm not kidding. I told Nicole . . . er, Miss Montgomery that I would do her a favor and give her a review." He didn't bother to elaborate on how Nicole had thought he was there initially to evaluate her B&B. And he didn't elaborate on how he'd turned down her offer.

"Okay, but why now? You're booked solid for a good six months. You're driving me crazy with this hectic schedule, and you can't physically keep up."

"I'm doing a favor." A favor that would turn out to be a necessity from what he could see. It would serve her purposes, but he couldn't deny that it would serve his, also. Another chance to be around the petite, sweet charm that was a major part of Nicole's personality.

"What do you want me to do to help you with this?"

Brad didn't have time to think through the details and blurted out what impulsively popped into his head. "I want to take a couple of the guys with me to the retreat."

"How will you decide which boys will go and which won't?"

"I don't know all the details. This is why I called you."

After he hung up, he could finally concentrate on the article waiting to be finished. Brad worked until early in the evening. A tightness in his neck finally made him grimace.

He rubbed the side of his neck in an effort to loosen up the muscle.

With no dinner plans, Brad opened the refrigerator and peered in. Leftover Chinese food in a carton, a half-eaten salad, and several bottles of water were the only tenants. He settled in front of the television with his scant selection of food.

The sitcom playing on the screen did little to stop his mind from wandering. Memories he had buried now resurfaced. Ever since he had come back from Hawaii, he thought about his grandmother constantly. He missed her warmth and safety that comforted him. How he had begged to stay with her at the hospital.

Brad looked around his apartment, staring at all the high-priced paintings and decorative pieces. He'd come a long way, but he'd never really noticed how empty it all seemed. Yet, he'd always proclaimed that he wanted to be alone. The reality wasn't as inviting, though.

His phone rang interrupting his thoughts. He leaned over to retrieve it. "Hello?"

"Mr. Calverton?"

Brad didn't recognize the voice. "Yes," he answered, hesitantly.

"This is Mr. Penbrook from the Community Center. It's about Big Ed."

"What about him?" Brad gripped the phone.

"He was in a fight and was stabbed."

"What hospital?" Brad cared for his boys deeply and his heart raced as the news unfolded.

"He was stabbed in his leg. The doctors are confident that he will have a short stay, but he's very agitated and is asking for you."

"Just tell me what hospital and I'll be there."

"St. Luke's on Hudson Street."

Brad dismissed Penbrook as soon as he had the necessary information. He called Freddie again to let her know where he was heading. Brad already started blaming himself for not being there to head off any altercation among his teens. Big Ed was known for his temper and, because of his size, he didn't back down easily.

Brad grabbed a taxi because he didn't trust driving himself in the middle of this ordeal. He offered up a quick prayer, steeling himself for what he would see. The driver earned his tip with each lean on his horn at another driver who wasn't swift on the gas when the light turned green. In due time, Brad stood in front of the automatic sliding doors of St. Luke's Hospital.

He stepped up and the doors swooshed open. Instantly, he'd entered another world, bustling with a sampling of people and various professions. Heading straight for the information desk, he swallowed his panic. After getting the room number, he aimed for the elevator.

A young woman walked up and waited beside him. He noted the pink balloon and white teddy bear she held. The simple gifts told their own story, but when she entered the elevator cab with him and they ascended, he tried to concentrate on the numbers indicating the floors. A soft sniff behind him sliced through his heart. The doors opened and his temporary companion slid past him. "I hope all goes well for you," he offered softly.

She wiped her nose and, with a tearstained face, gave him a weak smile. "Thank you. Hope all goes well for you, too."

Brad took a deep breath when the elevators closed again. He tried to keep positive thoughts in his head. On the eighth floor, he stepped into a hallway with corridors shooting off in every direction. He walked toward the nurse's station.

"I'm looking for Edward Thomas's room."

An older woman at a computer looked over the top of her glasses at him. "He's in room eight-twenty-two." She tilted her head to her right.

"Thanks." He turned in the direction that she indicated.

He walked in the door, taking in the empty bed closer to the door. "Big Ed, are you decent?" He passed the curtain to see his favorite protégé who now looked diminished under the covers.

"Hi, Mr. Calverton." The ready smile drooped at the corners. "Are you here to yell at me?" The young boy's eyes searched his face.

"Heck, no!" Brad looked at the teenage boy's bandaged thigh. "Must hurt quite a bit."

"Yeah." Ed grimaced. "Guess I'm the man now. Battle scar and all."

Brad restrained his critical comments. Instead, he smiled broadly and placed his hand on the boy's shoulder. "Hurry up and get better. I have a small trip planned for a couple of the guys."

"Really? Where are we going?" A frown creased Ed's forehead. "I can't do anything hard. The doctor says I have to rest my thigh." His eyes grew round. "You know, I was lucky that the knife didn't go an inch to the right or my artery would have been cut."

Brad didn't want to think about the near miss. "What happened to the other guy?"

"The police picked him up. Mr. Calverton, I wasn't trying to get into trouble. Since I made that promise to you, I haven't been doing nothin'."

Brad nodded. "I know and I'm proud of you. Lots of witnesses said that you didn't even fight back."

Ed laughed. "I was going for that nonviolent thing that you're always preaching. So much for that."

"Don't say that. By not getting into a fight, both of you were able to walk away."

"I'm not sure I wanted him to walk away. But I understand what you mean."

"Well, I'm taking you to Maryland for a short respite. You can heal your body and strengthen your mind."

"Uh-oh, sounds like one of those feel-good camps. But I'm game as long as you're there."

"Any word on when you'll be released?"

"Probably by tomorrow. The doctor will tell me today."

Brad looked up when a nurse came into the room. She nodded at him and then went about her duties without interacting with Ed. She treated him as if he weren't person. Then he noticed her frown when she looked down at his tattoo of a tombstone with R.I.P. on it and the name Joey underneath.

He glanced over to Ed to see if he picked up on the distant vibes from the nurse. The teenager had leaned back on the pillows with his eyes closed. He had pulled away from the immediate scene and he didn't look at either of them or talk at all throughout the mini-exam.

"Dr. Hartoff will stop by around nine."

Brad noted that at least she patted his hand before leaving.

"Mr. Calverton, can I stay at your place?"

The soft question had a powerful impact on Brad. He hesitated, not sure how to respond. "I'm not sure that I can do that. There are rules. Plus, it'll be hard enough getting permission to take you guys out of state for a weekend."

"But they like you. They'll let you do anything you want." Ed struggled to sit up, wincing at the pain. "Please, Mr. C, let me stay with you."

Brad rubbed his hand through his hair, weighing his options. His lifestyle really didn't lend itself to looking after a child. But he knew that the group home wasn't exactly the most inviting place for Ed. "How about this: Let me work on getting permission ASAP and then we can see if we can get a compromise on your situation."

Ed's face fell. "Okay, Mr. C, I'll wait."

Brad wished that he didn't have to leave, but he still had work to do. "I'll see you soon, Ed. I'll see if I can come back tomorrow. But if you leave, make sure to call me." He leaned down and touched foreheads with the boy. He closed his eyes and wished him well.

Outside the hospital walls, the fresh air was a relief. Brad inhaled to get the smell of disinfectant out of his lungs. The cool night air energized him so he was smiling by the time he reached his door. He put the key in his door and turned the knob, already unbuttoning his coat. Soft jazz played in the background. He stopped in the doorway, looking for any signs of danger. There were a few flickering candles around the dining and living room areas. Then he caught a whiff of a familiar perfume. At that moment, Shaunice stepped out of his bedroom with a bloodred silk robe on her tall frame.

"Hi, baby."

"What are you doing here?"

"I see you didn't change the locks. Could it be that you wanted me to come back? An unspoken invitation, so to speak." She trailed a lazy hand along the back of the sofa as she slowly walked toward him.

Brad squinted at her, trying to read what this unexpected visit was all about. He didn't feel an electric buzz or any kind of interest in her. Instead, he felt stiff with pent-up anger and hurt.

They stood face-to-face, a few inches apart. Her eyes searched his face and he kept his expression carefully blank. "Brad, we must talk. I've got so much to apologize for."

"Don't bother with the apology. What about my replacement? Can't imagine that he'd be happy that you're here, minus clothes."

"It no longer matters what he thinks. I'm stupid and impulsive, honey. What I thought that I needed was right under my nose, but instead, I went looking elsewhere." She touched his cheek and he pulled away from her.

"Shaunice, I don't know what game you're playing, but I'm not interested."

"I'm not giving up, Brad. No, I don't mean to sound psychotic, but we had a year together where we shared secrets and dreams." She walked over to the sofa and sat. "I'm not going to believe that you're willing to throw it all away."

"You did that already." Suddenly Brad felt the tiredness seep through his muscles. Having a conversation with his ex-girlfriend was the last thing that he wanted. He walked into his bedroom and closed the door.

A soft knock sounded.

"Leave me alone. You saw yourself in, you can see yourself out."

She opened the door and stood in the doorway. "Can I fix you dinner?"

He shook his head. Although she was a fine cook, there was no way that he was going to give her any encouragement. "I've already eaten."

"Okay. Can I stay here? I just want to get away from the media and their stupid probing questions. I'm only here for another day and then the shoot will be on the move."

Deep down he didn't think it was a good idea. But he didn't want to sound mean. "Sure. You can sleep on the sofa bed. Linens are in—"

"I know where they are." She smiled. "Thank you."

Brad dropped his head in his hands. His life didn't need complications, so why on earth did Shaunice show up in his house?

Later that night after climbing into bed, he tossed and turned in the dark, fluffing his pillows in between until he settled down under the covers.

He heard his bedroom door open and he stiffened.

"Psst, Brad, you still awake?"

"You'd better get back to that sofa. I'm in no mood for your games."

He felt the foot of the bed lower with her weight. "Got too much on my mind. What went wrong with us?"

Brad remained under the covers speaking in her general direction. "Your amnesia isn't scoring points with me. You kicked me to the curb once, and there won't be a second time."

Shaunice's voice turned hard. "Must you live in the past? You were never around when I needed you. Jetting off to these godforsaken places, dealing with the heat and extreme cold, gets to me after a while. Dustin was there. As the photographer, he could see what was happening to me and offered me something close and tangible."

By the time she had finished her speech, Brad was sitting propped up against the headboard. He clapped slowly. "If I was a magician, I'd make the violins appear and play for you. Did you ever stop to think about anyone else outside of yourself? Did you ever feel compelled, obligated to tell me that I'd been replaced? No. Instead, I have to read about it in a damned tabloid magazine."

He turned on the light and held up his hand. "It's my turn to unload. Then, I called you and your ditzy publicist treats me like I'm an insignificant reporter trying to win a chance at an interview." He got out of the bed and paced. He didn't know where to go, but he didn't want to be near her.

"I don't mean this in an offensive way. You came from nothing, Brad. When I met you, you were rising and I recognized that talent and tried to help you gain more confidence. But you sucked me dry. When I took you among my friends, you didn't fit in. All the education and sudden fame doesn't make someone classy. And I needed a break. But now I'm ready to help you. All you need to do is admit that you're out of your league and that you need me."

Brad stood rooted to the spot. Then he leaned back so that the guttural laugh could escape and also give his mouth something to do, after falling wide open. "You are a piece of work. But nothing you say will change the way I feel about you and where I want you in my life. To get things moving in that direction, I'll do you a favor. I'll call a hotel out of the limelight right now for you. I'll even put it on my tab."

"Don't be stubborn, Brad. You men always have to take things to the extreme. We need each other. I'm woman enough to admit it. Are you man enough to admit it?"

"You have ten minutes to get some clothes on." Brad walked out of the room, battling with himself to keep his temper in check. The gall of her to talk to him as if he were beneath her on the social scale. He gritted his teeth, frustrated for feeling the stinging venom of her nasty bites.

The phone rang and he looked at the machine with no desire to talk to anyone. He'd used up all his energy on Big Ed and Shaunice. The idea of dealing with someone else and their problems overwhelmed him. The ringing stopped in midring.

He swore under his breath and slammed the bedroom door open. Shaunice sat on his bed, her face contorted in rage. Brad barely heard the end of the discussion before he stormed over and snatched the phone. "Hello?" Only the dial tone was audible.

"What are you doing?"

"Taking care of business. One of your bimbos called here, but I set her straight."

"What bimbo . . . er, person?"

"Nicole. Sounded kind of mousy, if you ask me."

"I don't believe this." Brad had had enough. He picked her up by her arm and herded her out of his bedroom. With a definite push, she ended up on the sofa as he went around the room and threw her stuff in an overnight bag.

"Brad." Now her voice took on the characteristic whine. "Brad, please. Stop overreacting. Okay, I'll behave. Just give me a chance." She placed a restraining hand on his arm, but quickly moved it away when he turned his icy gaze on her. "What if I told you that I was pregnant?"

Seven

Be a man.
Say something meaningful.

The news floored him.

His reaction shamed him. He and Shaunice sat in his car in front of the hotel. She had delivered the news through tear-laden eyes. And all he could do was to stare out into the darkness, spying the cars between the screen of trees whizzing past on the nearby highway.

As the numbness ebbed, his thoughts settled and the sound of her constant chatter penetrated. He could now speak intelligently, but what to say? He didn't want to offend her with the wrong comment, like "Are you sure?" or worse, "Is it mine?"

"I know what you're thinking," Shaunice said softly. "And, no, it's not yours."

First, relief. Then, anger. "You were seeing someone else while you were seeing me?"

She wiped each corner of her eyes. "Yes."

"So, how the hell do you know that it's not mine?"

"Because I had broken it off with you before you officially found out. Think about it. We hadn't slept with each other for about four months." She looked out at the hotel. "It was easy. I was on my modeling shoots and you were on your book tours."

"You know how to deliver a punch." He couldn't look at

her. "Do you think telling me all of this now is going to make me want to be with you?"

"Let's not pretend, Brad. We were never the romantic type. Remember how we talked and discovered that neither of us believes in fairy-tale endings? We both had screwed-up childhoods, with no mother—well, mine was missing in action—and no father. It's just you and me trying to make a living in this world." She reached for his arm.

"Why, Shaunice? You're single and you have a career." He shook his head trying to understand her logic. "Why would you let yourself get pregnant?"

"I was comfortable. I liked the lifestyle he offered. I thought that he would want me—"

"If you got pregnant? My God, Shaunice, this isn't a case of a bad flu bug that will go away in a couple days." He stared at her, wondering what had ever attracted him. "What's the new daddy saying?"

"He doesn't know. He made it pretty clear last week that nothing could come of our relationship." This time the tears slipped down her cheeks. "He's still married to a wife who is sickly and he feels too guilty at the thought of leaving her."

"I bet. Wifey probably holds the purse strings. He used you, Shaunice."

"But there's nothing between him and his wife. They don't share the same room, and he said that he can't stand the sight of her." She raised her hand. "Hear me out." She paused. "I want you to seriously consider what I'm about to ask. Would you be interested in raising the child together? We could start over our relationship. Be a family."

First, Big Ed with his plea to live with him and now, Shaunice and her half-baked plan.

"Look, don't answer me right away. Sleep on it." She stepped out of the car before he could answer. With a small wave, she mouthed "Thank you" and walked into the lobby.

***

He looked over at the clock and groaned. In four hours, he had to be up and out the door to talk with the producers for the London deal. How in the world could he think about anything? So far two persons had approached him as if he exuded nurturing vibes. He didn't want the responsibility for a grown teenager, much less a newborn.

He thumped his pillow and flipped onto his back in an attempt to get comfortable. Folding his hands behind his neck, he stared up at the ceiling, counting the cracks in the paint.

"Oh, crap!"

He sat up and swung his legs over the side of the bed. Nicole. He'd completely forgotten that Shaunice had spoken to Nicole. What must she be thinking?

He grabbed the phone and punched in a familiar telephone number.

A sleepy voice answered.

"Freddie?"

"Brad? Is that you?"

"Yeah. I guess it's a little early to be calling." He glanced over to the clock.

"You're damn right it's too freakin' early." Freddie sighed. "Just for the record, you need to make some friends. That way, you won't be calling me at these ungodly hours. Okay, what's got you up at this hour?"

"You're my friend."

"No, I'm your assistant who has befriended you. But stop paying me and you will be out of an assistant and the friendship."

"You're mean."

"So I've been told. But you still need some friends."

"Friends are overrated. Are you going to listen to my crisis?"

"Oh, hell, another one?"

"I've been asked to be a father of sorts, twice today."

Freddie let out a deep belly laugh. "Okay, back up. You must have been a busy boy."

"Big Ed wants me to take him in." He pinched the bridge of his nose and squeezed his eyes shut. "It's such a responsibility, but when I looked in his face, I felt as if I should do something."

"Brad, listen to me. Big Ed needs more than a home, he needs attention and he will need professional help to overcome what happened to him as a kid." Freddie paused. "What did you say to him?"

"What could I say? I feel like the bad guy because I can't say yes unequivocally."

"Let's leave Big Ed for the moment. What's the other situation?"

"Shaunice."

"Oh, no."

"Exactly. It's a gigantic problem packaged in a skinny body."

"Yours?"

Brad chuckled with an edge of bitterness. "It's not mine."

"What? Then why are you trippin' over it?"

"Because she wants me to marry her and raise the child as ours."

Brad heard Freddie drop the phone. Her voice alternated between being near and then farther away from the phone. It was obvious that she was pacing, while the explicatives spewed from her mouth. Finally, she retrieved the phone.

"What did you say?" Freddie emphasized each word.

"Nothing. I said nothing." The guilt cut through him and threatened to choke him.

"I know how you are, Brad. You can't save the whole world. There's nothing else I can say without sounding heartless and cold." She paused. "Brad? Are you listening?"

"Yeah."

"Look, go to that retreat of yours. I know you will think about it and agonize, but maybe away from it all you can figure it all out."

Brad nodded, and although Freddie couldn't see him, she continued.

"Now that I'm up, let me work on your schedule. I'll make the arrangements. You can probably leave in about three days."

Brad nodded again.

"Brad, say something."

"That'll work." Brad knew that no matter how long he thought about it, it wouldn't matter. Either decision had major consequences.

Nicole stood at the top of the stairs and looked down on the sitting room area. She had spent the two days scrubbing, polishing, and rearranging. Her muscles ached from the endless household tasks, yet a strange sense of anticipation fired through her.

Brad's assistant, Freddie, had called her to finalize the arrangements. She imagined that she'd hidden her anger very well. After having her head bitten off by his crude girlfriend, he could have had the decency to call her back and apologize. Unless the girlfriend never told him. But this was no time to be proud and call the whole thing off. She needed him on her side.

Besides, what did she care if he had a girlfriend, crude or otherwise? It had nothing do with what she needed him to do. Obviously he wasn't going to make it easy. Not only was he coming, but he was bringing three teenagers with him now. She'd balked at first, but Freddie's skillful negotiating had her agreeing to the expanded guest list.

She raced down the stairs, pulling off the scarf tied around her hair. The grandfather clock in the hallway chimed, signaling four in the afternoon. They would be arriving within the next hour.

The aroma of spaghetti sauce crept through the house. Dinner was Italian fare with spaghetti and meat sauce, garlic bread, salad, and tiramisu. Gertie had cooked earlier and now Nicole had the meal warming, ready for the hungry youths.

After a quick shower, she slipped on a turtleneck and jumper. She had just fluffed her hair with her fingers when the doorbell rang. A once-over in the mirror, a quick dab of berry-colored lipstick, and she headed toward the door.

Taking a deep breath, she pasted on a wide smile and opened the door. "Hello." Nicole surveyed the group in front of her. "Please do come in. I think the temperature dropped a bit more today." She shuddered and stepped back.

Each teenage boy towered over her. As they sidled past, they gave her a quick "Hi," not allowing their eye contact to linger past a few seconds. Nicole bit her cheek to hide her amusement of their teenage gawkiness.

After the third boy had come in, she raised her eyes to the man who stood in the cold, as if waiting for his own special invitation. Nicole stared at his chest. This time she was the one to keep her eyes averted. His shoulders had the same broad strength. Then he walked forward and still she kept her eyes pinned to the top button of his coat.

"Hi, Miss Montgomery."

She closed her eyes at the sound of her name rolling off his tongue. The memory of their kiss sprang up and Nicole had to resist leaning into the expansive chest. "Hello, Mr. Calverton." Then, she raised her eyes past his neck to his square chin, full lips, wide nose, and dark eyes.

He looked down at her and his eyes flicked over her lips before a soft smile spread. She blushed, knowing that he also remembered the kiss.

She stepped aside for him to enter and then she shut the door. "Follow me. I'll show you to your rooms. I'm sure you must be starved. I've got a big home-cooked meal laid out for you." She kept up her idle chatter as she walked up the stairs and down the hallway. The boys were talking among themselves, with an occasional laugh. She hoped that she wasn't the butt of any of their jokes. "Okay, guys, you give me your names and I'll show you your rooms."

"I'm Tyrone."

Nicole smiled up at the boy, his face sprinkled with acne. He had a mischievous chuckle that instantly brought a smile to her face.

"Move over, young'un. I'm Vincent, the Magnificent." The boy was all arms and legs. He high-fived his way into the room and threw an arm around Tyrone's shoulders. "I got the bed near the window." Then he ran and flew into the air to land on the bed, which emitted a loud squeak.

"None of that, Vinny." Brad's voice had dropped an octave and held no amusement for the teenage antics.

"Yes, sir." Vinny hurried off the bed, straightening the covers.

Nicole looked over to Brad and was rewarded with a wink. She continued down the hall. "Who's next?"

"Me. I'm Big Ed."

Nicole looked up at Big Ed and wondered if he had stopped growing. He was a few inches shorter than Brad, but already had a solid frame. Instead of the usual cornrows, he had his hair in twists. "This is your room. I saved the full-size one for you, Big Ed."

"Fine with me, ma'am." Big Ed strutted. "All this is fine with me. Your place is off the hook." The boys slapped five and walked into their rooms.

"Ahem." Brad rocked onto his toes, his hands behind his back. "Forgot about me?"

Nicole noticed that he'd opened his coat. With his hands behind his back, his shirt was pulled against his chest. For some reason, she couldn't resist looking at his chest. Her imagination kicked in and she remembered the sheet of hard muscle when she kissed those gorgeous full lips.

"Stop daydreaming and show me to my room."

She gasped and felt flustered. "Right here. Same one you

had on your last visit. One new thing, though. The roof is fixed." Her face was still on fire from being caught staring.

"New scatter rugs? I like them."

"Thank you." Ordinarily she would have given her customary hostess smile, but his compliment was like a soft hand stroking her, and her smile radiated to another level.

"Well, I'll let you get settled and see you and the boys downstairs in a few." She exited the room and closed his door behind her. Her B&B was full of life and sounds. With a satisfied smile, she went on her way to get ready for dinner.

No sooner had she put down the last piece of silverware than Big Ed appeared in the lead with the others close behind. Chairs were pulled out and each got an occupant. Brad was the last one in the dining room and walked over to one of two empty chairs at the head of the table.

"After you." He motioned to the other chair opposite his.

She took her seat and then passed the bowl of salad around. Only Big Ed helped himself.

"Salads are good for you. Roughage and all."

"Yes, ma'am," they answered, but no one made a move toward the salad bowl.

"Just means more for me." Brad took a double helping. "Looking forward to the roughage."

"Eew," Tyrone snorted.

"Can we change the subject?" Nicole glanced around the table. "How about you tell me something short and sweet about yourselves, while I serve the spaghetti?"

"I'm going first. I'm Vinny. The girls love me. I can't be away too long or they'll get lonely. I was born this sexy."

Nicole had to hand it to the boy. When he became a man, which seemed to be right around the corner, he would be devilishly handsome. His skin was a cocoa brown and he had sharp features with a wicked smile that could land him on an advertisement for toothpaste.

"Enough with the crap. Miss Montgomery is too old for you."

Nicole appreciated Big Ed's protective nature, although he could have been more diplomatic.

"I'm Big Ed. I want to be a basketball star. When I come out on the NBA court, I want people to say 'Shaq who?'"

"Good for you. I hope you're working on your grades, too."

He patted his chest proudly. "Yup, my math grades have gone up, haven't they, Mr. C?"

Brad smiled at the teenager. "Yes, they have. As a matter of fact, all the boys' math scores went up. I'm proud of all of you."

"Well, I guess that means more garlic bread, spaghetti, and the surprise dessert for all of you."

"Ma'am, I'll be full after this helping." Tyrone patted his stomach.

"He eats like a bird," Vinny said.

"What about you, Tyrone? Tell me something about you."

Tyrone squirmed in the chair. He looked miserable with all the attention. Nicole didn't want any of them to be offended by her curiosity. "It's okay, maybe later."

"Listen to this." Big Ed laughed. "Some people call Tyrone Worm because he swallowed a worm on a dare."

"That's disgusting and I don't think I'll ever forget that." Nicole wrinkled her nose in distaste.

"It was no big deal and I got twenty dollars," Tyrone said. "Now that stupid TV show has people eating worse than that and they get hundreds of dollars."

"Well, let me say this now. There will be no crazy dares while you stay here." Nicole shuddered at the thought of what their active minds could come up with.

For several minutes, the sounds were of silverware hitting the plates. The bread disappeared and only a broken piece of crust remained. Most of the spaghetti had been eaten and what was left was barely enough to put away for another day.

"Looks like everyone is stuffed. How about if we wait for an hour or so before dessert?"

The boys nodded and immediately got up.

"I know you're not going anywhere without taking your plates to the kitchen," Brad said in that now common authoritative tone.

"Please. There's no need," Nicole objected. After all, it was her job.

"It's good for them. They need to realize there's no free ride," Brad argued.

Nicole understood what he meant, but still felt guilty at having them work. She went into the kitchen to direct them before they piled the dishes haphazardly into the sink.

"You boys can go into the family room. There are games, videos, and magazines."

"They're going to be spoiled by the time they leave here." Brad leaned casually against the doorway.

"Tell me about how you are connected to them." She rinsed the dishes and stacked the dishwasher.

He walked over and leaned against the counter. He stared at the floor for several seconds, causing Nicole to pause and look over at him. The glass that she held under the faucet overflowed and she turned off the water and set it down. Wiping her hands on the nearby dish towel, she studied his face, surprised to see some decision weigh heavily on his mind.

"Brad?" She called his name softly.

He didn't look up. "Had to think about it for a second. After I had moved into the neighborhood, I had ventured out to see what was in the immediate surroundings. I walked past the boys' home and felt an immediate pull. Although I'm busy and travel a lot throughout the year, I knew that I could still donate my time to them. These boys are my family. I care about them and I look forward to seeing them move out into the world."

Nicole listened and was touched by his words. "I feel so insignificant and trivial. What have I done? Nothing."

He pushed himself off the counter and walked over to her. He traced the outline of a curl in her hair before his hand dropped to his side. "You've done more than others would do."

She clicked on the dishwasher and followed him out of the kitchen.

"Join me on the porch."

"Yeah. We can sit out there. Do you think the boys are ready for their dessert?"

"Probably."

"We can put it on the table with paper plates and they can help themselves."

"Grab a couple of pieces for us. I'll brew some coffee."

Nicole wondered if he was this familiar at the other B&Bs he reviewed. Not that she was complaining, it felt nice to have a man around the house. After the dessert was served and the coffee brewed, she made her way to the porch.

"Have a seat in your favorite chair." Brad pointed at the chair where she'd fallen asleep that night months ago.

"Not many stars to see tonight." Nicole looked up at the sky.

"Feels like snow weather to me." Brad cut into his tiramisu and took a bite. "This is good." He gobbled up another piece.

Nicole sipped at her coffee, pleased that her tiramisu was a hit. "I wish you were staying longer." What the heck was wrong with her? That came out of nowhere. She set down her cup, trying to think of something.

"I can come back," he responded. His back was to her and his head tilted up toward the sky. "I like it here . . . with you."

Nicole looked down at her hands, feeling her heartbeat speed up and her breathing race.

Suddenly he turned and dramatically flopped down on the floor next to her legs. "But only if you make me more of this."

She laughed at him. "It's all about the food."

"Well, you know, I'm a growing boy."

"Would you please get up off the floor and sit in a chair?"

The casual brush of his shoulders against her legs was doing crazy things with her nervous system.

"So, Miss Montgomery, you've learned a little about all of us. Please tell me something about you. I'll edit for my review."

"Nothing like pressure. I'm the eldest in a line of over-achievers, fashioned off our parents. There are no black sheep, no jezebels, nothing, just a successful, boring brother and sister. Although that changed when I quit my successful job as a lobbyist and opened a country-style B-and-B in the middle of nowhere."

"Any regrets?"

"Sometimes. Like the day when I found out that you were a famous reviewer."

He chuckled.

"Of course, I wasn't good enough to be reviewed, then."

"I was here on R and R. I was suffering from a heartbreak."

"Ah, yes, the famous Shaunice."

He groaned. "Looks like I owe you a very deep apology. Shaunice paid an unexpected visit, things got a bit heated. She took it out on you."

"She said you were in the shower." The image that came to mind caused tiny quivers deep in her stomach.

"I wasn't . . . and it's not the way it sounded."

"No explanation needed."

"How about you? Broken any hearts lately?"

"Nice segue." She raised her coffee cup. "No, there hasn't been a someone special since college. There were several false starts after that. Work was my constant companion." Aloud, it sounded pathetic, she thought.

"Hard to believe that there's no one."

"Why?"

"Just figured that you would be settling down with a few children."

Nicole stiffened. "Is my biological clock ticking too loudly for you?" It might be her plan, but she didn't like the thought of him putting her down.

Brad cringed. "Looks like my mouth got me in trouble."

"You can say that again. Do you believe that a woman shouldn't own a business and be an entrepreneur?"

"I didn't say that."

"No, but you basically expect me to be wedded and bedded."

Brad took refuge in the remaining mouthful of tiramisu. He held up his hands in surrender. "You are truly a wonderful cook."

"It's the woman in me," she answered smartly.

"Are you going to continue stinging me all night?"

Nicole glared at him. If he only knew, he threw the logical side of her in a crazy mess.

He leaned forward and gave her a quick peck on her cheek. "Sorry." His eyes twinkled mischievously. "And thank you."

"For what?"

"The kiss you so kindly shared with me. Couldn't think of much else for several days."

Her face grew warm. "You're no gentleman. How could you remind me?"

"Maybe I was hoping that it wasn't a onetime experience."

Nicole drained her coffee cup and then stood. She knew they were both flirting, but this wasn't the time or the place. He was on assignment and she had a house filled with teenage boys who didn't need to see their mentor in any compromising situations.

"Good night, Mr. Calverton. Breakfast will be at eight, so that you won't miss the tour bus to the harbor." She walked past him, when his hand shot out and caught her wrist.

"You can't run from me, Nicole. Tomorrow we have to sit down and talk. I'll interview you for the article." He took her hand and brought it to his lips. Softly, he kissed the back of her hand. She pulled it away because the impression of his lips lingered. He tempted her and she had to concentrate to resist him. Without another word, she left the porch and went into the kitchen.

Tyrone slammed the refrigerator door closed. "Oh, didn't hear you." He looked around guiltily.

"I'm heading for bed. I see you got an apple. Good, I'm glad. I can never eat all the apples that I buy and then they go bad."

"Thanks, ma'am." He headed toward the doorway. "I like it here, thanks."

Nicole was touched and only nodded. She knew that by the time they left, her heart would be affected. Turning out the kitchen light, she went into her apartment, quiet and still.

She performed her nightly tasks of checking the voice machine. The message light blinked once. She pushed the PLAY button and listened to her girlfriends screaming over the phone on their way to brunch. She'd missed lots of these impromptu girlfriend outings ever since she bought her B&B. Hopefully, they wouldn't pop up at her doorstep while Brad was here. A giggle escaped at the havoc they would create.

Now that the day was finally at a close, she felt exhausted. In her robe and bedroom slippers, she headed back through the house to make sure the house was secured. She noticed a light on in the sitting room and went into the room to turn it off.

"Oh," she cried. "I didn't see you."

Big Ed started and closed the magazine he was reading.

"What's up, Big Ed? Can't sleep?"

"No. It's too quiet." He laughed. "New York never sleeps."

"Hmm. That's why I like it here. It's quiet and peaceful. I get to think about things."

"You're lucky."

"I think you're lucky, too, because you've got Brad."

"He is a nice guy." He sighed.

"What is it?"

"I wish he could be more than just Mr. C who comes to play basketball with us." He looked down at his hands. "I wish . . ."

Nicole didn't know whether to push him to reveal what he

seemed to want so very much. She waited to see if he would say anything else.

"You know, he's falling for you."

"Excuse me?" Nicole heard his words, understood his words, but they blew her away.

"Mr. C. He really likes you." He looked over at her with a wide grin. "I can see why. You're pretty and all that."

"I think you're mistaken. Your Mr. C is already quite taken." She recalled the angry voice of his significant other.

"Maybe." Big Ed shrugged. "Never heard him talk about anybody, except you." He chuckled. "I thought he'd never be quiet on the bus. It was like he was nervous and stuff."

"You flatter me, Big Ed. I have an early day tomorrow and so do you. I booked a trip for you to go see Baltimore Harbor. Don't stay up too late. I'm going to head to my room and crash."

"Okay. I'll go up in a few minutes. Thanks for talking with me. Sweet dreams."

As she walked around turning off the lights and making sure everything was locked, she heard Big Ed softly sing: "Nicole and Brad sitting in a tree, k-i-s-s-i-n-g . . ."

An Important Message From The ARABESQUE Publisher

Dear Arabesque Reader,

I have some exciting news to share....

Available now is a four-part special series **AT YOUR SERVICE** written by bestselling Arabesque Authors.

Bold, sweeping and passionate as America itself—these superb romances feature military heroes you are destined to love. They confront their unpredictable futures along-side women of equal courage, who will inspire you!

The **AT YOUR SERVICE** series* can be specially ordered by calling 1-888-345-BOOK, or purchased wherever books are sold.

Enjoy them and let us know your feedback by commenting on our website.

Linda Gill, Publisher
Arabesque Romance Novels

Check out our website at www.BET.com

THE "THANK YOU" GIFT INCLUDES:

- 4 books absolutely FREE (plus $1.99 for shipping and handling).
- A FREE newsletter, *Arabesque Romance News*, filled with author interviews, book previews, special offers, and more!
- No risks or obligations.

INTRODUCTORY OFFER CERTIFICATE

Yes! Please send me 4 FREE Arabesque novels (plus $1.99 for shipping & handling). I understand I am under no obligation to purchase any books, as explained on the back of this card. Send my **FREE Tote Bag** after my first regular paid shipment.

NAME _____

ADDRESS _____ APT. _____

CITY _____ STATE _____ ZIP _____

TELEPHONE ( ) _____

E-MAIL _____

SIGNATURE _____

Offer limited to one per household and not valid to current subscribers. All orders subject to approval. Terms, offer, & price subject to change. Tote bags available while supplies last.

Thank You!

AN063A

THE ARABESQUE ROMANCE CLUB: HERE'S HOW IT WORKS

THE ARABESQUE ROMANCE BOOK CLUB
P.O. BOX 5214
CLIFTON NJ 07015-5214

PLACE
STAMP
HERE

Eight

Brad boarded the van with his boys. The temperature had fallen and the day was overcast and dreary. Hopefully they would get through touring the Baltimore Aquarium and the Inner harbor stores before it rained.

The harbor in February was relatively low-key. Stores had been open for just over an hour. Brad walked through the main concourse taking it all in. The boys had split up and two went to the lower level. The pizzeria had been selected as the restaurant of choice for lunch.

Brad approached one of the teenagers who lingered. "Why didn't you go with the guys?"

Big Ed shrugged.

"I've been thinking about what you asked me." Brad sat on a bench near the escalators.

"Look, Mr. C, I didn't mean to push you into a corner. I appreciate what you do for me and all. I've got two more years and then I move on."

"And the rate that you're going, you'll be able to pick what school you'd like to go to."

"I guess so. Let's make a deal? If I can visit you during the holidays, then I won't bug you about living with you."

"Are you sure, Big Ed? I'm willing to make some alterations to my life. Like you said, it'll only be for two years."

"Don't get me wrong. It's not like I want to stay in that place, but you need to think about you. When you get married, no woman is going to want to deal with me."

Brad laughed. "Marriage! I'd better hold my tongue with someone who is yet to discover life."

"Don't try to fake it. I know you believe in all that stuff and then some, especially with Miss Montgomery." Big Ed wore a wide silly grin.

"Now, that's where you are so wrong. I'm not Miss Montgomery's type. When she settles down, it'll be for a business-suit, nine-to-fiver."

"Whatever. But you've got big dollars."

Brad didn't have a comeback. Somehow he knew that Nicole wasn't the type to be impressed or bought by his "big dollars."

After lunch, Brad and the boys walked toward the aquarium. A line had already formed with other school-aged kids. Thirty minutes later they had worked their way into the building. Brad was always impressed by the massive and mysterious sea creatures behind the thick glass. He envied the fluid movements of these graceful animals. They had no family ties, no obligations or commitments, no expectations. Besides, they didn't get their hearts broken.

He watched the shark swim around the tank. Its permanent toothy grin displayed rows of jagged teeth. It was king of its domain and didn't have to face Mrs. Shark declaring that she was pregnant by another shark. Suddenly he needed air.

"Vinny, let the others know that I'll be outside waiting for them."

"Sure thing, Mr. C. Did you know there's an all-girls' school in line around the corner?"

Brad shook his head. He debated and then came to a decision. "Maybe I should stick around."

"I'm just kidding, Mr. C. I promise, I'll behave."

Brad wasn't one hundred percent convinced that Vinny had control over his teenage hormones, but they were near the exit, anyway.

The brisk air hit his face and he involuntarily pulled his coat closer. It was definitely colder. Maybe he would have to cut his stay short, again. He'd check the Weather Channel before stating his new decision. The boys would be so disappointed. Not to mention that he wanted to soak up all the available time with Nicole.

Unable to stand still because the frigid temperatures cut straight to his bones, he paced. He surveyed the harbor, amazed at how much it had changed since he was a young boy. A mere few blocks away was the heart of the inner city where his grandmother's row house stood.

If he stayed one more day, he would have to go through the neighborhood. It had preyed on his mind ever since Hawaii and he knew that if nothing else, he had to fulfill his grandmother's request to visit the neighbors. Hopefully, he wasn't too late with his visit.

"Mr. C," Tyrone shouted. "It's cold out here." He shivered on cue, clearly distressed.

"I guess you should have listened to me and packed a thicker coat," Brad chastised.

"I'm going to get frostbite and die."

Vinny ran up and popped Tyrone on the back of his neck. "Stuff will start falling off before you die, stupid."

"Mr. C, think we can head back now?" Big Ed inquired through clenched teeth. In between the words, his jaw clicked from the cold. His limp was more pronounced.

Brad surrendered without a fight, only too pleased to be in a warm, covered haven. They marched back to the van parked in a close-by parking lot. As the driver pulled out onto Pratt Street, Brad couldn't help looking back. Maybe as early as tomorrow, he would relive the nightmare of losing his grandmother and having the state be his only guardian for more years than he cared to remember. The deep sadness stirred within his heart.

Nicole really needed an extra pair of hands. She had just come back with a new set of curtains and little ceramic knickknacks to decorate the kitchen walls. With the house empty, she had no one to ask for help, but that didn't ever stop her.

She climbed onto the counter and edged closer to the end. A nail poked out of her mouth, the hammer tucked under her arm, and the ceramic fish in her other hand. Just a few more inches and she'd be centered over the window.

"Yo, Nicole. Are ya home?"

Nicole started at the loud greeting. Her foot slipped off the edge of the counter and the fish twirled up into the air before crashing to the floor. A hot flash of pain raced through her when the hammer fell across her foot. By the time the chaos had ended, she was seated on the floor nursing her foot.

"Damn, Toni, why can't you knock like everyone else?"

"Because I didn't think family had to knock."

"Especially family," Nicole snarled.

Donna came over and helped Nicole up. "Sorry about that, hon. You know how Toni is, anything for a laugh."

"Toni, you owe me a ceramic fish."

Toni pushed a fragment with her foot. "Looks cheesy to me. Why the heck are you trying to make this place all country? You know I don't like country."

Nicole rolled her eyes. "Remind me to go look at my mortgage and see whose name is on it." She picked up the pieces and threw them in the trash. "You can either go to the store and buy me another piece or you can leave the cash."

Toni smirked. "I'll do the cash thing. Here's fifty cents, don't spend it all one place."

Nicole limped over to the telephone, picked up the receiver, and dialed.

"What are you doing?" Toni asked, clearly alarmed.

Nicole turned her back. "Shirley? Hey, it's me. Remember prom night—"

"Aah," Toni screamed and lunged at the phone. She pulled the receiver from Nicole's hand. "Shirley, let me explain . . ." Confusion marked her face and then realization dawned.

"You called the weather." She slammed down the phone. "Ha, ha, very funny."

Donna doubled over with laughter. "Serves you right. Now pay up."

Toni fished out a twenty-dollar bill and threw it on the counter. "This is robbery," she muttered.

"You'd better cough up another forty bucks. These things didn't come from the dollar store. I bought them from a specialty shop in Annapolis."

Toni took out her purse and emptied its contents onto the counter. Coins rolled and spun in scattered directions. Several bills floated down. "That's everything that I have. Now, leave me alone. This is what I get for coming over to see if you needed anything before the storm hits."

"You shouldn't have startled me. When I gave you the key, it was to be used if I wasn't here. And what storm are you talking about?"

"You haven't listened to the news," Donna declared. "There's a snowstorm heading this way. You know how those weather people are, they can never tell a straight story. So it could snow from as little as five inches to twenty-four inches."

"We didn't know if your guests left. So we came over."

"How the heck did you get out of work?"

"The snowstorm did it. The head guys decided not to press their luck, so they allowed folks who lived more than thirty minutes away to leave early."

"But you live fifteen minutes away," Nicole countered.

"And I don't do snow." Toni looked out into the dining room. "So if it snows, do you have room for me?"

"As a matter of fact, no." Nicole couldn't hide the triumphant smile at declaring her B&B had full occupancy.

Toni and Donna looked expectantly at Nicole for further explanation.

"Remember, I told you that the reviewer was coming for another visit?"

"I remember you saying that he didn't think your place was good enough to be reviewed," Donna stated.

"Yes, well, he had a change of heart. And he's not my only guest."

"Looks like we need to chat over hot chocolate."

Nicole hooked arms into each of her friends' arms and marched into the kitchen. She busied herself with the preparations, deliberately staying quiet until she had poured the warm milk.

"Oh, come on, Nicole, I'm dying. You can be so irritating." Toni reached for the coffee mug, inhaling the rich cocoa scent.

"Hold on, now. Brad brought his protégés with him, young adolescent boys."

"So, now it's Brad. Hmmm."

"Get off it, Toni." Donna waved on Nicole to continue.

"How long is the happy family staying?"

"He has to be back by Sunday." Nicole fought to keep her voice upbeat. Sunday was a mere two days away, but she really didn't want to face the fact that Brad wouldn't be around, nor was there an excuse for him to remain.

"Toni, let's get out of here as soon as we're done with this cocoa. I've got to head across town to pick up my mother. I'm not sure if this snow will wait."

"You lucked out, Nicole. We aren't going to get to meet your fabulous bed-and-breakfast reviewer."

And Nicole thanked fate for that.

She headed back into the kitchen after they'd left, sighing at the few shards of ceramic pieces still lying on the floor. Grabbing a dustpan and short broom, she swept them into a pile. A piece spun under the refrigerator, but its edge still showed. She dropped to her knees and slid her fingers under the grill. Her fingers did a crab walk to reach more than the tip of the piece. She felt a prick and drew back her fingers.

Blood dripped down her index finger. "Damn," she muttered. Just then she heard voices in the front hall and she hurriedly grabbed a paper towel and headed out of the kitchen.

"Hi, guys," she greeted Brad and the boys. "I'm a little pre-occupied, so come on in and relax. You can tell me all about your day when I'm finished playing doctor."

The guys headed upstairs, the chatter lively with descriptions of their visit. Nicole shook her head at their enthusiasm to outtalk each other.

"That looks nasty." Brad looked down at the soaked paper towel, bright red. "What happened?"

"Dropped something in the kitchen and when I tried to pick it up, I cut myself."

He pulled back the paper towel. "That's a nasty gash. Run cold water over it and then let's get it bandaged."

His touch made her warm all over, but it also scrambled her thinking. "I can manage on my own, thank you."

"For once, can you give up the driver's seat?" He held her hand until they walked over to the sink. "Okay, the gash isn't as bad as I thought." The water had cleared away the blood. The cut was long, but not deep. "You're just a bleeder." He opened and closed several cupboards. "Where are the Band-Aids?"

"In my place. I'll get one." She headed for her door. "Why are you following me?"

"We're going to get the Band-Aids?" He grinned.

"I can manage. I don't have guests in my quarters."

"I thought I had graduated from that status."

"What gave you that idea?"

"This." He pulled her hard against his chest. His arm wrapped around her body and she could feel his open palm burning an imprint onto her back.

Her heart was about to explode. "Brad." His name came out in a whisper.

"Shhh. I love the way you smell."

"I'm going to bleed to death."

"Then we'd better go get that Band-Aid."

Just like that, he had conquered her. Together they walked

into her apartment. He waited outside her bathroom while she went in to get the bandage from the medicine cabinet. She looked at her reflection in the mirror over the sink. Her eyes shone back at her, she could see the electricity in her face. Not that it was unpleasant, but her head and heart went into a tailspin whenever he looked her way or touched her.

She emerged from the bathroom, bandage in place. "Finishing snooping?"

"I had the kitchenette left, but maybe another time."

She sized him up, thinking that he didn't have to be so damned gorgeous. "Maybe."

Brad's cell phone rang. He pulled it off his waistband and looked at the display panel. "I have to take this call." He tried to bring a smile to his face, but he knew it came out as a grimace. He walked past Nicole and headed back into the house. "Hey, Freddie, what's up?"

"A whole lot."

He didn't respond. He sensed bad news.

"It's Shaunice."

He stared out of the kitchen window at the twilight descending.

"She called here a couple of times, looking for you. This last go-around, I guess she was getting desperate. She threatened to go to the press and accuse you of abandoning her because of the baby."

"Did she forget that she was the one who left?" he hissed, looking around him for any eavesdroppers, and walked purposefully through the sitting room to the porch. He paced the length of the porch, jabbing the air with his finger.

"She said that she'll cry in front of the cameras." Freddie paused. "I think she means it."

"What does she want from me? She was the one who said it wasn't my child." He felt a noose tightening around his neck.

"I asked her that and she said it's not yours, but you will take care of her and the baby one way or another."

"Has she lost her mind?" His temper flared. "I'm being blackmailed to look after a baby that's not mine."

"You could say no."

"I know, but then what will she do with the baby? I don't want to be responsible for the consequences." He had too many nightmares from being an unwanted child. "What did you finally tell her?"

"I told her that you'd be in touch." Freddie sighed. "Think before you commit to anything, Brad."

"I don't want to be anyone's father. I can barely get myself together and I'm still a work in progress. I don't need this crap."

"Especially with your trip to England."

"Damn. I'll talk to you later." He snapped the cell phone shut and stormed out of the porch. He felt caged. He grabbed his coat and walked out the door, slamming it shut behind him.

Nicole emerged from her hiding place in the dining room. She had walked up on the last few seconds of the conversation and could make out most of the words despite the dividing wall. The raised voice made her think that the boys had come back down and were chatting about their day. Instead, she heard anger and frustration in Brad's voice. Ready to take charge, she'd planned to offer her listening skills if he wanted to talk. The force of the door being flung back and his determined walk toward the front door gave her pause.

"What the hell." She'd made her decision. Grabbing her coat and gloves, she followed him out the door. The blast of icy air blast stung her cheeks. She huddled into her coat and ran to catch up to Brad's tall frame.

"Hey, looks like you need an ear." She chanced looking up at his face, hoping that he wouldn't be angry by her assertion.

He looked out past the wooden fence surrounding the front of the property. "I'd say that I need the great wise King Solomon."

Nicole watched the muscle in his jaw tick. The corners of his eyes crinkled as he squinted. "Can't say that I fill that role, but I do have my moments of brilliance."

He looked down on her with a soft smile. "I won't argue with you on that one." He sighed, the sound weighty and long. "I feel hemmed in." He balled his hands into fists. "Every available direction has the potential to blow up in my face."

"Are the consequences so bad, whether you do something or not?"

"Oh, God, yes." He kicked at the snow. "It's the most gut-wrenching dilemma."

Nicole sensed from the firm set of his lips that he was not ready to share any further information. "I sense that if you were the average man, it might not be such a dilemma. I think that you work on a higher set of standards that leaves you sec-ond-guessing yourself."

He turned his intense gaze on her. "That's pretty intuitive. What're your credentials?"

"Nothing in psychology. But I do recognize an over-achiever when I see one."

"Lady, compared with you, I've done nothing." He turned her around by her shoulders. "Have you stepped back and taken a look at your enormous success?"

Nicole did as he directed. She looked at her B&B. She had to admire the wintry scene with her bricked home and busi-ness sitting on farmland, smoke curling out of its chimney. "I'm not sure I'm successful, but I'm heading there." She looked up at him. "No changing the subject. We've got to get that frown off your face." She allowed an unrestrained shiver. "Besides, my ankles are now numb."

He laughed and Nicole melted against his frame where she could hear its rumble in his chest. "We can't have that." He promptly picked her up and bundled her with little effort against his chest. "There's something about you that makes me want to be your knight."

"I guess I've been a perfect damsel in distress every time

we meet." She chuckled, slightly embarrassed that he thought of her as needy.

Nicole enjoyed being carried into the warmth and coziness of the foyer. "Thank you, I'm fine now." She didn't want the boys to pop up with her dangling in their mentor's arms. When Brad didn't surrender to her wish, she wriggled and was rewarded with his arms tightening around her.

"Not so fast. I'm placing you in front of the fire. I'll take off your boots and I'm sure your socks are probably damp."

Sensory overload hit her system. "Um, I think you're over-doing the land rescue operation." She grinned to keep her words light. *"You're* the one who needed rescuing and, quite skillfully, you've turned the tables on me. I'm afraid to read what you'll say about me in your article."

He settled her in the oversize armchair and pulled it in front of the fire. Gently he touched her hair and traced a curl down her forehead. "It'll be the truth." He leaned into her, staring into her eyes.

Nicole raised her head off the chair, deciding that the warmth of Brad's arms proved more satisfying than the fire close to her feet. "The truth hurts."

Softly his lips brushed her forehead and he kissed her lightly on her temple. "I'll never hurt you."

"Mr. C, have you seen my CD?"

By the time Vinny came into the room, Brad was standing at the mantel and Nicole was reading a magazine. She hoped the precocious teenager wouldn't notice that it was upside down.

Audra sat behind her huge oak desk. The phone was wedged between her shoulder and neck as she leaned back in her leather chair. She was so close to making a deal with an-other developer for a strip mall. The taste of success added fuel to the adrenaline rush.

Her client had her on his speakerphone and she could hear the buzz as he and his lawyers discussed her terms.

"Okay, Miss Washington, you've got a deal."

A wide self-satisfied grin broke through on Audra's face. "Good news, I'll get in touch with Mr. Fitch; then his lawyers can finalize with yours." She pulled out a cigar and clamped the end between her teeth. "Get ready, Mr. Andrews; you're about to make tons of money."

"Let's hope so, Miss Washington."

Audra rang off and swiveled her chair around to admire the view. Instead, she looked at her reflection and admired her latest purchase of a navy suit. The earrings and matching bracelet were handsome accessories. She didn't need to check her makeup, it was always flawless. It took money to create the picture of confidence and status.

With the first item on her To Do list crossed off, she still had the nagging task of tracking down Brad. Her meeting with the investors was in a few hours. She sensed their unease that the plans weren't rolling out quickly.

She stabbed the intercom button. "Mildred, get me a cup of coffee."

An audible sigh answered her.

"Is there a problem?" She frowned down at the offending instrument.

"I don't do coffee, Miss Washington."

Audra hung up without acknowledgment or replying. A sarcastic quip came to mind, but her assistant was an enigma. She had seen her put the other senior managers in their place with the same soft voice that brooked no nonsense. At others' expense it was mildly amusing. For her, she could do without it.

She walked over to the coffee urn in her office and poured a cup. Her assistant probably expected her to burst out of her office in full indignation. She took a sip of the robust brew and smiled. Not today or at least not at this moment.

She picked up the phone, this time dialing Brad. After his assistant answered, she identified herself. "I need to get in touch with Brad. It's urgent."

"He's not available."

"Not good enough," she declared, frowning at the scuffed tip of her polished nail. "It's about the B-and-B in Maryland. I need to know when he'll be returning to review it."

"He's there as we speak."

Audra placed her hand over her chest and breathed a sigh of relief. "Do you have his number, other than his cell?"

"Only the contact number to the B-and-B. I've been communicating by his cell. He's due back this way in a day or so. That storm on your side of town really did a number on his schedule."

Audra didn't want to engage in idle chatter now that she'd gotten her information.

"Well, if you talk to him, please tell him that it's beyond urgent at this point."

Although she didn't get to solidify any plans with Brad, she was more willing to face her partners. Audra walked into the room, quickly surveying the faces of her partners. The air around her lay thick with tension. It didn't help that she didn't have any good news to tell. She poured herself a cup of water and took a sip to calm the jitters in her stomach.

"Miss Washington, I hope that I'm not wasting my time." The man sitting closest to her spoke, but he didn't turn to address her. Instead he stared straight in front of him.

"We're only experiencing a hitch," she offered, trying to give an easy smile to the other men. No one smiled back. "I have someone working on the inside for me, but if that doesn't work, I'm prepared to do whatever is necessary."

"I hope it won't come to that, because it involves more cost. Cost that will be taken out of your share." Again the man addressed the group. This time the men sitting around the table nodded.

Audra hated to be manhandled, but Mr. Druthers's reputation preceded him.

Nine

Brad stretched under the covers, his eyes closed, inhaling the aroma of freshly baked biscuits. The bed, this house, the woman who tantalized his senses intoxicated him into drunken slumber. Most mornings at home he awoke hours before the sun crept over the horizon. His sleep was rarely restful as his inner demons wreaked havoc on his mind.

Opening his eyes slowly, he stared up, mentally counting the beams crisscrossing the ceiling. The sturdy retreat proved safe and comforting for him. Although Audra rubbed him the wrong way, he could be grateful for her turning him on to this oasis.

His priority was to complete his interview with Nicole. He sensed her pride in the place, but he questioned her passion to care for it after the honeymoon phase wore off. He swung his legs over the side of the bed, stretched, and yawned once more. Then there was her apparent attraction to him and he couldn't help wondering when that would start to fizzle.

The bright morning sun peeped through the drawn curtains. At least no storm clouds were in sight. He pulled back a drape and had to shield his eyes from the startling brightness. A thick bed of crisp white carpeted the surroundings. The pine trees lining the front were postcard perfect with snow accenting each branch.

Now the scent of bacon and eggs filled the air and his stomach rumbled. By the time he left, Nicole would have spoiled him rotten with home-cooked meals. His days of frozen dinners or Chinese takeout were long forgotten.

After breakfast, the boys headed outdoors. Brad followed them and stood on the porch watching them play as he admired the expansive space of covered snow. The whiteness was so startling that the sun caused flakes to twinkle. New York's crowded city life didn't afford such panoramic views. His breath caught when a buck strolled out from the edge of the trees and sniffed the air. Maybe the eggs and biscuits reached him, also.

"Isn't it beautiful?" Nicole said softly beside him.

She stood next to him, bundled in a large jacket with a steaming mug of chocolate.

"This place is so perfect."

"I thought so when I purchased it. I felt an immediate connection that provided a type of comfort to me." She handed him the mug. "I wanted to share its special quality with others."

"Isn't that what a family is for?"

"There you go again. I have to be married, not a businesswoman."

Brad frowned, kicking himself for not choosing his words carefully. "It was my way of trying to find out if there is a special someone."

"Next time just ask."

"Yes, ma'am."

"No, there is no one. I told you that last night." She looked in the direction of the boys' loud exclamations. "Hasn't been for a long time." She cast a critical eye on him. "They all seemed a bit intimidated by little ol' me." She pointed at him. "Like you."

She didn't surrender an inch to him and he admired her even more for that. "Looks like all I can do around you is apologize," he said.

"At least it's not as frequent as when I first met you." She smiled and automatically he smiled back at her.

"I'm constantly amazed that you don't have a boyfriend." Brad watched the steam from his mug curl past her profile. He admired her features, even her ear with its diamond-studded earring. What lay beneath the cocoa skin? Was she an iceberg or at the other extreme, a hot-blooded seductress? The latter evoked a response that sent a warm rush through him. He shifted his weight, embarrassed by his body's traitorous reaction. He was here for a review, nothing else.

"Do you want to be my boyfriend?"

"Huh?" He shuffled, moving closer to the door. She hadn't moved an inch, but he could see from the stiffness in her body that she wanted his reply.

"Don't bother answering. I know you want an old-fashioned girl. One that will wait for you to ask her." Then she turned and gave him a bright smile, leaving him to feel as if he imagined the intense, emotional moment. "I'm getting cold, let's head back in." She walked past him and he meekly followed. "Mr. Calverton, what do you think of my B-and-B?"

Grateful for her switching subjects, he replied readily, "I'm pleased with what I've seen." He surveyed the interior. "I'm interested in a place like this."

"Really? Just for yourself?"

"Why is that so strange?"

"Not strange, just a little crazy because you can probably afford any residence in a ritzy neighborhood. Why would you want a B-and-B?"

Her curiosity rolled over him like a swift current in a roaring river. She always seemed to have that effect on him with her directness. "Don't mind me, I'm just talking."

"Well, it's just that . . ." To explain his reasoning would mean baring a part of himself that he'd rather shield from prying eyes, even Nicole's beautiful brown eyes.

"Hard to put into words, right? Same for me in the beginning. I knew once I had visited one that it was the right thing for me to get into. It's not about money." She sat on the stairs looking up at him, her eyes alive with her newfound passion. She ran her hand along the banister and post. "It's got potential, don't you think?"

"Yes, and you're on the right track. But only if you're in it for the long haul." He looked around the foyer and let his imagination run with the possibilities. Was it really the B&B or its petite owner who had more than a little spunk that he found intoxicating and addictive?

"One thing you should know, Mr. Calverton, is that once I've set my mind on something, only a miracle can make me back off."

He saw no hesitation. "What if I said that I was interested in buying it?"

"What if I said you could go to hell?" Nicole's eyes narrowed and the smile vanished. She stood on the step meeting Brad at eye level. "Is that why you came for a second time? Are you going to stiff me and write a nasty review and then try to take this place from under me?" Nicole placed a hand on her hip and jabbed at his chest with her other hand. "If you want to mess with me, then come on. I'll rip your b—"

"Whoa. Down, girl." Brad was torn between laughing at Nicole's indignation and having to defend his privates. "From being your boyfriend to being your first homicide victim— my, my, the options are scarce."

"Don't try to play me. I worked hard to get this place and I plan to work even harder to keep it."

"Do you know how utterly adorable you are when you're angry? Passionate and dangerous, what a rush!" He couldn't resist teasing her, although she partly discovered his motive. "I admit that I was curious about why you wanted a B-and-B, because you said you had a successful career. And I'm always on the lookout for a good investment, that's all. Didn't mean to give you any reason to fear me or my intentions. Friends?" He stretched out his hand as a peace offering.

"Friends." She offered him a familiar wide smile and he felt his heart loosening up at its radiance. "So does this mean that you're now my boyfriend?"

He shook his head, chuckling. "And you were a lobbyist, right?" He walked upstairs past her and said, "I can handle being a boyfriend." She didn't know it, but she was way out of his league for him to be *the* boyfriend.

"Okay, I'll just go cook and clean." She dipped a curtsy and left.

Nicole really didn't have much cooking and cleaning to do. But she had to give the illusion that Brad's retreat at her brazen declaration hadn't hurt. There were no regrets for her forthrightness. She only wished that she could penetrate Brad's defenses.

By the end of the day, her young guests were snapping at each other. Each person's little idiosyncrasies plucked some-one else's nerves. Brad had to step in on several occasions before a heated argument escalated into something physical. Nicole sighed. It would appear that the recuperative effects of the retreat had come to an end. Her city-born-and-bred guests were ready to return to the Big Apple.

After dinner, Nicole set her mind on the task of coming up with some kind of activity since the roads were still too icy to go into town. She loaded the last dirty dish into the dish-washer and punched in the washing cycle. What would her mother do in a time like this?

She hadn't thought about her mother in this way in a while. Yet, she could tap into many wonderful memories of the fam-ily at their vacation home having face time. Her mother had taught her many life skills that she had resisted in her quest to be her own woman. What a role model her mom had turned out to be. Funny that when she was younger many of her friends had their mother at home full-time and she had envied the privilege.

When it counted, it was her mother's fiery independence and strength that served as her source of strength when she waited for the results from the doctor.

Lately, Nicole realized that the efficient, dependable workaholic was only one side of her. She'd taught herself to be focused and committed to the cause. It took a random guest to walk into her B&B and shove logic aside. In a matter of minutes after meeting him, her imagination knew no limits. She found herself in an emotional state that she had never experienced before.

With limited entertainment options available, Nicole grabbed an armful of videotapes from her apartment and headed back to the family room. "Hey, guys, got a few movies for you." She dumped them into a heap on the couch.

"Got *Cops and the Original G's*?" Vinny asked. "It just came out on video." He formed his hands into a gun and acted out a scene. "You think you're the law of this neighborhood, punk? I'm the law. I'm judge and jury. And on this day, I'm your executioner, mothafu—"

"Whoa, whoa." Nicole frowned at him, wondering who the heck would go to the movies to see something with that title. "Do I look like I would have that tape?"

His scrunched face still in his bad-boy role was answer enough for her. "Guess not." Vinny took his place on the floor, no longer interested in her offerings.

"Dawg, that was on the money." Tyrone slapped a high five with Vinny.

"Obviously, Vinny can't handle anything intellectual. I, on the other hand, am open to new experiences." Big Ed smiled, all teeth. "So what you got?"

"He's just cheesin', Miss Montgomery," Tyrone offered. "I think he's got a crush on you." Tyrone slapped his knee and rolled around in the chair guffawing at his revelation.

Big Ed's head snapped up obviously surprised by Tyrone's admission. "You better stop with all that. I ain't interested in Miss Montgomery. She's way older than me."

"That's enough, before either one of you insults me any further." She counted the tapes. "Pick a number and you'll get whatever that tape is."

Vinny groaned.

"Vinny, go make two bags of popcorn for us. That's your

punishment for groaning." Nicole watched him go, and hid the chuckle at his lanky figure hurrying off to the kitchen.

Brad walked into the room, his eyes only on her. Nicole blushed, loving the way his huge frame filled a room. He looked heavenly in faded blue jeans and a sweatshirt. If she wasn't mistaken, it looked like he had a slight bow in his leg. Some might see imperfection. She found the added touch an ingredient for a totally sexy package. "Brad, pick a number."

"Nope." He surveyed the despondent faces staring back at him. "You're not going to blame me for making us watch some public television, highbrow documentary."

"We've decided." Big Ed motioned to the other guys and himself. "We're picking number three."

She pulled the number three tape and hid the label. "Keep your eyes on the screen." Quickly, she slipped the tape into the machine and started the movie, bracing herself for the protests sure to follow.

The opening title popped into view—*Out on a Limb*.

"A love story?" Vinny held his head in distress.

"I don't think it would have mattered what was picked. I'm sure Nicole only has romance stories in her stockpile," Brad teased.

They were the only two standing, with the boys sitting on the floor sharing a bowl of popcorn. "It wouldn't hurt to balance all that testosterone with some social graces." Nicole cast an irritated glance their way. "Pretty soon you'll be taking girls out on dates. At least you'll know what women want. As for you . . ." She pointed at Brad. "You could do with a few brushup tips." Quite grandly, she sat in the armchair and pulled the lap cover over her legs and stared at the screen.

Half an hour into the movie, everyone had relaxed. The few comedic spots brought laughter and the soft romantic scenes drew the usual groans.

Nicole wondered what Brad thought about the underlying message of the movie. This was one of her favorite movies because it spoke to her on different levels. She easily identified with the lead character, Joni, who took charge of her life with focus and planning. The turmoil came, however, when a stubborn, ill-tempered man, Seth, moved in as her new neighbor. Immediately he upset the balance in her life, until she struggled with what or whom she desired most of all.

Nicole barely suppressed her satisfied sigh when Joni opted to follow her heart and go after her man. Only movies have a happy ending, but she was willing to settle for its hopeful themes. Before the credits could start rolling, the boys popped up.

"Thanks, Miss Montgomery. Ah, we'll just be heading upstairs now." Big Ed turned to Brad. "We have to start packing, right?"

"Go ahead." Brad waved them away, laughing as they hastily retreated.

"Regardless of what they say, they will thank me later." Nicole pushed the REWIND button on the remote. At least Brad didn't run up the stairs, leading the pack, although she could do without his constant snickers.

"On behalf of all men, stop analyzing me."

"Me?"

"I can feel the effects of your brain whirring away as you compare me with that sap in the movie." Brad pointed at the dark television screen.

"Oh, really? And what is wrong with that sap?"

"He had no backbone. Looks to me like he gave up a lot for nothing in return."

"Oh, my gosh!" Nicole exclaimed. "How can you say that? No one gave up anything."

"Joni sure didn't give up a darn thing."

"And Seth had to reshift his priorities, but he certainly didn't give up anything either," Nicole defended.

"Reshift? Is that what you call it. He got whipped. If there were an additional twenty minutes of footage, it'd show her taking over his life, and pressuring him until they get married."

Nicole glared at Brad, debating cracking his head with the remote. "You're dark and depressing."

"Dark, but realistic. Then the kids come into their messed-up world as a captive audience having to deal with all that drama."

Nicole sighed. "Well, that makes my life difficult."

"What?"

"That philosophy of love. You're like an atheist of love."

"And you're the exact opposite. Like a fanatical cheer-leader. And what the heck do my views have to do with your life?" He leaned back against the cushions with an arm thrown on the back of the chair.

Nicole rolled her eyes. "Men are so dense. I'm attracted to you, Brad." She pointed at him with the remote. "Are you attracted to me?"

"What's that have to do with anything?" he asked, frowning.

"If you find me attractive, then we need to do something about it. So . . ."

"What does love have to do with it?"

"In your case, not a thing, but let's take baby steps. Answer me: Do you find me attractive?"

Brad drew himself up from his relaxed position on the love seat. His expression was neutral. He eyed her warily.

"Someone must have done a number on you," Nicole declared.

"I told you . . . don't analyze me."

Nicole got up and walked behind the love seat, stopping behind him. When he didn't move, she gently held his head and leaned it back on the couch. No one spoke and she stared straight into his dark eyes, trying to penetrate whatever barrier he erected to keep her out.

He shifted slightly, his breathing a little harder. Nicole didn't let her gaze shift, but noted his chest rising and falling more. It wasn't time to let up, though. She slid her hands down the sides of his face and cupped his chin. By her stepping forward, his head now rested against her stomach.

"What is it, Brad? Why are you afraid of me?"

"Afraid? My attitude shouldn't be mistaken for fear. It's called being realistic. I have nothing to offer you. One day, you'll grow tired of me, the real me, and discard me in your recycle bin with all the others."

Nicole stopped looking into his eyes, and instead focused on his lips, where a moment ago he had licked. "You'd rather fight the mutual attraction and starve your soul?"

"I don't mean to hurt your feelings, but the mutual attraction may be a figment of your imagination."

She walked around and sat next to him, this time keeping her hands to herself. "You are a tough case. While I come up with plan B, tell me about yourself."

"No."

Nicole raised an eyebrow. "So now you're resorting to rudeness." She threw her head back and laughed. "I must be having an effect. I'll go first. I'm the youngest of three. My mother is a pharmacist and my father is a surgeon. My brother is in the military and lives in Germany with his family. My sister is also married with children, living in the Bahamas. So with them out of the way, my parents spend their time on me, waiting impatiently for me to fall in line and get married."

"Is this where I come in?"

"Maybe. I'm wondering if you're worth the fight." She examined her nails. "I'm not used to doing the pursuing. There was a time that I wouldn't have given you the time of day." She shook her head when his eyes narrowed. "Not that I thought I was too cute for you. Nope. Instead it was because all I thought about was work, work, and more work."

"And what happened?"

"Let's just say that I suffered a small crisis and it reshaped my priorities."

"You're like vanilla flavoring, a little goes a long way." Brad took her small hand in his and stroked the lines of her veins.

"And you like vanilla?"

"Love it."

"Then come here."

He leaned forward and covered her mouth with his lips. Nicole wanted to swallow him whole and enjoyed exploring his mouth with her tongue. When he gathered her up into his arms, she relaxed and allowed him to take over with soft, deep strokes of his tongue. She pulled away first. "I see you like to nibble and sample the merchandise. Are you willing to stick around for seconds?"

He pulled away, not meeting her eyes.

The hesitation, his withdrawal, spoke louder than his denial. It had the sobering effect as a dash of cold water. "Take your boys home, Brad. I'm a woman with needs, physical and emotional needs. I think you are all the man that I need, but you've got to meet me halfway."

"What do you want from me, woman?" Brad's voice sliced through the air, filled with a raw edginess.

At the moment, she wanted only him. Nicole stood and walked up between his legs, bumping each thigh apart with her leg. A sly grin crossed her lips when she saw his stomach clench. "You're safe for the moment, Brad," she reassured him in a husky whisper. "I won't teach you a lesson that you'll never forget, just yet." She tilted her head toward the door. "Can't with the boys here."

His hands moved to the sides of her hips. She took one hand and gently guided it over her buttock. Her devilish smile merely deepened. With her other hand, she put it against her lips and kissed each finger tip, leaving a moist memory on each finger.

"You ask me what I want? Is it clear now?"

He gulped. "But is that all you want from me?"

She laughed, still husky, arching her neck. "Not at all. But since you're into sampling, I thought I'd give you a taste of what a real woman is like. I'm not sure what you've been dealing with, but you don't know your worth." In an instant, she snapped out of the sultry seducer and slapped his thighs closed. "Sleep on that." She reopened the doors and stood in the doorway with her arms folded across her chest.

She had issued a challenge and he wished he could have a snappy comeback, but the telltale bulge in his pants prevented him from jumping up. Instead he chose to pretend that he was in control. "You're a beautiful woman, Nicole, but the timing isn't right for me. Maybe one day . . ."

He saw the spark of anger flash, but she retained her sentry post at the doorway. "It's a shame that you hold your heart a prisoner."

Before he could reply, a flurry of excited voices caught their attention. "Where are the boys?"

"I hear sounds coming from the basement."

They headed to the open basement door.

"Miss Montgomery, you won't believe what we found!" Big Ed stood halfway on the stairway, looking up at Nicole and Brad.

"What is it?" Brad's heart pounded. Who had gotten hurt?

"Come on down. You've got to see it for yourself." Big Ed disappeared down the steps and around a wall.

Brad looked at Nicole, mirroring her concern. "You lead, I'll follow."

Nicole hesitated on the top step. "That's really macho of you. What if something jumps out at me?"

"Exactly!"

"Men." Nicole rolled her eyes and stomped down the stairs.

Brad followed closely behind, ready to throw her to the floor, if necessary. They heard the boys' excited chatter down a narrow hallway. "What's down here?"

"Nothing really. I haven't gotten around to cleaning it up. I was thinking about making it into a gym and putting the massage room down here."

The narrow hallway prevented him from walking alongside Nicole. He kept a hand on her hip, wanting to maintain some kind of body contact as they approached the source of the excitement.

"Okay, guys, what's up?"

The three boys were on their knees, peering into a dark room. Big Ed came over to Brad and Nicole, his hair dotted with cobwebs and his T-shirt and jeans covered with powdery dust.

Nicole stepped past Big Ed. "Move over, guys, let me see." She stuck half her body into the dark space. Brad forced himself to wait for her to emerge and say something.

"It's some kind of room." She brushed her clothes. "I'll need a flashlight."

Brad stepped up to make his own assessment. "How old is your house?"

"I'm not sure. I think about a hundred years or so. Why?"

Brad wasn't sure whether he should voice his opinion before further investigation. But it would fit, given the location of the farmhouse, this room, which he was sure had another exit, and the town's history. He ran his hand around the doorway. "How did you find this room?"

"We got kinda bored," Vinny said, clearly agitated. "Then we came down here, just to look around."

"We were pretending that we were in a rap group. So we were dancing and rapping," Tyrone joined in.

"My foot hit the wall and the door popped open." Big Ed pointed at the slight dent in the wall. "I'll pay for it, Miss Montgomery."

Brad scowled at the group. "See what horseplaying does?"

"It's okay, Brad. One of you go upstairs and look in the kitchen for a flashlight." Nicole placed a calming hand on his arm. "What do you think about this?"

"I'm not sure."

"I think you have an idea, though."

He nodded. "A secret room."

"Why would anyone have a secret room, other than in stories with castles and dungeons?"

Brad ran his hands over the opening reverently. His heart beat excitedly. "Because it was a place for the slaves to hide."

Ten

Sunday morning rolled in with lots of excitement from the previous night. Nicole knew they had unearthed a monumental treasure laden with history. Late into the night, she had walked into the windowless room. There was another short door that led through a tunnel that had now caved in. Brad thought that maybe there was another structure that camouflaged the trapdoor that was sure to be the escape hatch.

Much work had to be done to verify the find, but municipal offices wouldn't be open until later in the day. In the meantime, her guests were departing, including Brad. Finding the hidden room overshadowed any further discussion between Brad and her. She finalized the paperwork for him to sign whenever he came down. She could hear the constant patter of feet and thuds from the suitcases. The taxi would be there in ten minutes.

"Looks like it's time for us to be heading back."

Nicole looked up and couldn't bring herself to give a smile, even a faked one. "I've got your paperwork for checkout ready." She slid the papers toward him.

"Thank you." He reached for the papers, his fingers grazing hers.

She pulled back, not wanting any lasting memories of his touch, scent, or anything that would imprint further on her subconscious.

"I think you'll be pleased with my write-up. I'll send you an advance copy."

"Thanks." She could feel him looking at her, waiting. But she had given all that she could and he had rejected her. At some point, a girl had only her self-respect left. She was determined to keep that intact until his taxi disappeared from view.

A car horn sounded. The boys thundered down the stairs and ran past her door. She hoped they didn't leave without a proper good-bye. Without glancing at Brad, she walked around her desk and left the office.

"Now I know you boys aren't gonna leave me hangin'." She stood in the doorway with arms outstretched.

They had already jostled for seats in the taxi. Looking chagrined, they stepped out, tripping over each other. "Sorry, Miss M, I truly had a good time," Vinny said, and gave her a shy hug.

"I liked it here," Tyrone offered. "It's quiet and pretty. Thanks." Tyrone smiled, but didn't step forward.

Nicole didn't violate his space and smiled back and waved as they loaded up and left.

If she didn't keep herself busy, the alternative would be to sit around and miss Brad. She'd also miss the boys who gave the house a lived-in quality. She went upstairs to strip each bed and open the windows for airing.

She dusted, vacuumed, and moved the dirty laundry down the hall as she cleaned each room. She saved Brad's room for last. Not only because it was the biggest one, but she wanted to take her time, enjoying the lingering scent of his cologne. She didn't know when she would see him again. They had made no promises, nothing that could remain unfilled.

There was no reason to have him return. He had made it clear that she wasn't reason enough. After cleaning the room, she closed the door, and the symbolism wasn't lost on her.

Her phone rang. She ran down the stairs and headed into the office for the nearest phone. She answered. It was the town's historian who also worked at the city's library, which she knew would be open today.

"I'm so glad you returned my call, Mr. Welsley."

"How can I help you?"

"Over the weekend I found a room; actually, I think it's a secret room."

"Where?"

"In the basement. Someone hit the wall, I guess in the right spot, and a door with no knob opened."

"Very interesting." He paused. "I'm not sure how I can help you."

"I need your expertise on the local history. My feeling is that the house was a refuge."

"I'm not sure about that. Most of those houses were closer to Annapolis. Not that it's impossible. I'll have to come and take a look."

"Sure, anytime. In the meantime, I'll be researching the history of the house. If you can help me in that area also, I'd appreciate it."

"Your best bet is to try the courthouse. Should have it there."

Nicole thanked him and hung up. She didn't have time to go to the courthouse tomorrow.

Grateful for the lull in guests, Nicole descended the stairs with her huge stack of laundry. She opened the basement door and tossed it down the steps. She'd deal with it later that evening when she was winding down. There was still grocery shopping to be done and Toni had arm-twisted her into meeting everyone for lunch.

Driving into the town, Nicole enjoyed the rare pleasure of just hanging out. The traffic was light as she drove along the winding roads to her friends' favorite restaurant. Green fields of rolling hills whizzed past with the occasional farmhouse sitting prominently on the property.

She pulled up to the former farmhouse, now an Italian restaurant. The parking area in front of the building was filled, so she drove around to the back. The Taste of Italy

158 Michelle Monkou

had a well-deserved reputation with the townspeople. Nicole pulled into the graveled lot and headed in.

Luckily the other women were already there, so she was seated immediately.

"Who's springing for me?" Nicole slid into the booth.

"What makes you special?" Shirley accused, shifting her body to make room.

The waiter stopped by and took their orders.

"What a cutie." Toni leaned back in her chair and admired the college-aged young man.

"Robbing the cradle again, I see," Shirley said, wryly.

"Whatever!" Toni waved her off.

The drinks arrived. Nicole had an iced tea.

"Shirley, what's happening with you?" Donna inquired.

"Everything's fine."

"Hmm," Toni said. "Seems to me that you're not talking about your most beautiful man anymore." She looked at Nicole and Donna. "I mean we haven't even seen him."

Shirley twisted her water glass around on the coaster, keeping her eyes downcast.

"We're all waiting for an answer," Toni prodded.

Nicole sensed Shirley's reluctance. "It's all right, honey. You don't have to say anything if you don't want. Toni is trying to live vicariously through you."

"You know, you may have a point," Toni conceded. "Things have been pretty lame on my end." She turned her attention to Nicole, piercing her with a stare, and pointed with a nacho chip. "You, I don't plan to back off because I'm liking that glow."

Nicole sighed. She knew that sooner or later she'd have to admit defeat. Then would come a healthy dosage of pity.

"Uh-oh." Toni slapped her hand on the table. "Don't tell me that you screwed that up." She sat back against the chair with arms folded. "Damn, Nicole."

Donna elbowed Toni. "Toni, shut up."

The orders arrived filling the lull in the conversation.

Nicole pretended to be absorbed in the television overhead.

"I want to hear about it," Toni insisted. "Stop looking at that boring car racing and talk."

Nicole sighed. "He came, he saw, and he left."

"Nothing happened?" Toni asked with doubt laden in her question.

Nicole shook her head.

"So you wasted a good opportunity to be sinfully wicked?"

"Sex isn't everything," Shirley objected.

"In your case that statement is correct because you pick men who just want you to be their mother."

Donna's fork clattered onto her plate. A deepening frown marked her forehead. "Pay her no mind." She squeezed Shirley's shoulder, which had slumped under Toni's on-slaught.

Nicole didn't always appreciate Toni's forthrightness. Many times, they'd bumped heads, not speaking for weeks because of Toni's sharp tongue.

Shirley was the most sensitive of the group, despite all the years of having to deal with Toni. She was always affected.

Something about Toni bothered Nicole, though. "What's really wrong, Toni?"

"What do you mean?" Toni stared back defiantly.

"Is it your mother?" At the possibility that her favorite "auntie" might be ill, her heart softened toward Toni.

"No." Toni took a long drink of her iced tea. "It's not any-thing."

"Liar," Nicole rebutted. She propped her cheek and waited.

It was now Toni's turn to squirm under the scrutiny. No one spoke, sensing that there indeed was news to share.

"Remember Clayton from last year?"

They all nodded.

"He's history, right?" Nicole had to state the question be-cause it delayed the reason for her dread.

"He *was* history." Toni played with the linguini, wrapping it with her fork. "About two months ago, he got in touch with me."

Donna sighed heavily and pushed her plate away.

Nicole caught her exasperated look, but decided to wait to hear Toni's version before casting judgment.

"For a while it was beautiful to have him back in my life."

"Unbeknownst to us!" Donna accused. "I can't—"

"What about his wife?" Nicole interrupted. Donna's raised voice had some of the patrons turning in their direction.

"He said they had finally separated and—"

"And you believed him? After all that big talk you do around us, you fell for the oldest line in the book." Donna rolled her eyes at her cousin.

"He *was* separated," Toni insisted. "At least I thought so because he'd come from work and spend the night."

"So when did you learn that he'd lied?" Donna wasn't cutting her a break.

"When I told him that I was—"

"Pregnant?" Shirley squeaked.

Toni nodded. When she looked up at them her eyes were flooded with tears.

"What did the bastard say?"

"He didn't say anything. I'd made the first prenatal appointment and he said that he'd come to the doctor's office." She sniffed and brushed a tear away. "But I went through the entire examination by myself. When I got home, he had moved all his stuff out of my apartment."

Donna placed her arm around her and hugged her close.

"There was no note." Toni sounded so small, unlike the aggressive, in-your-face presence that was her usual self.

"Bastard," Shirley hissed.

"I bet you haven't had time to think about anything," Nicole said. Her heart went out to Toni, knowing how hard she'd fallen for Clayton.

Toni nodded. "You're right. I'm not sure what my next step will be. But I do know that in seven months I'll be a mother."

Nicole recognized the familiar determination in her friend's voice. She was willing to support her no matter what her decision. "It's going to be tough when you tell your family," Nicole warned.

"Tell me about it. Not only did I get back with the enemy, but I'll have a lasting consequence. Most children are conceived through love. But in my case, my child was conceived in a moment of stupidity."

Donna rubbed her cousin's shoulders. "Don't be hard on yourself." She paused and winked at Shirley and Nicole. "After all that's our job."

Shirley placed her hand, palm down, on the table. "Ladies, it's time for our usual oath."

Donna placed her palm on Shirley's hand with Nicole following suit. They waited for Toni. The sight of seeing her eyes laden with tears brought them to an emotional, teary-eyed discussion about love's blindness.

A week ago news about Toni's life had shaken up Nicole. It reiterated that she wasn't where she wanted to be in her life. Her heart had the answers, but that wasn't enough. There was no way around being in love with someone who wouldn't, or couldn't return her love.

Although her days were busy and she had accomplished another goal, she couldn't overcome the loneliness. Ever since Brad and the boys had left, she couldn't shake missing them . . . and him. Whenever she had the doldrums, she'd take on a physical task that punished her muscles and made her so exhausted she slept without having to deal with the pining of her heart.

Nicole pulled the ladder from the shed and dragged it to the back of the house. Charles wasn't available until Thursday and there was no way that the gutters would hold up if there was another heavy rain shower. As she propped the ladder against the house for the task at hand, she thought about how far she'd come. From the power-brokering political bull pen to the exacting duties of a B&B owner.

Although, lately, her B&B's plight had become very political, it amused her that people like the mayor and Audra underestimated her reaction. She'd spent time building her reputation by maneuvering among the empty promises and manipulating the players.

Nicole gave the ladder a shake to ensure that it was on firm ground. She mounted it, remembering not to look down. The snow was long gone, but the air was still nippy. Once she got eye-level to the roof, she carefully swung her leg onto the roof and pulled herself up. Gingerly standing up, she didn't make any sudden movements. Her breath caught at the fantastic waterfront view of Annapolis. A sense of awe overcame her as she stood over some of the biggest trees in her yard. She felt so small in relation to everything around her.

She edged forward and stooped to hammer in first one nail and then another. It wasn't as bad as she'd imagined. By the time she'd made it halfway across, however, her fingers had become numb. Their stiffness made it difficult to hold on to the hammer. Barely any breeze blew, for which she was thankful because of the low temperature.

A sound from the other side of the house made her stop. She stood, trying to determine exactly where it came from and what made the sound. Then it stopped and after a while, a door slammed. Someone had arrived. Wondering who it could be, she inched along the roof to get to the front.

From the angle where she stood, she couldn't see who was at the door, but she could hear the person knocking. "Hello," she yelled, cupping her mouth. "Who's there?" She had to repeat the call before the person stopped knocking.

Nicole saw the shadow on the ground appear first, getting larger. Then a familiar face looked up at her.

"What brings you here, Mr. Calverton?"

"It was something you said."

Nicole couldn't claim that she wasn't excited, that her heart didn't race, that it took all her self-control not to stand with her legs apart, hands on her hips, and shout from her rooftop.

"I said a lot of things, Mr. Calverton. You may have to refresh my memory."

"I'll refresh more than that."

"So, you're ready to meet me halfway?"

He bowed with flourish. "At your service, ma'am."

Nicole took her gloves off and threw them down at him. "I'll be right there." She stepped quickly along the edge back to the ladder. She had been so angry when Brad left, but one look at his face and she couldn't stay that way.

Her heart soared with anticipation. She stepped onto the ladder and began her descent looking down to see if Brad was there. There was still a long way to go. Her foot missed a rung and she slipped, holding on tightly to the sides of the ladder.

"Honey, be careful."

Nicole's hands hurt, but she put on a brave smile and wave. "I'm fine." She continued on down and halfway down stepped on her shoelace. It jarred her momentum.

"Nicole."

She chanced looking down at him to give him a thumbs-up sign and her hand slipped. This time there was no chance for recovery. Nicole felt as if someone had plucked her off the ladder and then let her go to free-fall to the ground. Just before she lost consciousness, she wondered why Brad hadn't moved out of her way.

Brad sat in the waiting room, impatiently looking at his watch, wondering when the doctor would give him an update. He didn't want to have to deal with his distress in public.

"Mr. Calverton?"

Brad looked up and quickly read the name tag. "Doc, how's she doing?"

"Let's go see her and we can talk. By the way, I'm Dr. Fenton." They shook hands.

Brad walked beside the doctor, holding back his questions that he knew would soon be answered.

"Miss Montgomery doesn't have a concussion. But she has some nasty bruises and a sprained ankle. It's my understanding that she lives alone. Under the circumstances, she'll need to make alternative arrangements. Not for long, just for a few days."

Brad had three days before he headed to England. That would give him enough time to set the record straight. "I can stay with her, Doc."

"Good. Well, here she is," the doctor said, pointing to the end of the row of beds.

Brad had allowed the doctor to go ahead of him. He wanted her to be prepared to see him. Maybe the excitement that he felt from her had all been erased from the fall.

"Brad," Nicole called to him, softly. She reached an outstretched hand to him.

"Oh, my gosh, you look terrible." He laughed, but only to keep himself from crying. Her face seemed so small on the pillow with a large purplish bruise on one side of her temple. Her bottom lip had a cut that had already begun to heal, but was swollen.

"And you look wonderful," she offered with a wincing smile. "Thanks for allowing me to land on you."

"My pleasure."

"Actually Mr. Calverton, if you didn't try to break her fall, it would have been worse. She might have had a few broken bones. By the way, have you been checked?" Dr. Fenton asked.

Brad raised his hands. "I'm fine." He probably did have a few bruises, but his phobia of doctors and hospitals was more overpowering.

"I'll start the discharge papers. You may stay here until someone comes to take Miss Montgomery out to the driveway."

Brad nodded, fully appreciating that the doctor allowed him to stay. He waited until she had walked away from the bed, before turning his attention to Nicole. "I'm staying with you for a few days."

"Oh, Brad, no. That's not necessary. I can get Shirley to come over."

"No argument. I was coming to see you anyway."

"Oh, yes, I remember now. Not that I'm not glad to see you, but why?"

"Because despite it all, I'm really a romantic at heart."

Nicole took his hand and kissed it. "I promise it won't be a painful experience. Would you kiss me before I go insane?"

"Gladly." He hovered over her face before kissing her gently on her forehead.

She groaned. "Try again."

"Bossy little thing, aren't you?" This time he kissed her on the tip of her darling nose.

"You're lucky that I'm not my usual self."

"Shh." He dropped a kiss on her mouth, flicking his tongue across her lips for the sheer thrill of it.

"Ahem, Miss Montgomery," a voice interrupted. "I'm here to take you out of the hospital."

Brad didn't pull away immediately. He didn't give a damn who saw him kiss Nicole. "Later, we must finish this."

She grinned back at him, wincing when her smile got too wide. "It's a promise."

Brad pulled up in front of the B&B. The porch light was on, as were a few lights in the house. He had made the necessary calls to Nicole's friends from the hospital, explaining what had happened. They were all equally interested in his coincidental appearance and interrogated him about his intentions. Donna reminded him that he only had tonight to take care of Nicole before they checked in. Bright and early, they were heading over to see if he did a good job nursing her. She also promised to go over now and turn on a few lights for appearance's sake.

"Stay put." Brad ran around to the passenger side, knowing that Nicole would give her best effort to get out without his help.

"I'm fine," she replied, through gritted teeth.

Her mouth was set in a thin line and her brow beaded with sweat. He scooped her into his arms.

"I wish I had the strength to resist you . . ." she said, her voice trailing off.

He carried her into the house and straight to her bedroom. "I'll draw you a hot bath for a good soak. In the meantime, here, take these." He opened a small white bag, pulled out a brown bottle, and shook out two pills. "I'll get you some water."

Once she had taken the medication, he ran the water.

"Your bath is ready, m'lady." He placed a robe within her reach. "Let me know when you're ready and I'll take you to the tub."

He waited just beyond the bedroom door, listening to her struggle and give an occasional groan.

"I'm ready."

She had the robe tied loosely around her. Fatigue was etched on her face. He scooped her up again and took her to the tub. Not sure whether to set her down and have her use her own strength to get into the tub or help her with his eyes closed, he hesitated.

"I'll need your help. Let me sit on the corner, here," Nicole said. "I don't think I can put my leg in and keep the other one from getting wet."

"Okay, but I promise I'm not looking." His words rang sincere, at least he wanted them to be, but deep down he knew that he might sneak a quick peek.

"Here, I'll make the first move." She pulled the sash and wiggled out of the robe, never taking her eyes off his face.

Brad was sure he'd stopped breathing. His groin tightened and he wondered if he'd ever come to life again. Smooth and creamy brown, her full breasts lay bare for his admiration. Their dark brown nipples tightened under his intense stare and he imagined what it would feel like to touch them. He expected to see Nicole laughing at him, but she remained still, waiting.

"I'll need you to support me, while I take it off." Her voice sounded small in the steamy bathroom.

He stepped up and held her. The robe dropped to her feet, revealing the rest of her. She leaned over slightly to hold on to the bathtub wall and her breast brushed his hand. He sucked in his breath sharply. There was no way he could help her with his head turned to the side.

"Brad," she called. "Look at me."

He turned slowly.

"It's okay." She kissed him. "I want you to see me. I want you to feel me. I want you to want me, like I ache for you."

Every time she mentioned the word "want," his groin reacted, keeping beat with her. He knew why he was still resisting. If he succumbed, then there was no turning back. No safety net in case he fell. All he had to do was to look into her brown eyes and let go.

Nicole placed her hand on his chest. "I'm ready. Are you?"

He nodded. Stepping back, he gave her room to step into the tub. Just as he admired her breasts, he admired her slim waist down to her wide hips. There was no missing the curly black triangle with its promise of erotic pleasure. She lowered her body into the suds and he adjusted her bandaged leg onto the side of the tub.

"Did you take your medication?" His mouth felt dry.

She nodded. "I think it's kicking in, thank goodness." She leaned back in the tub until the suds modestly covered her chest. "Give me your hand," she ordered.

He obliged, wondering what she was doing. She pulled his hand beneath the suds, not caring that his sleeve was now wet. His hand moved along her thigh and then she placed it between her legs.

"Pleasure me, baby."

His fingers acted on their own volition without all the inhibitions that he seemed to be experiencing. He rubbed the moist patch, playing with the short curls. Then he let his fingers trail down around her inner folds. Nicole arched against his fingers, rubbing the sensitive skin against his hand. Her eyes were closed and her head tilted back. He leaned forward and made a path from the base of her neck to her chin with his tongue. The water slapped noisily against the tub as her body continued rocking against his fingers, inviting him inside. He slipped a finger in, testing, exploring, enjoying the exclusive tour of her hidden treasure. Pulling away from her mouth, he wanted to attend to another part of her. He cleared the suds away from her breast and lifted it out of the water.

Once his tongue touched her nipple, he sucked deeply, loving the moans that escaped from Nicole. He continued playing and teasing her beneath the water and slipped in two fingers to intensify the torment.

"Take me now," she whispered.

"I'll dry you off and then we can finish in the bedroom."

"No. Now."

He pulled towels off the rack onto the floor. "I'll be right back." He undressed in her bedroom, and slid on his protection.

He lifted her out of the tub and set her on the towel. "Are you sure?"

"Turn on the heat lamp."

He dried her off, lingering over each part of her with reverence. "You're so beautiful." He placed a kiss on each breast, loving their softness against his face. His kisses continued down her stomach, with a quick flick of his tongue on her belly button. He saw her fingers convulsively grab and release the towel. Continuing on, he kissed a trail until it reached her patch. He pushed her legs up, supporting them with his shoulders. He wanted to take his time. With soft flicks of his tongue he worked the outer folds and then grazed his teeth against the clitoris, for which he was rewarded with Nicole's thighs clenching his head in a vise grip. Saving the best for last, he lazily licked her inner sanctum, tasting her sweet juices that were ready for him.

He carefully lowered her legs and pulled back to adjust himself, supporting his weight on his arms. He lowered his mouth to hers and kissed her deeply, shoving his tongue with all the force of his pent-up passion. Nicole grabbed his butt, sinking her nails into each cheek. She guided him in, writhing with abandonment with each stroke.

Brad grunted loud and hard, but he didn't care. She wanted him to pleasure her, but it sure wasn't a one-sided deal. With long, artful strokes, he drove deep into her. Not every woman could handle his size, but Nicole fit him like a glove.

He was sure that he would have an aneurysm trying to make her come before him. She raked his back with her nails, but the agony mixed with the heady sexual act made him want to please her even more. He took her breast into his mouth, pulling at its nipple. Then he rubbed his stubbled chin against the sensitive peak and that broke the dam of Nicole's pleasure point. He felt her insides pulsate against his penis and then he released with a guttural groan.

Eleven

Audra hit the END button on her cell phone. She'd had it with Brad. Ask the man to do one thing and he couldn't follow through. She'd left another message with no trace of diplomacy or tact. "I'll be back this afternoon. I've got business to take care of," she snapped at her assistant.

Her black pumps tapped sharply as she stormed out of the building to her car. She hit the gas pedal and shot out of the parking lot, wheels squealing.

Ten minutes later she drove down the lonely stretch of road. Before long she turned into the driveway of her latest heartburn. She noticed that several cosmetic touches were in evidence. The place had its charm and she knew that Nicole could make it into a success from sheer determination. Therefore her job was to shake things up. Charm versus a multimillion-dollar payout wasn't much of a decision.

She got out of her car and walked up to the door. She drew in her breath, bracing herself against Nicole's feistiness. She rang the doorbell, listening for any signs of activity. At length the door opened and Audra took the first step in declaring war. "Nicole, how the heck are you?" She breezed into the house before Nicole could react. A quick glance around revealed no activity in any part of the house. No need for any witnesses. "I see that you're damaged goods." She pointed at Nicole's bandaged foot.

Nicole remained standing at the opened door. "Now is not a good time."

Audra waved aside her objection and walked into the family room. She took off her coat and threw it over a chair. "Have a seat." She gestured to a nearby chair. "We need to discuss this issue."

Nicole, with much struggle, picked up the coat and dropped it on Audra's lap. "You're not welcome here and there is no issue for discussion." She rounded the couch and faced Audra with her arms folded across her chest.

"I beg to differ," Audra explained, taking great pains to keep cool. "A great offer came your way and you rudely threw the opportunity back in my face. You're standing in the way of progress. I'm at a loss as to why you would be so difficult and pretend to care about development when you weren't born and raised here."

Nicole's hand tapped a beat while Audra spoke. Frankly Audra was surprised that the other woman hadn't interrupted her speech. As a matter of fact, she appeared distracted.

"It doesn't matter what you say, I'm not selling this house—my business."

"Pressure will be put on the mayor to push for rezoning."

Nicole sighed and put a hand on her hip. "Next year is an election year, Audra. Can you imagine the fight when I lead the citizens of Glen Knolls on a campaign to save their city from the clutches of the evil land developers and their greedy minion, the mayor?"

Audra felt the panic rise. She stood up and fidgeted, picking imaginary lint off her clothes. "Any other time I'd say that you're making a good point." She accepted Nicole's roll of her eyes. "But these men are not to be messed with. They want this property and whether or not I can assist them is irrelevant. If it means sacrificing the mayor, then so be it. Audra took a deep breath to calm herself and she lowered her voice. "Some of these men don't take rejection well." She walked ahead of Nicole, her stomach churning at the level of her stubbornness. "Your life could get very interesting in a short while," she tossed over her shoulder.

Audra listened to Nicole's limping gait behind her. She slowed down so that she could catch up at the front door.

"Audra," Nicole called. "Don't throw out threats without being ready for the consequences. You're not the only one with connections. You and your gangster entourage aren't invincible." She walked in front of Audra.

Audra took a step toward her. "I will make it my personal mission to close this place down." It gave her great pleasure to see Nicole back away from her. Despite her cockiness, the other woman still feared her.

A floorboard creaked overhead. Audra's head snapped up. She didn't think that anyone else was there. One look at Nicole spoke volumes. Audra narrowed her gaze, paying attention to Nicole's attire for the first time. Nicole wore blue baggy sweatpants and an oversize T-shirt with a football logo. "Dress code for the business seems to have taken a downward slide."

"Good-bye, Audra."

Audra accepted the cue, and walked out the door. After it closed behind her, she walked away and then abruptly turned around, looking at the window that was situated over the foyer.

"I do not believe this!"

The figure stepped back from the window, but not before she saw the unforgettable face of Brad Calverton and his bare-chested physique.

His betrayal burned a bitter trail from her mind to her heart and back again. She clenched and unclenched her fist, fighting the temptation to knock on the door. Even she was afraid that she wouldn't be in control of her emotions if Nicole opened the door.

No tears came as she stormed her way to her car. Instead the seeds of retribution were sown. She backed out of the driveway and headed for her office. When she returned there, no one came near. Her dark expression shot sparks at anyone bold enough to catch her line of vision.

She picked up her phone. "Larry, hi, it's Audra. Need a

favor. I want a B-and-B inspected inside and out." She paused to catch her breath. Her heart still thumped from her anger.

"There has to be a complaint, a written one that is with some kind of documentation or at least more details."

Just to be a pain to the prissy witch made Audra feel victorious. Because of her connections with the local bed-and-breakfast registry owner, she could hinder Nicole's chances of getting accepted. "Don't piss me off, Larry. You owe me, several times over. Don't get short-term memory. I am not to be messed with."

"Calm down. Fine. Give me more details."

By the time Audra had explained her mission, she felt much better. She hung up, satisfied that Nicole's life would be hell for a little while. But she wasn't done with Brad. As a matter of fact, she hadn't begun. She leaned back in her chair, flipping her pen while thinking of the possibilities.

"Brad, dinner's ready."

Brad finished tightening the washer on the bathroom faucet. He slipped on his sweatshirt, washed his hands, and walked out of the honeymoon suite. He really didn't want to face Nicole, guilt weighing on his conscience. "I'm coming," he answered, attempting to keep his voice light. That damned Audra arriving unexpectedly floored him. He'd overheard most of the conversation and almost got caught when she looked up at the window.

Nicole slipped her arm around his waist when he came down the stairs. She looked up into his face with a small smile, laced with a smidgen of sadness. She limped beside him as they walked into the dining room. "Gosh, it smells good." His stomach growled. "What's for dinner?"

"From the sound of it, it doesn't really matter what's for dinner." She remained standing until he sat. "What have you been going on about for the past two days?"

He thought about it, then smiled. "Crab cakes?"

She nodded.

"Cheddar cheese biscuits?"

She grinned. "I also did my carrot soufflé."

He wrinkled his nose.

"You've never tried it." She pushed his shoulder playfully.

He grabbed her around her waist and pulled her to him. "Honey, you could cook mud pies and I'd eat them." He puckered and she answered with a quick peck.

"Remember that when you make me mad."

"Will do, ma'am."

The mood had lightened with the banter, but it didn't take long for Brad to feel like a heel. He debated telling her about Audra. She deserved to know that the woman didn't mean her any goodwill, but what exactly was his role? He couldn't come out of this little drama clean. Maybe he'd test the waters. "Did I hear the doorbell earlier?"

A small frown played on Nicole's forehead. "Um, yes. It was this woman named Audra."

He watched her take a bite of her biscuit. The visit unnerved him for obvious reasons, but he was surprised by how closed up Nicole appeared to be over the matter.

"Did she need something?" When Nicole looked questioningly at him, he continued, "It's just that it sounded like you were arguing."

"Sorry, didn't mean to make you feel like you're barging into my life. Audra has been a constant pain in my behind since I opened for business. She and I both wanted this property and I got it because my personality and reputation didn't precede me like Audra's did."

Brad took a forkful of crab cake, enjoying the highly seasoned flakiness of the meat. He wished that he could really savor each mouthful under different circumstances.

"Now Audra is pushing me to sell and—get this—she basically threatened me." Nicole shook her head.

"What?" It was past the time that Brad should have stepped in, but enough was enough.

"Remember when I saw you that night at the hotel? I was very upset. Audra had corralled me with some business owners. Now those business owners may run me out of my B-and-B." She dropped her fork onto the plate and put her head in her hands. "I can't believe it."

Brad loved his crab cakes and biscuits, but his heart ached for Nicole. "Do you think that there's any truth to her threats?" Even as he asked the question, he couldn't chase the dread.

"I don't know. Audra is a little witch, but I never thought that she would use violence."

"She might be all talk."

"I know, I know. And you're leaving in two days?"

"Well, I wanted to talk to you about that."

This time, Nicole shoved her plate away. "Please, Brad, don't break my heart. I'd rather you didn't say anything. I know that you don't have as intense feelings as I do."

"Stop right there. All I was going to say is that I have to go to England for a business trip. I do expect to be back and then I'm seriously considering moving back to Maryland."

"Would you?" Nicole scooted her chair back and limped over to Brad.

"I want to be with you. Maybe we can see how things go for us and all." He kissed her softly, parting her lips with his tongue, expertly dancing with her tongue.

"I don't want you worrying about that woman. Everything will work out," he said. There was a lot on his plate for the next day, but another agenda item had now been added.

Early the next morning, Brad headed out, telling Nicole that he had to conduct business. He'd borrowed her car so that he could get to where he needed to go without too much hassle. His one drawback, however, was getting hopelessly lost among all the new housing developments that proliferated in the county.

Brad finally pulled into the Stratford Condominums and

parked. He walked to the concierge desk, which was strategically placed to block any unscheduled visitors to its tenants. "Good morning," Brad greeted the uniformed attendant. "I'm here to see Miss Washington."

The attendant nodded, picked up the phone, and dialed. "Miss Washington," he announced, "you have a visitor." The attendant looked at him expectantly.

"Brad."

"Mr. . . . er . . . Brad." The attendant replaced the hook. "Apartment 3031. Take the elevator to the third floor, turn right, and go to the end of the hallway."

"Thanks." Brad wasn't surprised that Audra hadn't balked at his unannounced visit. He was not in the mood for any of her tricks or silly attempts to get his attention. She had crossed the line.

He stepped into the elevator cab and stared at the red LCD numbers. The doors opened and he stepped into the hallway. There was no need to follow the attendant's directions because Audra stood in her doorway with her robe draped loosely on her body, adding nothing to the doll-sized negligee that barely passed her hips.

Neither spoke as he walked toward the door. He hadn't planned a speech or even a snappy opening. But he did know that by the time he left, she would understand that if she didn't back off, she'd have to deal with him.

"Come on in, cowboy." She stepped back so he could enter. "I'm brewing coffee." She walked into the kitchen, the open robe swaying along with her walk.

"I'm not interested in any." He didn't want to sit and chat.

She remained in the kitchen. "What brings you here so early, especially when I've been leaving tons of messages on your phone? Didn't even know that you were in town."

"Well, I'm here and I figured it's time we concluded business."

She walked back into the living room with a steaming mug. "I don't plan to talk to you standing. Have a seat." She sat back on her sofa and crossed her legs. "So you want to end our business arrangement. I didn't know we had one."

"Actually we didn't, but I'll get to that in a second. First, you lied to me."

"Really?" She sipped her coffee, revealing no emotion.

"When you sent me information on the B-and-B, what was your real intention?"

Her forehead wrinkled with a puzzled frown. "You've lost me. I gave you the information so that you could visit it. It seemed like a good place for a future retreat facility for your boys."

He blew out an exasperated sigh. "Yep, that's what you'd have me believe. But after I met Nicole I realized that she has no intention of selling. So why set me up? Better yet, why set her up?"

"Strong words, Mr. Calverton. I thought we were friends. I do you a favor, and now you're coming to my house to pick a fight with me."

"Admit that you had ulterior motives for my going to the B-and-B. You didn't give a fig about what I wanted, my boys, or anything else."

She set down the mug, her eyes sparkling with barely contained anger. "I gave you an opening, it was up to you to make it happen."

"Make what happen?" he exploded. "Nicole isn't interested in selling. She was never interested in selling. All you managed to do was make her feel threatened with my presence."

"Looks like she got over that fear, though." She stared at him.

He refused to let her make him feel like he'd blown it. He suffered his own guilt at being duped. "Well, let me put an end to all this, right here, right now. I am not interested in using that B-and-B for my retreat. Nicole is not interested in selling it. I plan to write a glowing article about the historic setting and its beautiful, intelligent owner."

"Come off it. How the hell are you selling it as historic?"

"You'll see," he offered.

She studied him and then pulled her robe closed. "You know, Brad, you can't run from who you are. Nicole will wise up, and then what?"

He stiffened. "I don't see you exactly embracing your past." He pointedly looked at the overstuffed leather furniture suite and the chrome and glass accenting pieces around the living room.

"Maybe, but I don't have a celebrity image to uphold with the media. What would they say about your mother and father? The foster home? I think they would hang on to every word," she added, admiring her nails.

Brad refused to defend or explain anything to Audra. As a kid, he had admired her spunk and survival instincts. Looking at her now, he saw a harsher quality to her eyes. They stared back at him with undisguised contempt. "I've been here long enough. The last thing I'll demand is for you to undo whatever transactions you've made with your shady partners."

"Or else?"

"I would use the same image and influence that you reminded me about to nail your butt to the wall. You like the high life and you'll do anything to keep it. You'd probably sell your own father." He got satisfaction when she flinched at his last remark. He walked to the door and turned. "Don't get greedy, Audra." He opened the door and walked into the hallway. She came up behind him so quickly that he figured she'd had to run.

"It's over?"

He stopped, puzzled.

"Between us?"

His puzzled look deepened.

She wrapped her arms around her body as if she was cold. "I mean our friendship."

"I'm realizing that we were never friends. We shared space in each other's life because of unfortunate circumstances.

Nothing has happened today to make me change that opinion. You've got me in your focus and, frankly, it's made you cold and unappealing."

Audra faced him. There were no snappy comebacks. She walked backward, not taking her eyes off him, and retreated into her apartment.

Brad left feeling much better about things. He wanted to believe that he'd paid his penance for not being truthful with Nicole. He also wanted to believe that he'd protect her from everything and everybody.

He turned on the radio and tuned it into a station that was playing a current hit. He bobbed his head to the heavy beat as he headed for Baltimore.

Audra woke up later stretching her stiff joints. Once again she had awakened on the couch in her den. Her body shivered when it was hit by the initial coldness of the room. She looked over at the clock; her coffeemaker should be percolating in five minutes.

In the meantime, she'd take her shower and get dressed for another day of showing five-hundred-thousand-dollar homes to potential buyers. The job still excited her and her commissions were getting higher as she developed her expertise.

She stripped off her clothes and turned on the shower, adjusting the temperature. She put her back to the pulsing water, enjoying the feel of the hard pressure. A few minutes later she stepped out of the shower stall feeling invigorated.

As she dressed, opting for a black turtleneck and gray wool pants, she settled her mind with a strategy for cinching the deal.

That afternoon Audra sat in her office with a satisfied grin on her face. She closed the file on the Gatewood Property. Her wealthy client was willing to pay the million-dollar price tag. But the sweetest part was his invitation for dinner in New York. She had to be ready in an hour because that's when his private jet would be leaving.

Ideally she would be on Brad's arm, but he'd blown that deal, breaking her heart in the process. There were years since when it all had started in the same foster home. Despite their lowly beginnings, they'd both worked their butts off to achieve their level of success. Once, Brad had told her that he never wanted to look back at where he'd come from, wanted no reminders. However, by hooking himself with that uppity slip of a woman, he'd also turned his back on her.

Determined not to be down for long, she took her bruised ego in hand and dressed herself in a stunning black pantsuit that hugged her full breasts and round behind. Tonight, she'd don the role of seductress, playing the perfect companion to her plastic surgeon date. She'd been having doubts about her insatiable thirst for the finer things in life. But a few hours of living the high life and witnessing the fawning effects of others would stir her appetite. By the end of the night, she knew, she'd have to pay up for the extravagance. It wasn't so bad when she kept emotions out of it. Her night on the town would probably culminate with the doctor opening his penthouse suite and bidding her entry. What the heck, she knew the deal.

Brad turned down the familiar street and drove through his childhood neighborhood. The row house still looked the same with familiar shrubs framing the small patch of land. He didn't have too many memories, except flashes of a birthday or his grandmother's ladies' auxiliary meeting, and the nightmare about his grandmother falling ill.

He didn't have a plan in mind, so he drove up the street, looking from one house to another. The exercise was mainly to familiarize himself with the neighborhood. He watched a small group of boys standing in front of the house he wanted. He rolled down his window and leaned out. "Is this where Miss Williams lives?"

The boys ignored him and kept talking.

Brad recognized their little game. Being a stranger in the

neighborhood wasn't to his advantage. He tried another tack by pulling a dollar out of his pocket. "Now can someone tell me where Miss Williams lives?"

The boys stopped in midconversation and pinned him with their stony stares.

Brad looked at each face, deciding very quickly that he'd offended them by producing not only a bribe, but a very weak one.

"Mister, what do you want? If you don't leave those boys alone, I'll call the police. You damned pervert." A stern elderly lady stood on the porch.

"Miss Williams? What's going on?" Another woman much younger leaned over her porch, peering around an offending shrub. "TJ, come on over here."

Brad didn't want any undue attention. Until now he wasn't sure that he wanted to reconnect with his past. That plan appeared to have fizzled under the curious buzz among the neighbors of Crampton Street.

He killed the engine and quickly jumped out of the car. "I didn't mean to alarm anyone. I used to live here a long time ago."

"What's your people's name?" the elderly woman asked.

"Thomson. I lived with my grandmother—Ada Thomson."

"And what's your name?"

"Brad. Brad Calverton."

She made her way slowly to the opening on the porch. Brad saw the silver cane by her side, which she clearly needed. "Come closer. My eyes aren't that good."

Despite her age, Brad didn't believe her, because she clucked her tongue before he approached.

"I always said that you took after your father, but you got the shape of your mother's face . . . her coloring, too."

"Are you Miss Mavis Williams?"

She nodded. "Come in." She directed with her signature cane.

His stomach and nerves quivered. In a few minutes he

would learn about his past, filling gaps in his childhood memories. He walked past the children up the few stairs into the house.

As soon as he passed through the doorway, it was as if he stepped back in time thirty years. He walked into the living room and sat on a couch that had seen better days. The cover was a floral print that was now faded and worn. Miss Williams was already seated in a chair with a table lamp lit near her. Brad followed her prompting for him to take a seat on the couch. His gaze wandered around the room, taking inventory of the framed photographs on the wall and on the mantelpiece. He wanted to see if any face would jog his memory.

"Turn on that lamp near you," Mavis said.

Brad obliged, squinting at the sudden light in his eyes. He shifted his position and waited.

Mavis sat like a queen with her hand on the cane. Her hair was pulled back in a severe bun, yet her eyes held a warmth that beckoned to him. She inhaled deeply and blew out her breath slowly. "You've grown up into a good-looking young man."

"Thank you."

"Where have you been all these years? Why have you come back now?" She tapped the cane waiting for his answer.

He shrugged. "Seems like the right time."

"The demons must be stirring." She smiled. "Brenda," she called out, "can you bring some lemonade and cookies for our guest?"

Brad didn't really feel like that combo, but everything he said or did was being evaluated.

The person he thought was Brenda walked into the room. She glanced at him shyly and offered a half smile. He reached forward to take the proffered lemonade and small plate of cookies. "Thank you."

"This is my niece, Brenda. She's staying with me for a few days. Thanks, honey."

Brenda smiled and left the room.

Brad took a sip of lemonade, surprised that it was quite tasty with the right amount of sugar.

"Good, isn't it?" She chuckled when he nodded. "Your grandmother and I used to play bingo at the church on this night. Then we'd sit on our porch and talk about our kids and our grandkids." The smile left her face and she looked away at the window. "They came here for you. Do you remember?"

Brad always thought they had come for him in his grandmother's house. With the houses having similar floor plans, it made sense that his memory got jumbled over time. "I know that I hated that day," he half whispered. "I never wanted to come back here."

Mavis laid her cane across her lap. "Been running a long time? Your grandmother wanted me to keep an eye on you. I failed you both on that one."

"Miss Williams, I don't hold any bad feelings against you."

"Don't blame your grandmother, either."

He shook his head. As he got older, he realized how much his grandmother had done for him and the sacrifices she must have had to make.

"Her heart had been bad for a long time. I think it was when Marcia died. Your mother was so young and so beautiful."

Brad leaned forward. He didn't have any photos of her and he was three when he went to live with his grandmother.

"No one knew that she was allergic to penicillin."

He wanted to hear every detail, but at the same time he cringed.

"And my father."

Miss Williams turned sad eyes on him. "I'm sorry. He and your mother had separated when you were an infant. I'm sure with a little effort, you may be able to find him."

"No." As his only living relative, his father had earned all his anger and bitterness. He had no desire to ever meet his father.

"Anger eats at the soul, young man," Mavis admonished. "One day you may need him or he may need you."

"I've gone through hell and back." He shook his head. "Some days I think that I'm still there. The only person I need is me."

Mavis rapped her cane on the floor. "Listen up, boy, because I've got a story to tell."

Brad had a feeling that what he was about to hear would change his life. Change wasn't something that he welcomed, especially if he had the control to walk away from it. All he had to do was scoot his butt off the couch and walk out the door. He didn't have to turn back, he didn't have to listen to Mavis, and he didn't have to deal with the longing that he kept buried. The thought of having a family, even if it was one other person, had given him a glimpse of a promise. It would blossom, unless he could stamp it out of his heart and mind.

"There's no family on this street that doesn't have a complicated life. And yet, I believe that in any other part of this here United States, it's not so different." She cackled for a long time. "Your father and mother got married very young. I think it wasn't too long after high school. Being so young, it didn't take them long to change their minds about each other. Your grandmother was fit to be tied because she didn't like Elroy one bit. Few months later, Marcia was pregnant—"

"With me," Brad finished.

"Nope."

"What?"

"Marcia had a boy. I remember the row with your father because he wanted the boy to be called Elroy Junior. Your grandmother stuck her nose in that one and convinced Marcia to call him Derek."

"Why?"

"No particular reason. She figured that it was bad enough the boy would have Elroy's last name." She cackled again. "Your grandmother was a pistol. Anyway, just like clockwork, your mother and father had their spat and Marcia and Derek were in your grandmother's house. Marcia went back and forth, never working up the courage to leave Elroy."

"Was he abusive?" Brad's hands curled into fists.

"Not in the way you're thinking. He abused her trust, though. He had so many women. They were too happy to flaunt themselves in front of Marcia. One day, I guess it got to be too much and Marcia moved back home, pregnant and with a four-year-old."

"I don't remember any brother."

"Marcia got sick and your grandmother's health wasn't the best. Elroy had remarried and he wanted Derek to come live with him. Your grandmother felt that he was at the age where he needed his father. When she got really sick she tried to get in touch with him, but no one knew where he was."

"The state didn't try to find him?"

"I'm sure they did the best they could do," Mavis replied.

"And he sure didn't try to find me."

"Maybe he got sick? Died?"

"I don't care about him."

"I can understand your feelings, but what about your brother? He never did anything wrong to you."

Except that he got the benefit of a father's love. "Not interested in him either."

Mavis got up from the chair and made her way to a closet in the hallway. "Brenda, come help me with this box." Her niece dragged the box into the living room and opened the carton. "Brad, take out those photo albums and the shoe box."

Brad did as he was told and placed the newly found treasures on his lap. He'd rather be in the privacy of his home to examine everything. "May I take these with me?"

"Yes, yes, of course."

Brad slowly opened the shoe box to get a preview of its contents. There was a letter addressed to him and his brother. The word jarred. A few hours ago, he thought of himself without any family connections. He'd denied having any connections with the many children he'd come in contact with at the state home. Now in the matter of a few words, a brother and a father had popped into existence. He fingered the letter, running his thumb over the delicate, curvy handwriting. His mother had written this to him. He wanted to put it to his nose to see if he could detect her scent.

He spied a red hardcover book and gently retrieved it. Flipping the pages, he figured it was a journal of some sorts. Between the covers were her dreams, fears, and thoughts. Stuck in between two pages were two envelopes. Brad turned them so that he could read the names. Brad Calverton. Derek Calverton. He laid them back down, his hands suddenly sweaty.

"Find him," Mavis prompted gently. "Give him his letter."

Twelve

"Brad, you're so quiet." Nicole pressed Brad for conversation. "Don't you like the meat loaf?"

"Oh, honey. Yes, I do." He kissed her hand and gave a bright smile. "Lots on my mind, that's all."

"How was your day? You were gone for such a long time."

"I had some business to take care of."

Nicole sensed that whatever Brad had been doing contributed to his dark mood. She'd hoped that he would have trusted her enough to share his burden. Instead he played with the meat loaf, swirling it around in the mashed potatoes.

"Are you still leaving tomorrow?"

Brad nodded and sighed deeply. "I've got to leave for England. But I promise, I'll be back. Here." He traced the outlined of her forehead, down her nose, and lingered at her lips.

Nicole loved the strength and warmth of his hand. She closed her eyes and gently kissed his palm, fighting back the loneliness that filled her heart. "I'll be here waiting."

"You know what? I'm acting like a gloomy bear. Let me do the dishes and tidy up and then, Miss Montgomery, I'll give you the attention that you deserve."

Nicole smiled, relieved that Brad was making an effort to lighten his mood. There was so much that she didn't know about him. She didn't want to push, but she really did wish that he would open up soon.

Nicole waited in bed for Brad. While he was out today, she'd gone shopping for a special gift. She hoped that he liked it.

"Is my sweet muffin decent?"

Nicole giggled. "That depends."

The bedroom door opened slowly and Brad leaned casually against the door frame. "Oh, my." He grinned wickedly.

"I take it that you approve." Her surprise gift seemed to be a definite hit. She was on the bed in a provocative pose on her knees wearing her two-piece lingerie set. "So what do you like about it?"

"Hmm. Let me come closer for an inspection." Brad stared at her body, his grin widening as he walked slowly behind her.

Nicole felt the bed give to his weight, but didn't turn around. She bit her lip to keep from giving way to a case of giggles. "I'm waiting," she said in a singsong voice.

"And I'm still looking." He trailed a finger along the bottom edge of her top and lifted it. "Oh, my, my, my."

Nicole turned her head.

"Nope, you can't turn around."

"Then hurry up and tell me what you think."

"Black is good. I like it against your skin. Good contrast. The lace adds enough camouflage to tease. And the thong action is an A-plus." He framed her body from behind with his.

Nicole bit her lip, but not before uttering a breathy sigh. She closed her eyes and allowed him to support her weight as his hand slid under the gauzy top. Her skin quivered from his touch. His hands slid up her stomach to her breasts where his fingers played with her nipples. He planted soft kisses on the back of her neck. "Oh, Brad," she sighed. Her body responded with an insatiable hunger for his attention.

"I love touching you." He slid one of his hands down to her panty and tucked a finger around the flimsy waistband. "I think thongs are the sexiest piece of clothing."

"All for you, babe." She turned around, not waiting for him to tell her. "I want to kiss the living daylights out of you."

He chuckled and grabbed her butt. "Go ahead, make my day."

She nipped at his full bottom lip and sucked it. Once she

kissed him full on his mouth, Brad took over, slipping his tongue into her mouth. Their tongues danced around each other, playing their own version of tag. After kissing him long and hard, she pulled away. "I need to breathe."

"Breathing is overrated." He pushed her back onto the bed. "Plus, I'd love to give you mouth-to-mouth."

"I bet you would, lover boy."

Nicole slid down her panty, teasing Brad with air kisses.

He growled at her, grinning at her sexy display.

"I want this moment to last. I hate to let you go. Whenever you leave, I wonder if I'll ever see you again. I wonder if you'll ever let me in here." She tapped his chest with her finger. "I don't think there's any room for me." She looked into his eyes for denial.

He blinked slowly and looked down at her chest. "Am I in yours?"

She nodded, noting that neither his eyes nor his mouth showed any lightness. She reached up and hugged him tightly. For now, she would settle. Right now, without thinking about tomorrow, in her semidarkened room, she had enough love for both of them. With the familiar rip of the foil packet, she was ready for him.

When he eased into her, she uttered a soft cry, surrendering all her fears to the unknown. She wanted him with a greedy abandon and arched her hips for the need to be satiated. She matched his deep strokes, wrapping her legs around his waist. Their erotic dance had its own rhythm and beat, reaching nature's peak that her soul craved each time she was with Brad. When her body was ready for its release, Nicole relaxed and rode each orgasmic wave, shuddering from the intensity. She held on to Brad's shoulder tightly, needing something firm and stable to keep her from floating up and away.

"I'm going to miss you," Brad said, as she lay against his arm.

"I'm going to miss you, too. Will you call me when you're in England?"

"Of course."

They lay in contented silence. Nicole wondered if she should admit to Brad that she'd fallen in love with him. But she didn't want to ruin what they'd just shared. Instinctively, she felt that Brad wasn't ready to commit and she didn't want to scare him away. She'd put it off for a little while longer.

The next morning, Nicole kept up a brave front. She willed the tears not to come forth. After Brad left, she could give in to her emotions.

The taxi's honk shook her out of the doldrums. "Brad, the car is ready."

Brad appeared beside her with his suitcase. He set it down and pulled her into a tight embrace. "I'll miss you more than you think." He kissed her, long and hard.

Nicole watched the taxi pull off as another car pulled into her driveway. A woman leaned out the driver's side. "Miss Montgomery?"

Nicole nodded.

"I'm the historian you requested. Mrs. Johnson."

"Oh!" Nicole stepped aside for the woman to enter.

"The person you spoke with had to attend a meeting, so I'm the next best thing."

Nicole noted the woman's embarrassment and quickly surmised that they didn't think her claim was valid.

"Coffee?" Nicole offered.

"No, thanks. I've got to get back to the university. I have a class in about an hour."

Nicole led the woman downstairs in the basement. There was no conversation, only the sounds of Mrs. Johnson's heavy breathing and their footsteps going down the uncarpeted stairs.

"I guess Mr. Welsley explained that this house isn't exactly on the path of the underground railroad."

"Yes, he did." Nicole flicked on the fluorescent light, which buzzed and flickered until it came on. "Like I told him, it's not a reach to consider that the house was simply a safe house."

Mrs. Johnson shrugged and walked around the room, running her hands along the walls. "I checked the history of the house. It was originally built by a farmer in 1852. Married a young thing who came from money. Even in that time, this house must have been expensive. Probably the wife's dowry."

"I'll need as much factual information as possible." Nicole had difficulty restraining her excitement. The possibilities meant a new phase for her B&B.

The doorbell rang. Nicole excused herself, wondering if she had a new guest. She didn't expect anyone to arrive until mid-March for a wedding.

The doorbell sounded again. "Coming. Coming." Nicole hurried to the door. "Yes?" She stared back at the face of a disapproving man.

"I'm Mr. Watkins with the state health office."

"Yes?" Nicole gulped.

The man pulled out a folded sheet of paper from his jacket pocket. "I have a letter reporting major health code violations. I'm here to inspect the property."

"What the hell are you talking about?" Nicole snatched the paper from his hand and skimmed down the details on the paper. "Who complained? I don't understand."

"I don't know who complained. I'm just assigned to conduct the inspection. I presume it was a guest, and from how quickly this got expedited, it must have been someone who was really pissed off."

"Show me your ID." Nicole knew that she didn't have anything to worry about, and it was easier to let this man do what he had to do. However, for her troubles, he'd have to deal with her prickly attitude.

She examined the ID, taking longer than necessary. "Okay, come in. But you'll have to make it snappy. I've got things to do today. If you ask me, all this is a waste of time."

Mr. Watkins held his hands up in surrender. "I only need to look in a few places. I'll start with the kitchen."

Nicole led him into the kitchen, opening cabinets and the pantry door. She stepped back and waited with her arms folded.

"Miss Montgomery?"

Nicole suddenly remembered that Mrs. Johnson was still in the basement. She hesitated, debating whether to leave Mr. Watkins unattended with his mission. "I'll be right back."

He nodded and she left to see Mrs. Johnson.

"I do have to be leaving, Miss Montgomery. I called Mr. Welsley because more needs to be done to verify the finding."

Nicole escorted her to the door. "What's your gut feeling?"

"Gut feeling can get you in trouble, but I'd say that you've got a real find here. Once the news gets out, you'll be beating off guests."

Mr. Watkins walked into the room. "Ma'am, when was the last time that you had this place fumigated?"

Nicole cringed as the smile from Mrs. Johnson's face eased away. "I have a contract with a company. I'll get you the paperwork," she answered, crisply. She turned to Mrs. Johnson, deciding that it would be better to get her on her way. "I'll be waiting to hear from you."

"Okay, it should be a day or two." Mrs. Johnson headed for the door, but not before giving Mr. Watkins a doubtful look.

After the door was closed, Nicole glared at the inspector. "The paperwork is in my office. Follow me."

"I'm not the enemy, Miss Montgomery. I follow orders."

"So, just like that, someone complains and I have Big Brother swooping down on me." She opened her file drawers and ran her fingers over the files, looking for the pesticide company.

"Like I said, it must have been a really irate guest or someone with influence." He shrugged. "I only follow orders."

"Here it is. See? The contract is for a year." She pointed to the bottom of the paper. "As a matter of fact, they were just here."

"Yep, you're right. Thank you. I didn't see anything in the kitchen or any of the other rooms. May I check upstairs? Then, I'll be going."

"Promise?"

Mr. Watkins didn't bother answering.

Nicole escorted him upstairs, following him into each room. Thank goodness she'd tidied up immediately after the boys had left. Everything was neatly in its place, and with the periodic airing of the rooms, they didn't have the usual mustiness that could settle on an unused room.

After looking in the last room down the hallway, Mr. Watkins approached her. "I'm satisfied. If you would sign this paper, I'll leave you a copy, just in case you get any more problems."

Nicole obliged his request. After his van backed out the driveway, she breathed a sigh of relief. Who would have called in such a false report? She'd had a number of guests since she opened, but no one had left unhappy. On the contrary, she had letters from past guests, promising to return. As for influence, none of her guests struck her as particularly rich or connected. Of course, there was Brad, but as quickly as his name popped into her head, she dismissed it.

Well, it was quite a morning. She stood on the brink of success if the new find in her basement was declared a hideaway for slaves. Then in a matter of minutes, she could have had a state health code violation slapped on her property, temporarily closing her doors and ruining her reputation.

A thought popped into her head. She walked into her office and searched for a business card. Then she picked up her phone and dialed. "Yes, may I speak to the mayor? It's Nicole Montgomery."

"Hold one moment."

Nicole leaned against the desk with the phone cradled between her cheek and shoulder.

"He's busy, may he call you back?"

"Tell him that he can talk to me or hear what I have to say on the six o'clock news."

"Hold."

A few seconds later, the mayor answered. "Miss Montgomery, you do realize that I have this city to run?"

"If it's a burden, then there's no need for you to do it for a second term."

He chuckled. "How may I help you?"

Nicole hadn't rehearsed any part of this conversation. Only in the last few minutes had she decided to call the mayor and play her own brand of politics. "I wanted you to be the first to hear the news."

"What news?"

"That my B-and-B was a hideaway for slaves."

"You have proof?"

"I'm working on it. Mrs. Johnson from the university has made her examination. Some experts will be coming over to verify her report."

"So, in other words, you're jumping the gun with this bit of news."

"Maybe, but it also wraps up any plans you had about this land. Even if this proves false, it will take a while for folks to believe that the land isn't worth conserving."

"You want to be responsible for holding back progress?"

"Another mega-mall is progress?"

"Money means better schools, better police enforcement—"

"Save it for your voters." She slammed down the phone, not really caring about diplomacy.

She picked up the phone again, this time calling the local television station. She could certainly fall flat on her face if the place wasn't a hideaway. On the other hand, it would be such a score in her favor.

She hung up the phone, pleased that the camera crew would come to her home later that evening to do a live spot for the news hour.

What to wear? Spurred to action, she limped through the house to her apartment. Her phone rang. "Hello?"

"Hey, whatcha doing?"

"Hi, Toni. Actually I'm looking for an outfit to wear for my television interview."

"Get outta here."

There was nothing like Toni's breeziness to bring a smile to her face. "Looks like I'll need to do an emergency shopping mission."

"I'm game. Donna's here with me, hovering and being a pain in my behind."

"I'll meet you at J.C.'s in half an hour?"

"That works. See you then."

Feeling much better, Nicole got ready for her shopping trip with the girls.

Brad sat in his hotel suite looking out at the busy traffic below. England's clock was five hours ahead and the jet lag kicked his butt. Evening had descended with him sitting against the headboard in a half-sleep state with only one shoe on. He glanced over at the phone, which blinked at him, signaling a message. He must have dozed off at some point, because he couldn't remember hearing it ring.

His stomach grumbled, reminding him that despite his exhaustion, he needed to tend to himself. He dialed room service and ordered a light meal of tea and scones.

He checked his message. It was Freddie making sure that he'd arrived with no problems. He called her back, but she wasn't there and he left a message.

There was one person he wanted to hear from and he wondered if Nicole was at home or busy with her B&B. Now he wished that he had told her about his brother. It was more than the fact that he had a brother; it was sharing something about himself. His hand hovered over the phone. So many thoughts raced through his mind, but they were more like doubts.

Before he could take their relationship to any higher level, he would have to tell her the truth. He didn't know how or when, but one day soon, he'd have to confess. He closed his eyes and ran his hand through his hair. He'd not only played games with her, but with himself.

In self-disgust, he stripped off his clothes and headed for the bathroom. He stepped into the tub and submerged himself in the soapy bubbles. Maybe he could wash off not only the day's dirt, but also the sense of shame that cloaked him.

Sipping tea and eating scones, he watched the BBC. He looked over at the telephone, hesitating for a moment before picking it up. It rang four times before the answering machine picked up and played Nicole's voice. He loved the way she spoke, lilting and husky. "Hi, Nicole. Just calling." He put down the phone, suddenly embarrassed by the depth of his emotions.

By the next morning, he wasn't feeling any better. There was no time to ponder, the driver would be there to pick him up for the meeting. Brad readied himself, trying to focus on what the network was about to offer him. All he could think about were the consequences.

While he rode in the sleek black car through downtown London, questions Ping-Ponged their way around in his head. To have his own talk show was a coup in any country, yet, over the last few months, the idea wasn't as exciting as it once was. He'd have to relocate here for the better part of the year, and in the first few months he'd be all over Europe boosting the show and making his name a household word. He sighed.

The car stopped in front of a gray, metallic structure. Brad stepped out, taking in his surroundings. No matter where he went, all the major cities had too many people, too many buildings, and too many cars. He smiled to himself. What the heck had come over him? For heaven's sake, he lived in New York, the model city of overcrowded development. A few months ago, it was his haven where he could slip into the cracks and be anonymous. After visiting a B&B in Glen Knolls, his safe lifestyle was dissolving around the edges. Now his soul craved a suburban, countryside living for peaceful reflection. More than that, he wanted a place where he could heal and rebuild who he was, because at this very moment, going up the elevator, he felt broken. And it hurt. It hurt like hell because he didn't know how to begin.

The elevator doors opened and he approached the massive semicircle desk of the receptionist. She offered a welcoming smile.

"I'm here to see Mr. Cooperstock. I'm Brad Calverton."

"Good morning, sir. He's expecting you." The receptionist pressed a button and announced his arrival.

A few seconds later, he was being ushered into a large meeting room already occupied with various suits. Brad took a deep breath to settle his nerves and began the process of greeting and exchanging pleasantries.

At the lunch break, he excused himself and asked for an office. He'd made some pretense that he had to make a phone call, but he needed some space. The extent of what they offered him boggled his mind. All that was left for him to say was "I accept." He poured himself a glass of water and took a long drink. When had things gotten so complicated? He called the receptionist and had her page his lawyer.

When the lawyer walked into the office, Brad motioned to the chair opposite him. "Mr. Fielding, I presume negotiations are over?"

"Sir, negotiations are never over until you sign on the dotted line." He studied Brad for a few seconds. "Is there something you'd like me to look into?"

"No. What's next?"

"Well, they want to take you on a tour of the studio and to meet some of the people slated to work on your team." He hesitated. "But if you'd like to postpone that until tomorrow, I'm sure it would not be a problem."

Brad shook his head. He didn't want to inconvenience anyone. The company's hospitality had been so outstanding that he felt the worse for delaying his decision.

"When are you leaving?"

"I was leaving at the end of the week, but I may shorten my visit."

Mr. Fielding nodded, his hands steepled under his chin. "May I ask whether you are having second thoughts about this venture?"

"Since I'm not prepared to give an answer today, I guess I am having second thoughts." Brad grimaced. "It's a lot to think about and there are some people that I need to talk to . . . about what it would mean . . . you know."

Mr. Fielding didn't show any signs that he could relate to Brad's indecisiveness. Of course not, he probably only measured life under "success" or "failure" by a sizable commission or not.

"What would you like me to tell the company?" Mr. Fielding asked with a sudden dryness to his tone.

"I will give them an answer in a week from this day. In the meantime, I will go on all the tours and participate in any discussions that they have planned." Brad stood and buttoned his jacket, feeling more in control.

"As you wish, sir." Mr. Fielding also stood and followed him out of the office back to the meeting room.

Nicole followed Donna into the third store. She hadn't planned on making selecting an outfit such an ordeal, but with her two friends in tow, they made the exercise torturous. "Look, ladies, I've only got two hours left. Why can't I buy the blue pant suit?"

"Because you'll look like a seventies geek with that shade of blue. Looks more like a bathroom color." Toni wrinkled her nose.

"Then how about the beige dress?" Nicole said, leaning against a rack of skirts.

"Your skin tone is already beige," Donna piped up.

"I like that coral blouse." Toni pointed at clothing above Nicole's head.

Nicole turned and looked up. It was a simple button-down cotton shirt, but the shade of pink was becoming. She tiptoed and a grabbed her hanger with her size. "Ladies, looks like we have to try again. This is way too expensive."

Toni gave an exasperated sigh. "How much is the freakin' blouse?"

"You shouldn't be using such words. The baby can hear you," Donna scolded.

"Freakin' isn't a bad word. Would you really like to hear the bad word?" Toni rolled her eyes at Donna.

"I can see that I'll have to be the one to teach the baby right from wrong."

"Would you two quit, please? I need help finding another blouse."

"I'm tired and I want to eat, so take the darn blouse to the cash register and let's go," Toni hissed.

"Uh-oh, Nicole, watch out. She's undergoing a mood change," Donna joked.

"I'm not paying sixty dollars for a cotton shirt. You can tell that to your other personality," Nicole stated matter-of-factly to Toni.

Toni approached her and with a sudden swipe took the blouse from her hand. She walked to the cash register, holding it over her head while Nicole tried to grab it.

"I'm not buying it, Toni."

At the cash register, Toni dropped it and whipped out her credit card. "You're right, Nicole. You're not buying it. Now shut up and let this woman do her job."

Donna pulled Nicole aside. "Leave her alone. She's been in this crazy mood. I think morning sickness is kicking her butt, because it's not only in the mornings."

Nicole sighed. "I'm not helping either. My mood stinks.

Come on over and then after the interview Toni can watch us drink wine, while she drinks milk."

"Milk? Oh, yuck." Toni handed the bag to Nicole and they hugged.

"I love the blouse, but you're still a pain," Nicole teased.

They hooked arms together and headed out of the store.

Nicole was glad that her friends had stuck around while the camera crew set up. Shirley had shown up after work and now the three women had made themselves comfortable.

"Miss Montgomery," the reporter called, "we're ready."

Nicole ran her hands down the sides of her clothes and stepped in front of the mirror for a quick once-over. Feeling satisfied, she followed the reporter's directions to stand in the designated spot.

"We'll be going live in a few minutes. I'll ask a few questions, but you'll have the lead. It's a sixty-second piece. The camera will be on me in the beginning, but after that, it's all you. I'll do this with my hands when your time is almost up." The reporter made a rollover motion with her hands.

The cameraman spoke into an earpiece. "Okay, we're going live in five-four-three-two-one." The red light on his camera blinked on.

Nicole froze for a second, her thoughts in a scramble. In her panicked state, she couldn't hear the reporter, only seeing her lips move with brief flashes of a smile. Everything around Nicole appeared to be in slow motion. She turned toward the chair where her friends sat. All she could make out were their lips smiling.

". . . tell us, Miss Montgomery." The reporter held the microphone in her face with an expectant expression.

"I . . . um . . ." Nicole took a deep breath. She was a lobbyist. She was on Capitol Hill testifying. She was the star. A soothing calmness descended over her. She was ready. "In my former life I was a lobbyist where everything was an emergency and everyone was important. It took a personal crisis to make me realize that life is short and it was time to take a step back and enjoy. I bought this old farmhouse and converted it into a bed-and-breakfast inn."

The reporter stepped in when she paused for a breath. "Montgomery's B-and-B is a wonderfully quaint getaway, but there's more to it than meets the eye, correct?" The reporter turned her attention back to Nicole.

"Yes, there is. I recently discovered a secret hideaway. I called in a historian from the university, who agrees with me that it may have been used to hide runaway slaves."

"Wow, so what's the next step?" The reporter stepped back and the camera focused only on Nicole. The reporter motioned that Nicole had ten seconds left.

"The university has agreed to send a team to look at the structure and history of the farmhouse. I'm sure that my claim will be confirmed and then I plan to have the house and nearby property recognized for its historic value."

"Thank you, Miss Montgomery. And now back to you in the studio, Phil." The reporter smiled until the camera was turned off. "You were excellent."

"Thanks. At first, I couldn't remember a thing." Nicole giggled and flopped down between Shirley and Donna.

"We kept trying to tell you to smile."

"I did, eventually."

"If that's what you want to call your grimace," Toni said.

"Don't listen to her, she's jealous," Donna accused.

Nicole escorted the reporter and cameraman to the door. She felt as if a weight had been lifted off her shoulders.

"Here, looks like you could use this." Shirley had a glass of chardonnay for her.

They headed for Nicole's apartment, wanting to be in a cozy environment. Shirley flopped onto her bed.

"Hey, watch that wine on my comforter." Nicole batted Shirley's feet off to the side.

Toni lay across the foot of the bed. "Ladies, are you thinking the same thing that I am?"

Nicole paused in the middle of squirming out of her skirt

to put on shorts. "Whatever dirty thoughts you're having, Toni, stow them."

"I wonder if lover boy visited your four-poster queen-size bed?"

"Toni, you're too much." Shirley sat up with her wineglass held high. "But I'm waiting for the answer."

"Me, too," Donna chimed in.

Nicole took her skirt and went into the walk-in closet. "Do I ask about your love lives?"

"Yes," they answered in unison.

Nicole sucked her teeth and emerged from the closet. "I'm giving you three questions. One apiece."

"Me first," Toni shouted, raising her hand. "Did you do it with lover boy?"

"Yes."

"I knew it!" Toni screamed, rolling around Nicole's bed in glee. "So was it good?"

"Next person and next question." Nicole ignored Toni.

"What's the plan for the two of you?" Donna inquired.

"Good for you." Nicole nodded approvingly. "You asked a leading question." She sauntered over to the chaise longue near her bed and sat back with her legs crossed at the ankles. "Brad is away in England." She sprang up. "Oh, crap! I forgot to check the machine." She pushed the PLAY button on the machine as four pairs of eager ears listened. When she heard his voice, a small smile spread over her face. Reclaiming her seat, she sighed. "He promised to relocate here."

"What?" Shirley asked.

"Aha, that's the third question." Nicole pointed at a very confused Shirley. "He promised to relocate here," she repeated.

Donna and Toni fell onto each other laughing. A few minutes later Shirley took a pillow and threw it at them. "That's not fair. My *what* wasn't a question. It was a statement." She came over to Nicole, crawling on her knees. "Please, please, Nicole, let me ask another question."

"Should I, girls?"

"Oh, what the heck, let her have second chance," Donna begged.

"Go ahead, Shirley." Nicole ruffled her friend's hair playfully.

"When are you going to tell him that you've fallen in love with him?"

The room suddenly went silent. Nicole looked down at Shirley's face for signs of amusement or derision. In her dark brown eyes, there was only sincerity. The romantic one out of the bunch didn't want her to break her romantic notions. She dared not look over at Toni, though. Toni with her penchant for the cold, harsh reality and practical philosophy wouldn't understand. "I'll probably tell him when he comes back."

"Probably?" Toni asked, frowning.

"I'm not answering any more questions." Nicole reached for her glass of wine and took a sip.

"Fine. I'm bored with lover boy anyway," Toni replied.

"So what are we going to do tonight? Let's have a slumber party." Shirley looked at the three faces expectantly.

"You mean that you won't be leaving tonight?" Nicole groaned. "I've got a couple of new movies. Pick one. In the meantime, I'll go make some popcorn."

Nicole pulled out the blender, knowing that orders for daiquiris would be forthcoming. She pulled out her bags of microwave popcorn and lined them up next to the microwave. Her phone rang. "Hello?"

"Hi, babe."

"Brad," Nicole sighed. She pulled out the bar stool near the counter and climbed on. "I'm sorry I missed your call earlier. How is it going?"

"Too British for me. I don't know what possessed me to think that I wanted to do a British talk show."

"You're planning on turning it down?" She had mixed feelings about the deal, but she knew what it would mean for his career.

"I have a week to think about it, but all I seem to be thinking about is you."

"I've been thinking about you, also. I can't wait for you to come back . . . here."

Nicole looked at the clock on the microwave. "It must be really late."

"One o'clock. Couldn't sleep. I think I need you next to me."

"Maybe we can take care of that problem when you return," Nicole replied.

"I'll hold you to that. Well, I'll let you go."

Nicole gripped the phone. She didn't want their conversation to end, but the sound of her friends giggling in her room forced her to end the call. "Okay, I miss you and I'll be waiting."

"Bye."

"Bye, honey, we love you."

"Shirley, Donna, Toni, get off the phone," Nicole shouted into the phone. She heard Brad chuckle. She dropped the phone and raced toward her room. The door slammed in her face and she heard the lock turn.

"Brad?" There was only a dial tone. She slammed down the phone. There were about to be three homicides in Glen Knolls.

Thirteen

Audra hung up from her phone call with Larry. The news wasn't unexpected that Nicole's B&B didn't violate any health codes. That wasn't the point when she had called. It was an impulsive act done to irritate Nicole. Since he had put his best man on the case, she had been reassured that he'd done a thorough job. She smiled at the image of Nicole hurrying after the inspector.

Her phone rang. "Yes?" At the sound of the mayor's excited voice, she came to attention. "Slow down."

"Haven't you watched the news?"

"No." She'd been at home, but feeling too lousy to watch any news. "What happened?"

"It's about the B-and-B."

"Yes?" Audra dragged the word out slowly. Her fingers curled around the phone and she gritted her teeth in anticipation.

"Apparently it's a historic property."

"I've heard that one before." She rolled her eyes, remembering that Brad had fed her the same nonsense.

"Did you know that it has a secret room for runaway slaves?"

"What?" Audra shouted. Instantly a sharp pain pierced the side of her head.

"Nicole Montgomery got the local television station to do an interview. Now my hands are tied. I've talked to the experts and there's very little doubt that it's a hideaway." The mayor exhaled noisily. "You know what this means, right?"

Audra sighed, closing her eyes to what she was about to hear.

"It's over. No more meetings. No more time with your development group. I've got to think about votes, so I'm pulling out." He paused. "Audra, I'd suggest that you pull out."

"Yes, Mayor Wallace." She hung up, feeling nauseated at the news. If she'd listened to Brad, she could have gotten the information much earlier and been able to act proactively.

She walked around her apartment rubbing her temples. The news was devastating, but even worse was the seed of fear that took hold. If the mayor knew, it meant that the other investors knew also. When she finally got hold of them, it would be like walking into a den of predators. They would not be happy at the turn of events.

She picked up her mobile phone and turned it on. If they did contact her, it would be through her cell phone. Her message icon popped on and she pressed in her code to retrieve the message. She bit her lip at the curt orders from Mr. Druthers. He was calling an emergency meeting at ten o'clock. A glance at her watch showed that she had thirty minutes to get to the meeting.

The fact that she was meeting at the Busby Hotel near the BWI Airport meant that some of them were flying in for this meeting. Audra walked up to the front desk to get directions to the meeting room. She walked into the room, happy to be the first one. She helped herself to water and took a seat.

The rest all arrived together and Audra wondered if they'd had a meeting without her. She sipped her water and pasted on a smile of greeting, but it quickly ebbed when there were no returning smiles.

"Let me get right to the point, Miss Washington," Mr. Druthers said. "I've got a lot of things to do today and I'm angry not only that I have to find out important news from

a television set, but that you weren't anywhere to be found."
His voice raised slightly.

"This is all new to me, also," she replied meekly.

"Didn't you have someone supposedly working on the inside? What the hell happened with that?"

"He said that he couldn't get her to sell."

"And you didn't see fit to tell us that either?"

"You didn't want to hear the truth."

Mr. Druthers stood and walked around to where she sat. Audra set her glass down because her hand shook uncontrollably. She'd learned a little too late that Druthers had a reputation that was as dark as his suit.

"Miss Washington," he hissed, "I've spent a bundle of money on your sorry town, that stupid mayor of yours, and the fund because of you."

"I . . . I didn't come to you."

He grinned. "You're right. You didn't. Vincent, here, came to me with your scheme."

Vincent squirmed as the blame seemed to have shifted.

"But, you see, I'm not quitting. I don't like losing one dollar, one thousand dollars, or one million dollars. So you see, darling, you'll go to Miss Montgomery and let her know that I want that property." The men around the table shifted, mumbling among themselves. "She's a pretty thing. If she wants to remain that way, I'd suggest that she follows your recommendation."

"Look, I want no part of this. I'm walking away from the deal," said one of Druthers's associates.

"Me, too." All the men voiced their dissension, gathering up their briefcases.

In a matter of minutes, only Audra and Mr. Druthers remained in the room. Audra looked up in his face, wondering how someone with great hair, soft bedroom eyes, and manicured hands could have such a deep cruel streak.

"I can't do what you're asking of me." Audra steeled herself against his wrath.

He looked down on her long and hard. "I think we're cut from the same cloth. You're just a newbie at being a taker of the world." He sat on the edge of the table. "Let me explain: There are two types of people, the givers and the takers. From the first day that I met you, I could see that gleam in your eyes. There's a hunger in your eyes that reaches deep into your soul. I'd hoped that this deal would go through so that you could get a taste of what it's like to conquer. It'll feed that hunger for a little while, but then you'll need something bigger for the growing appetite."

Audra shook her head to break the hypnotic stare. His words rang true, but she refused to have this mobster freak identify her with him. "I'm sorry." She got up and walked past him, half expecting him to put her in a stranglehold.

"It's not over, Miss Washington. Somehow, I believe you'll be coming to me before too long."

Audra looked over her shoulder at him.

"It's the gleam." He pointed to his eye.

She ran out of the room and continued running out of the hotel until she got to her car. Breathless, she fumbled with her keys until she got into her car and started the engine. She headed for home wanting to take a shower and scrub her skin to cleanse herself of his evilness.

After a night of bad dreams and bouts of sleeplessness, Audra awoke with puffy eyes. Her head throbbed and her thinking was fuzzy. She opted for a cold shower that shocked her system and strong, freshly brewed coffee for the caffeine kick. She placed her coffee cup in the sink and cleared up the kitchen. Today she was visiting her father. She'd already called in to work to tell them that she'd be working from home and then showing a few houses.

As she drove toward the nursing home, she had to concentrate on keeping her mood light. Driving through the wrought-iron gates, she felt as if she was leaving the madcap buzz of her world and entering an artificially created paradise. So many tired souls behind the painted shingled facade that made her teary-eyed every time she visited. She pulled into a parking spot and turned off the engine, resting her head on the steering wheel until she could get herself together.

"Okay, Audra, pull yourself together." She wiped away her tears, repairing the black eyeliner smear as she walked toward her father's room.

"Dad," she whispered, sitting on the edge of his bed, "I'm here." The pink and white carnations that she'd brought a few days ago still looked perky. She added more water to the vase and returned it to the windowsill.

She heard him stirring behind her. "Which one is it?"

"It's Audra." She turned with a bright smile and walked over to the edge of his bed. "I came to see how you're doing." She bent and kissed his wizened cheek.

"Audra?" He frowned and touched her cheek. Then as if someone had pulled aside a curtain, he offered her the biggest smile that she'd seen in a while. "You're my eldest."

"Yes, Daddy." She blinked back tears and held onto the tiny shred of hope that his lucid moment would last a little longer than a few seconds.

"I'm tired."

"Well, you got to stop whooping it up with the nurses."

He chuckled. "You know how it is, every night is party night." He struggled to sit up. "Do you think that I could go outside for a bit? We can have breakfast on the porch."

Audra paused in the middle of helping him up. Did he really mean the porch, because their home did have a wrap-around porch? She wanted to talk to her father a little while longer. "Daddy? The nursing home has a sunroom where we can eat."

"That's what I mean. Could you help me change my clothes? I think it's bad manners to be walking around in sleeping clothes."

"No problem." Audra took out a fresh shirt and pants, socks, and his loafers.

A few minutes later, she helped him up and they made their way to the sunroom. Although she'd eaten her breakfast, she selected a cherry Danish and a glass of orange juice to keep her father company.

"You're looking tired."

She nodded. "Didn't have a good night."

"Shouldn't let your demons get to you." He turned his gaze away from the windows and the surrounding view on to his daughter. "I can see them."

"Excuse me?" Audra patted his hand, figuring that he'd veered off again.

"You work hard for what you've got. I can tell because you never come here with any man, no children. But you're looking mighty fine. Something's got to keep you so focused. I figured it's demons."

Audra didn't want to look in his eyes. Instead, she focused on the grounds and the morning activity. "How did you do it, Daddy? How did you keep going even after we were gone?"

A sigh shuddered through his body. "It was like a nightmare that wouldn't end. I felt like a failure. Hell, I still feel like a failure. But I was determined to have my family back together."

Audra wiped his tears away, while holding hers back. "We're a family again, Daddy."

"When was the last time that you saw your sister, or your brother?"

She didn't respond immediately, wondering what brought on all this reflection. "I've been really busy, so we've been missing each other."

"Well, here she comes."

Audra looked over to the doorway and sure enough her sister and her husband came in waving. "Oh, my, Joi is getting big."

"I hope that I will live to see my grandbaby. My first."

"You'll do more than live to see the baby, Daddy. You might be delivering it," she joked.

Audra looked across the room at her sister's family approaching. They could be a poster pinup for the successful African-American family. The only item missing was a dog, which the last Audra heard was an Irish setter.

At the rare times that they bumped into each other while visiting their father, Audra realized how much she missed her family. From the look of things, Joi was well adjusted and radiated the elation that her name signified. She knew Joi was pregnant, and from the size of her stomach, she was due any day.

"Hi, sis." Her sister hugged her head to her round belly. Audra swore the baby kicked her in the head.

"Hi, Daddy, are you doing well today?"

Audra hugged George, Joi's husband, and her nephew, Jason, who seemed to have grown another foot since she last saw him.

"As well as can be expected. I'm glad all of you're here. We're missing Greg."

Joi patted his hand, and cast a surprised look at Audra. She'd noticed their father's sense of awareness also.

"Greg is at school. He's got another year."

"And then my son is a doctor." His chest swelled with pride. "All of you have made me so proud. You were able to achieve success despite me." He shook his head and bowed it onto his chest.

Of all the times that she'd wanted her father's approval, this wasn't it. The warm family atmosphere of sharing and caring had no place for the dangerous game she was currently involved in. Joi owned a hair salon. Greg was studying to be a pediatrician. What had she accomplished?

"Sis, what's up with you? Can't even get you to come over for dinner."

"It's been hectic."

"Never too hectic for family."

Her sister's words rang true; nevertheless they irritated the heck out of her. As a matter of fact, Joi's always sunny disposition caused many arguments that Audra initiated.

"Don't get all prickly on me," Joi admonished, seeing Audra's grimace. "It's just that I haven't seen you in months and I have something to ask you."

Audra sat back, wondering if Joi was about to hit her up for money—that was more her brother's style. "Do we need to go somewhere private?"

Joi shrugged. "It's nothing bad, but I know you, so let's go for a walk." She stepped aside for Audra to join her. "George, keep Daddy company. We've got some talking to do."

Quiet, dependable George nodded and pulled up a chair next to his father-in-law's.

Audra followed Joi out into the courtyard. The day was warming up, letting them know that spring was around the corner. Audra shielded her eyes from the direct sun and followed the path toward the covered patio.

Joi didn't speak to her on their short trek, leaving Audra to imagine the worst. She and her sister had a similar build, but she wore her hair at her shoulders and Joi wore hers in a neat bob just below the ears. Audra looked over her sister's hip, suede, purple skirt suit and matching tights with black chunky-heeled shoes. Thank goodness, she still maintained a sense of style with her conservative preferences.

Joi pulled out a plastic chair and took a seat.

Audra followed. "Okay, you made me jump through hoops for your bit of news. Spit it out."

"With the baby coming, I've been thinking about a lot things, including the family." She looked over to the sunroom. "I want us to be close . . . again."

"Were we ever close?" Audra didn't want to talk about the past with her sister. Her feelings were all in a jumble and she desperately wanted to be the big sister and share her words of wisdom.

"I'd like to think so. You took care of Greg and me. You made sure we ate, even when there wasn't enough for yourself. Mama would have been proud." She offered a shaky smile, blinking back tears.

"For the little I've done, you've turned out well with your husband, son, and the business. How is it going? Do you need money?"

Joi wiped away her tears. "Money? Is that what you think I need from you?" Joi reached over, took her hand, and clasped it between hers. "The only thing I need from you is a yes."

Audra leaned forward, waiting.

"I know I'm being dramatic. I want you to be the god-mother."

"What?"

"I want you to be the one to take care of my children if something happens to me. I want you to be the one to teach them how to be wonderful, caring people. You were my role model and I want you in their lives to be a role model to them."

Audra gasped and leaned away from her sister. She could only open and close her mouth repeatedly. Words failed her. Her sister was so wrong about her. "I don't. . . . Can I think about it?"

Joi sighed. "Don't do this to me, Audra. Don't shut me out," she pleaded.

"I'm not all those things that you said. If you only knew," Audra explained.

"I'm not saying that you're perfect, sis. But I know that for me, you are the one I always looked up to and wanted in my corner when things got rough. Well, things are far from being rough. I don't want to wait for the bad times to reach out to you."

Audra nodded.

The sisters hugged tightly, crying on each other's shoul-ders. Then they erupted into laughter, each dabbing her nose and face.

"Let's go back and rescue George," Audra prompted. She'd agreed to her sister's request in the beautiful setting of the artificial paradise. The place had a sense of make-believe and playing a role for her sister fit the bill. But if her sister really knew what she'd been up to and how far she was willing to go to get what she wanted, there would be no chance that she'd want Audra to be in her house, much less as godmother. She didn't deserve the sisterly devotion that Joi held for her. Maybe it was too late to change.

Fourteen

Nicole woke up early and wired. Brad was due back from England and he'd promised to come to Maryland first. She tried to downplay the intense happiness that filled her. Luckily she had a full day with the historians and an architect. It was all out of pocket, but the rewards would be great when she had the official confirmation about her B&B.

By midday, Nicole's B&B hummed with activity. She was busy in the kitchen preparing lunch for the group now examining her basement. Her phone rang incessantly. No doubt the newspapers and television stations all wanted to have the exclusive for when the news would be relayed. For the most part, she allowed the calls to roll to the answering machine.

"How's it going?" Nicole handed a chicken breast sandwich over to Mr. Simmons, the architect.

"It wasn't difficult to get the title information from the courthouse. The house was definitely built in the 1850s. Even for its time, this property is top-quality construction. There've been a lot of renovations, like the kitchen and your apartment. However, the framing throughout the house and especially upstairs is characteristic of that period."

"And the tunnel?"

He bit into the sandwich and gave her a thumbs-up sign. In between chewing, he answered, "The tunnel was part of the original house, which is interesting, don't you think?"

Nicole wasn't sure what his point was. She gave a slight nod, waiting for him to explain.

"It's interesting because it meant that the owner had planned to do this or some other secretive thing. Making a move like that with a family—and I'm assuming he had a family, because the house is so large—could be very risky."

"The other end of the tunnel comes up in the field over there." She indicated with a slight gesture with her head. "What was over there?"

"Probably a barn of some sorts. It wouldn't have been odd to have a huge barn. This was farm country, after all."

Nicole stared out of the little basement window to the spot where the barn would have stood. She tried to imagine what that time was like with the house bustling with activity. How many children did the farmer have? How did he even get involved in the abolitionist movement? Did he do it for the money or for some higher moral obligation?

"I don't think we could begin to imagine what it was like," Mr. Simmons stated. He walked up next to her and leaned against the windowsill. "I imagine that they came in through the barn and made their way over to the house. The family would then feed and clothe them until it was time to hit the road again."

"What a responsibility!" Nicole pictured little children running beside their mamas, scared and hungry. She turned away from the window to break away from the direction of her thoughts. She'd lived a pretty selfish life, one that gave her lots of material rewards. Having someone depend on her terrified her. Heck, depending on someone terrified her. It was unknown territory, but strangely appealing because of one person and one person alone.

"Miss Montgomery?"

"Over here, Mrs. Johnson."

The historian had returned with another specialist. "Based on the town's history and its citizens, we can surmise who the first owners were. It seems they were a northern couple who moved south of the Mason-Dixon line and took up antislavery activities immediately. They were supposed to stand trial, but before the trial a mob came after them."

"Were they killed?"

"No, they were tarred and feathered and chased out of town. Someone else took the house." She looked around the room. "I wonder if the slaves came to the house thinking that they would be given safe haven. What if the new owners didn't help? I can't even imagine."

"I can't even begin to think about it."

"By the way, have you ever heard of Julia Stoutman?"

Nicole shook her head. "Should I have?"

"She's about one hundred years old and is featured in the local newspapers because she knows the town's history. You should talk to her."

"She's in a nursing home?"

"Yes. She doesn't have any family; basically outlived them." Mr. Simmons chuckled. "I know what you're thinking, that she's a lonely old woman. Maybe a little, but she has a regular spot twice a week on a radio station in Silver Spring. Plus, she does an advice column in the weekend papers."

"Wow." Nicole was truly impressed. Even if Julia Stoutman wasn't able to shed any light on the B&B's owner, she sounded like a fascinating woman to chat with.

Mrs. Johnson got her pocketbook and retrieved a piece of paper and a pen. "Here's her number, just give her a buzz. Tell her Thelma gave you her number and it's about the B-and-B."

Nicole looked down at the number, wondering what fascinating stories she would hear. She tucked the piece of paper in her pocket and promised herself she'd call Julia later.

"I think we can wrap it up here," Mr. Simmons suggested. "Have you decided what the next step will be?"

"The mayor is waiting for a report from you. Then if I want it to be officially documented as a historic property and under the protection and coverage of the town's historic preservation fund, a hearing has to be held for the community's input."

She paused, surveying the room and the people standing around her. "I'm not sure."

"It's a big decision with advantages and disadvantages. Being under the fund would give you the publicity that you want for your B-and-B."

"But—"

"But, then you can't make any repairs, renovations, or enhancements without their permission. The rules would apply to landscaping, also."

"You've got to be kidding me." This was her B&B and when she'd bought the property, it was in need of major work just to get it livable, much less get it ready for business. All her savings had gone into it and now that it stood a good chance of being a hot tourist spot, a selected few would have some say.

"Don't make any hasty decisions. Sleep on it."

"Thanks, Mr. Simmons. I'm so glad that you all were able to come and check things out."

"I'll write up my report and if you decide to have a hearing, let me know."

Mrs. Johnson gave her hand a reassuring pat. "We'll come out and support you. What you have here is pretty amazing. It's a piece of history that brought so much happiness with a fresh new beginning to people's lives."

Nicole shook their hands warmly, grateful for their passion to unlock the mysteries and tell the stories of the past. Once they were gone, she rearranged the furniture in the basement. She lingered over closing the door, feeling compelled to say something or do something reverent. In the semidarkened room, alone and subdued, she followed her heart and knelt in the doorway.

"O heavenly Father." Her voice was a mere whisper. "Thank you for touching the hearts of those who stepped forward to help my brothers and sisters. Thank you for leading so many onto the path of freedom. Thank you for inspiring others to care, to love, to feel the power of your love and transcend the evilness that permeates the souls of the weak and cowardly. Amen." Nicole's voice echoed eerily in the darkness.

When she walked upstairs, she felt as if she were reemerging into a new world. She remembered how it felt when she had walked through the house after she closed on the property. This was her new home, a place to feel comfortable and to feel inspired to be a better person. Her utopia was a sanctuary that she wanted others to enjoy. Now she faced a dilemma, whether to fight for recognition by the historic preservation fund or just be a B&B owner of an old farmhouse.

A knock on her door startled her, but she quickly relaxed when she heard the key being inserted in the lock. She peeked through the window for confirmation of her guess—Toni.

"What's up?" She was glad to see her friend, but surprised at the unexpected visit.

"Nothing, driving through." Toni strained her neck, looking into the other rooms while standing in the foyer.

"No one's here." Nicole frowned, noticing that her friend didn't have that usually sassy behavior. Come to think of it, Toni hadn't been herself since announcing the pregnancy. "Is everything okay . . . with the baby?" She held her breath for some indication of impending sad news.

"Yes. I'm feeling fine and the baby is doing okay." She walked past Nicole and went to the family room. "Could I get a cup of decaffeinated tea?"

"Oh, sure." Nicole immediately went to the kitchen to prepare the hot beverage. Toni wanted to talk and, frankly, she'd rather focus on someone else than her basement and its mysteries.

"Any guests coming your way?" Toni shouted from the other room.

"I had one, but he canceled. I guess that's the way of the business." Nicole stirred in the right amount of sugar, knowing Toni's sweet tooth. "I am expecting a nonpaying guest, though."

Toni popped her head around the corner. "Don't tell me," she squealed. "Mr. Cool and Handsome is returning. He might as well move in."

Nicole handed her the tea. "We've decided to take things slowly. He's going to stay in Maryland for a while, but not here."

Toni took the tea. "Thanks." She sipped gingerly, giving Nicole a thumbs-up sign. "You're okay with that?"

"Yep. Considering my track record with the opposite sex, I'd better keep things moving slowly." Never mind that her heart screamed for the fast track.

"Don't let too much time go by before you tell him your feelings."

"What's there to tell? He knows that I like him." Nicole shook her head. "Boy, does he know that I like him!"

"What about love?"

Nicole didn't answer; instead she stared at a grape jelly stain on the linoleum near the refrigerator.

"You do love him," Toni pressed. "I see that sparkle in your eyes when you talk about him and the soft smile you wear when you're daydreaming."

"I think I fell in love the first time he came through that front door." She sighed. "But one thing my mother taught me is that love ain't enough. I want his trust, his confidence. I want him to see me as his life partner, soul mate, whatever you want to call it."

"Be patient, maybe he's had a rough go at things."

Nicole nodded. "Yeah, I guess." She pushed off from the counter and walked toward Toni. "Enough about me. Bring you and your tea to the family room. It's time to talk to me."

Nicole led the way to the family room and plopped down on a couch. Pulling her legs under her, she hugged a few of the toss pillows and watched Toni get herself comfortable.

"My car is packed."

"Packed?" Nicole sat up straighter. "Where are you going? What about Donna?"

"Slow down. I'm going home for a month or so. I resigned from my job. I just need time to get my head straight before the baby gets here." Toni held the cup in both hands. "What scares me is that I don't feel any nurturing vibes. I might not be a good mother. Heck, I wasn't even planning on being a mother."

"It's okay to feel panicked about something that wasn't planned. I know you, Toni, and I know that you'll be a loving mother. Besides, you'll have Shirley, Donna, and me playing backup." Nicole saw that her words had some effect, but Toni's shoulders were still slumped. "How did your parents take it?"

Toni groaned and laughed ruefully. "Mom knows. God, she was so supportive. I just knew that she'd go ballistic. I had my speech about how old I was and that I could look after myself and my child. But she said to come home at once. I guess the old me would have balked at that offer, but right about now I'm feeling so fragile that I want to be with my mother."

"And your father?"

"He doesn't know. Mom advised me to wait until I got there. Daddy's little girl not only did the *nasty,* but didn't use protection. But I have to be willing to face the consequences."

"I'll miss you."

"You could visit. It's not that far away."

"I know. The girls and I will head south to visit."

"I'm leaving early tomorrow morning. Think I could bunk with you for the night?"

"No problem." She could share Brad for one night when he arrived.

Twilight descended and Nicole walked around the house and turned on a few lights. She wanted the house to look hospitable when Brad arrived. In her excitement, she'd baked a pan of his favorite cookies, which were now cooling on the rack.

"Mmm, what smells so good?" Toni sniffed the air and headed for the oatmeal raisin cookies.

"Touch those and die," Nicole warned, appearing out of the pantry closet.

"Just one, please?" Toni whined, her hand creeping over to the stack.

"Only one." Nicole marched over and handed her a cookie, then took the stack with her. "I'm putting these in a safe place until Brad arrives."

"What time is he coming?" Toni asked, munching.

"He'd said around six." Nicole looked at her watch, a frown creasing her forehead. "It's now eight."

"Maybe his plane got delayed or he had to stay over one more day."

Nicole sighed. "Yeah, maybe."

The phone rang and she sprang for the receiver. She answered breathlessly, hoping to hear one particular voice.

"Hi, Miss Montgomery, it's Mrs. Johnson. I was so excited with the secret room that I couldn't let it rest. I called Ms. Stoutman and she's willing to see you tomorrow."

"Oh, wow, that's great. What time?"

"Around noon."

"Thank you so much. I look forward to meeting her." Nicole took down the address and then rang off.

"Looks like you won't have time to think about Brad."

"All the better for him." Nicole's eyes glittered angrily.

After a night spent tossing and turning, Nicole gratefully welcomed the sun and daylight. No word from Brad worried and angered her. Her fears stoked the fires of her anger as she imagined that he'd changed his mind, but didn't have the common courtesy to call her. She'd come to the conclusion that his feelings weren't as intense; therefore, he had opted to stay elsewhere.

"Hey, lady, I'm heading out now." Toni scooted her chair back from the dining table and carried her dishes into the kitchen.

Nicole felt terrible that she was spending the last few minutes of her friend's visit to think about Brad and his no-showing, no-calling, Mr. I'm-afraid-of-commitment butt.

"I'll miss you." Nicole hugged Toni and followed her out to the car. "Please call one of us every so often, okay?"

Toni blinked back tears and nodded.

"You'd better get your butt back here when it's time to push that baby out."

"I will, I promise."

Nicole stepped back and watched Toni drive off. She didn't envy Toni's position, but she'd be there for her. Inhaling deeply, she decided to go for a walk. It would clear her mind and help her refocus. She buttoned the light jacket and headed down the road.

It was Saturday morning and she had a long list of tasks. As she strolled down the road, a few cars whizzed past her. She couldn't help looking at the passengers to see if there was a familiar face. Why did she have to go over the deep end? Focusing on Brad's absence instead of enjoying the walk was getting old.

At least the day wasn't very cold, but a refreshing cool breeze drifted over the hills. She'd walk to the beginning of the next property and then turn around to head home. It was quiet with only the cows for company. If nothing else, she had her visit to Julia Stoutman to look forward to. She turned around at the specified point.

As she walked down the road, she looked at her new property. She tried to imagine herself as a guest and tried to use an objective view of what she saw. The house with its fresh paint and new siding gleamed in the morning sun. Her garden was well tended, and soon she'd be able to plant flowers along the footpath. Even her white picket fence added a special touch that made her B&B cozy and comfortable. As her sign swung slightly in the breeze, she couldn't help feeling proud of what she'd accomplished. Swinging her arms up and down, she took a few more deep breaths, shaking off her mood.

"Are you going to stand out here all morning and admire your place?"

"Brad?" Nicole ran toward the man who had claimed her heart. He met her halfway across the path with arms outstretched. She jumped into his arms. He was actually here and she was in his arms, kissing him madly on his face.

"I missed you, so much." She blinked with the surge of emotions and tears that had been ever present. "I thought you'd changed your mind."

He carried her into the house, her arms wrapped tightly around his neck. "I told you that I was coming on Saturday."

"You said Friday."

"I said Friday first, but then I left a message on the answering machine."

"Oh."

Brad pursed his lips. "I think I need an apology because I'm so sure you and your girlfriends were cursing me out."

"Only Toni and me." She smirked and kissed him before he could say anything further.

He kicked the front door closed with his foot and Nicole slid down from her perch. "Any visitors?"

"Just us."

"Good because I really, really missed you."

Nicole giggled and snuggled against Brad's neck. "Where's your suitcase?"

He went outside to retrieve his cases. "I need a shower and then let's eat. I'm starved."

"You take a shower and I'll take care of the food." Nicole bustled around the kitchen happily preparing a small plate of fresh fruit to munch on while they waited for their frittata to bake. When Brad rejoined her in the kitchen he placed a soft kiss on the back of her neck.

"I feel so much better."

"Dig in. How was the flight?"

They made small talk over the fruit and eggs with Nicole keeping him company at the dining table.

"Nicole." Brad's countenance turned serious. "I need to tell you something."

Nicole held her finger against Brad's lips. "Not now. You're scaring me and I'm not sure that I'm ready for bad news." She looked into his eyes. "It *is* bad news, isn't it?"

Brad didn't answer and he didn't keep eye contact. Nicole pushed away from the table and stood. "Okay, Brad, but wait until I come back from my appointment." She walked out of the room and then stopped, keeping her back to him. "Please don't break my heart."

Nicole bowed her head, her brain already echoing the *I told you so* statement. It was time to get ready and she made each step of her preparation a major decision to force her mind from thinking about Brad and his potential bad news. If it wasn't something that was so devastating, he would have come right out and said what he had to say. Instead, he gave enough forewarning to alert her that what he had to say wasn't any ordinary news.

"Will you be here when I get back?"

"Yes, I will." Brad walked over to her standing at the door and kissed her softly on her cheek.

Sitting in Ms. Stoutman's apartment, Nicole felt as if she were in a museum. Walls, tables, and bookcases were dotted with memorabilia spanning one hundred years and more.

"Miss Montgomery, I've been looking forward to seeing you."

"Please call me Nicole."

"And call me Julia." The little old woman handed her a glass of iced tea and then sat in an armchair that dwarfed her already small frame. "So you want to know information about your house. My mother was a midwife and delivered a few babies in that house." Julia chuckled. "My father worked in a steel factory in Baltimore. A few times I accompanied my mother and would help keep the younger ones occupied. I loved it because the Patterson family was well off, the father owned the largest grocery story in the city."

"Did you know about the secret room?"

Julia shook her head. "We were never allowed to go in the basement."

"Do you think they knew about the room?"

Julia shrugged. "How long did it take you to find the room?"

"I spent so little time down there, but the boys that were staying with me saw it. You could see the doorway cut into the wall. You would have had to have furniture in front of it to miss it, especially if you were looking for someone. So I do believe that they knew about it."

Julia took Nicole's hand. "Enough with the past. What are you going to do about it?" She clapped her hands. "I'm so excited about the possibilities."

"I'm faced with registering it as a historic building." Nicole shrugged.

"That's great. Think of all the publicity."

"That's what I'm afraid of. Once I register it, then I may have to jump through hoops to do anything with it."

Nicole arrived back at the house and slowed down when she saw Audra's car in her driveway. She slapped the steering wheel. "What the heck does she want?" Nicole pulled up next to the car and noticed that Audra was in the driver's seat.

"Audra, what are you doing here?"

"I need to talk to you, Nicole. I didn't see your car and figured you were out. So I waited." Audra stepped out of the car.

"I don't have time." Nicole slammed the car door, exasperated at having to deal with Audra. "I have company, so don't think that you're coming in to make a scene."

"I'm here to apologize."

Nicole stopped midway to the door and turned around to see if Audra was kidding. "Should I jump out of the way for the lightning to strike? Audra, don't try to play me." Nicole spun around and marched to the door.

The door opened and Brad stood in the doorway. "I heard you shouting."

"It's nothing. Audra, you've got five—" Nicole's words died as she looked from Brad's shocked face to Audra's angry countenance.

"Well, hello, Brad."

Icy dread slithered down Nicole's body. "You know each other?" Her voice was a mere squeak. She coughed to clear away the lump in her throat. "Come in, Audra, it looks like you may have more to say to me than originally planned." Nicole flinched and jerked away from Brad's movement toward her.

Fifteen

Brad wasn't sure where or when Audra had shown up, but that didn't matter now. Nicole's face had been enough to let him know that he was in big trouble. All his plans to tell her about his unintended role in Audra's plans were up in smoke. He knew from looking in Audra's eyes that he was about to go down. "Nicole, allow me to explain."

Nicole tilted her head to the side and studied him. "Not yet, I think that I'll have Audra go first."

Audra hadn't moved from her spot just inside the door. "I knew Brad from our days at a foster home. It was a brief stint for me, but I'd gotten to know Brad. We became friends."

"Friends?"

"Over the years we kept in touch with occasional visits."

"Don't try to make it sound like something that it wasn't. I came down for conferences," Brad declared.

"You came for conferences all right, but you didn't have to call me and invite me to dinner when you came to town." Audra looked at Nicole. "I thought we were friends."

"Continue." Nicole bit her cheek to keep the tears at bay.

"Anyway, I came across this property when it was for sale . . ."

"For heaven's sake," Nicole grumbled. The warehouse supermarket parking lot barely had any spaces. Nicole pulled into a space at the other end of the lot. To make matters worse, she had a lengthy list of food items for three couples celebrating their reunion.

She pushed the cart methodically down each aisle, selecting food. She scratched out rice, sphagetti, and green beans. Three down, about seventeen more items to go.

"Excuse me, but don't I know you?"

Nicole turned to see who addressed her. A stocky young man wearing sunglasses smiled at her. She had no idea who he was, unless he was some jerk trying to make conversation. Well, now wasn't the time. "I don't think so."

"Sorry. I was just so sure. Nicole . . . um . . ." He snapped his fingers and tapped his head.

"Montgomery. Nicole Montgomery."

He gave her a winning smile and pointed at her. "I knew it." He walked over to her with his hand outstretched.

Nicole still didn't know this beefy man, but he looked friendly enough. She offered her hand for the handshake. He grabbed her wrist and pulled her against him. Nicole could smell the tuna fish on his breath.

His face carried a savage sneer. "I have a message for you from my boss."

"And who is your boss?"

"You'd better reconsider selling that B-and-B. You've got twenty-four hours to decide."

"Your boss must be one of the developers. Well, you can take my message back to him." Nicole gritted her teeth at the painful grip he had on her wrist. "Tell him to go to hell." She got emboldened when her reply clearly stumped him. "You've got three seconds to take your hand off me or I will scream this place down."

Her threat brought a smile to his face. "You call the police and your mother on 1101 Pearl Street, Jacksonville, Florida, may not be able to evacuate her burning house."

Nicole gasped. Words failed her. This whole episode was something out of a movie, except there was no director sitting off to the side waiting to say "cut."

Her beefy intimidator let go of her hand and without another word, turned and walked down the aisle. Nicole stared at the place where he had stood. Her mind raced with terrifying images, while her limbs were rooted to the spot.

She pulled out her cell phone and dialed. Her mother answered. "Hi, Mom. Just checking up on you. Is everything okay?"

"Yes, dear. Your father and I are spending the day on the lake. He says we're fishing, but I'm going to have dinner prepared just in case." Her mother's light laugh reassured Nicole. "What's wrong, dear? You sound a bit strange."

"I'm fine, really. I'm on my cell phone, it distorts the voice."

"Well, you have a good day. We've got to run."

Nicole snapped the phone shut. It took her a few seconds to let the relief sink in before she could think.

"Nicole?"

She jumped at the sound of her name, afraid that her nightmare wasn't over. "Brad," she answered. "What are you doing here?" She wanted to run to him and let him hold her against his wide chest. Instead she backed up against the store shelves, needing that firm support to keep her from sliding into an emotional puddle.

"Who was that?" he asked, looking in the direction of her tormentor.

"Who?" She looked around as if she didn't have a clue.

"The man who was three inches away from your face," he elaborated slowly. "It looked like he was threatening you."

"Oh, him . . . he was asking where the canned corn was."

"Are you finished here? We need to talk."

"I still have other items. And there's nothing to talk about."

"Suit yourself." He followed her as she walked down the aisle, selecting food items.

Nicole chanced a quick glance out of the corner of her eye whenever she stopped to take an item off the shelf. She noted that he didn't even push a cart to blend in with the other shoppers. He simply walked two feet behind her.

"I can't take this anymore. What do you want, Brad?" she asked through gritted teeth.

"I'm insisting that you give me a chance to say my piece." He waited. "You owe me that much."

"Owe?" She shook her head, laughing. "Why do you think that I owe you anything?"

"Because we have something special between us. You have a right to be angry, but you're overreacting about the entire situation."

Nicole sucked her teeth and pushed her cart down the aisle and around the corner to the next one. The man was unbelievable. She didn't have time to play any games, and no man was going to lead her down some stupid road. Despite his charming personality and good looks, she wasn't going to be drawn in.

"Nicole," he called, drawing the attention of other shoppers. "Nicole."

She refused to turn. Since he was having difficulty accepting that it was over, it was up to her to be firm. All the passion-filled embraces and steamy lovemaking were in the past.

Nicole finished shopping, expecting to see Brad appear with another plea. She had to admit to feeling a bit disappointed when there was no sign of him. Now that he had left, she had other business to attend to before heading home.

Her errands completed, Nicole drove to see the one person that she'd hoped never to have to see again.

Sixteen

Brad sped down the road, his mind racing along with the scenery whizzing past the windows. He had screwed up big time. He banged the steering wheel with the heel of his hand. "I knew I should have told her," he muttered.

The whole episode made him mad just thinking about it. If Audra had kept her fat head out of Nicole's business, he wouldn't have played superhero. In his somewhat tarnished armor, he'd willingly played the knight off to slay a dangerous dragon.

Brad parked the car in haste, crossing the thick white line of the parking spot. He didn't care. A few minutes later, he was pounding on Audra's door.

She opened it, clearly shocked to see him.

He pushed past her and stood in the living room, arms folded. "Audra, we need to talk."

"I guess you're coming to blast me from breaking up your little tea party with Nicole." She offered a sad smile. "Actually, I didn't know you would be there."

"Then why?"

"I went to warn Nicole." She sighed. "Then I saw you. But more than that, I saw that look in your eyes when she walked through the door. I guess I just snapped."

Brad digested what he'd heard. "Audra," he said without anger, "you and I were never going to get together. Be honest, I'm not your type."

"What exactly is my type, if it's not you?"

He shook his head. "I can't keep going back and forth with you on this. I came here for another reason. Someone threatened Nicole today."

"What? Is she okay?"

"Scared, but I think she's going to try to handle it on her own."

"And you're here to save the day."

"Yes."

"What do you want with me?"

"You know who is behind this mess, so you are going to take me to this person."

Audra waved her hands. "Nope. No can do."

"You said that you came to warn Nicole. So under that snakeskin of yours—"

"Low blow."

"I'm sorry." He ran his hands over his face. "Audra, I'm tired. The woman I love hates me right about now. I'm not going to lose her." He ticked off each item on his finger. "Now this person that you have forcing her to sell—and now threatening her—will have to deal with me."

Audra clapped after his heated speech. "Glad to see that your survival skills have surfaced. As much as you turn your nose up at your childhood, it just might get your sweetheart out of trouble."

"Call him and set up a meeting now."

Audra walked toward her bedroom and then hesitated.

"I don't have time for any of your bull, Audra."

She turned slowly. "I'll help you, Brad. Things got out of hand. I'm sorry."

Brad saw the sincerity in her eyes. He'd like to pretend that he didn't feel a connection with Áudra. It was nothing remotely similar to the way he felt about Nicole, but she reminded him of his roots. By denying her, he'd shoved his childhood experiences in a black hole. It was this obsession with keeping his past a secret that got him in trouble with Nicole. "Audra, there can't be anything between us. I'm sorry, too, for dissin' you. Right now, though, I need you to help me."

She nodded and went into her room.

Nicole drove through the gates of the condominiums, her stomach churning at her gutsy move. There wasn't any guarantee that her idea would meet with success. Maybe she could feed off her anger to give her the confidence to head off a dangerous enemy.

She circled the area, looking for a closer parking spot. No luck. It would seem that she had to go for the spot on the far end of the lot. After parking the car, she walked toward the building, fumbling in her pocket for the piece of paper with the condo number. A soft breeze stirred up, catching hold of the paper and lifting it out of her hand. It landed a few feet away from her and Nicole squatted to retrieve it.

Wisps of a conversation drifted toward her. It wasn't exactly what was being said that caught her attention. Instead it was the familiar deep rumble of Brad's voice. Her hand stilled over the paper, listening to him. In a split second, she felt as if someone had punched her in her stomach. The other voice replying to Brad was Audra's.

Nicole looked up from her crouched position and saw the couple walking away from her. They walked, shoulder to shoulder, engaged in deep conversation. Nicole stood, not really caring if they saw her. The searing pain in her heart scorched any reservations that she had had.

She turned away and headed for her car. There would be no confrontation, no false promises, no lies. Even her tears didn't spout like Old Faithful. She was dry and empty.

Somehow, she drove back home. As she pulled up, the warm cozy feel of her B&B seemed far away. Thank goodness her guests hadn't arrived. She went through the mindless task of putting away the groceries because she was preoccupied with the vision of Brad smiling down on Audra's face.

The doorbell sounded. For a moment, she hesitated. "You still have a business to run," she said to her reflection in the hallway mirror. She didn't look too bad, simply unhappy. If these were her guests, then she had to play the perfect hostess.

After a dinner of meat loaf, steamed broccoli and carrots, and a garden salad, Nicole served a simple dessert of deep-dish apple pie to her newly wedded couple. She cut herself a thin slice of the sweet temptation.

"How long have you been doing this?" Alister questioned, his sharp blue eyes full of curiosity.

"It's been about ten months now." Ten long months, Nicole wanted to say.

"This must have been a dream of yours," Janet said, her face reflecting all the love she could hardly contain for her new husband.

Nicole thought about the origins of this venture. "I think it was an impulsive act more than a dream." Looking around the dining room with its country charm, she knew she had stretched herself beyond even what she thought she could do.

"Do you think we can see the room?" Janet inquired, playing with the end of her silky red hair pulled back into a ponytail.

"The room?" Nicole turned from husband to wife for clarification.

"We heard on the news about the hidden room and its history," Janet gushed, her freckles standing out against her pale complexion. "I would love to see it. This is a treasure of our past."

"I'll show it to you later in your visit," Nicole said slowly.

Alister sipped his drink, hiding a small smile. "I know what you're thinking."

Nicole didn't say anything, but looked at him.

"Janet's words, 'This is a treasure of our past,' made you

flinch. It's all of our pasts, regardless of race, sex, or religion. I think it's important to share it with everyone."

Nicole nodded, but still didn't speak. Her guests looked like the perfect models for midwestern kindergarten teachers.

"I hope Alister hasn't offended you," Janet said, her voice laden with worry. A soft blush suffused her face.

"No, not at all," Nicole said at last. "I was just surprised that folks would have come to see it so soon."

"But of course, I consider it some sort of pilgrimage." Janet smiled and reached for a second helping of apple pie. "And it's all yours. You are so lucky to discover something so important. I'm sure you've had lots of offers for the property since the announcement."

Nicole didn't feel like confessing her problems to the happy couple. Janet was too close with her guess, and this conversation was much too close to the heartache that she currently suffered.

After Alister and Janet had retired for the night and Nicole had cleaned up the kitchen, she retreated to her apartment. She glanced down at the answering machine and saw the light blinking slowly. There were three messages. She hit the PLAY button and listened, knowing that she really only wanted to hear one voice in particular. The first message was from her former boss. She only left a brief message for her to call, whenever she could. Nicole didn't erase the message and waited for the next. It was from Toni. A smile crossed her face as her friend cried for help while her mother scolded in the background about her messy room. The last message played and Nicole held her breath at the sound of Brad saying her name. He apologized again and said that he wanted to see her tomorrow before he headed for New York. She wrote down the meeting information because once and for all, she was going to give him a piece of her mind. And then he could go back to New York for good.

***

Brad followed Audra with his car. He wanted to be alone, and after he dealt with this guy he might not be in the mood to deal with Audra. He noticed that they were heading into Washington, DC. After he drove around the third traffic circle, he decided that he'd have to follow Audra out of the city or be hopelessly lost. Eventually she pulled up in front of a large brownstone that fit into the neighborhood of other large town houses.

The mysterious man had his thuggish ways, but didn't live the lifestyle. Brad stepped out of his car, taking an assessment of his wealthy surroundings. "You've been here?" Remembering how she had expertly weaved around the traffic and turned down streets without hesitation, he had his opinions.

"No. I knew where he lived, but I've never visited." She rubbed her arms briskly to minimize a shudder. "He's not exactly someone that I would claim as a friend."

Brad was surprised that they were able to walk right up to the front door without interference. He kept looking over his shoulder for one of the man's henchmen to jump out from behind the sculpted shrubbery. Audra used the heavy brass knocker.

"May I help you?" a uniformed maid asked.

"I'm here to see Mr. Druthers," Audra stated.

"Is he expecting you?"

"No, but he will want to see me. Is he here?"

"Your name and the nature of your business?"

"Audra Washington," Audra replied.

"My business is Nicole Montgomery," Brad added.

"Step in and have a seat. I'll be back shortly."

Brad didn't speak to Audra while they waited. His stomach had tightened in anticipation of the fight ahead. He had no idea what he could say to sway this man. There was also the unpleasant scenario that he'd have to pay dearly for his presumptuous gesture.

"Miss Washington, Mr. Calverton. Mr. Druthers will see you now. Please follow me."

Brad allowed Audra to be in between him and the housekeeper, giving him time to study his surroundings even more as they moved past a formal dining room and an expansive sunken family room to sliding wooden doors. When the housekeeper slid them back, Brad saw the head honcho behind a large, highly polished desk. He figured that it was a study, decorated with huge floor-to-ceiling bookshelves.

"Audra, what's your problem?"

Brad stepped in front of her. "I have the problem."

"And who might you be?"

"That doesn't matter," Brad answered. He'd decided to take the offensive. "This is about Nicole Montgomery and her B-and-B."

"Ah." Druthers leaned back in his chair. "You're pretty ballsy." He pointed at Brad. "And *you* are wearing on my nerves." He pointed at Audra.

Brad wanted the attention back on himself. No need to turn the spotlight onto Audra, regardless of her role. "Your man threatened Nicole."

Druthers nodded.

"She's not selling the B-and-B. That is her home. Why do you want it so badly? Is it an ego thing?"

Druthers slammed his hand on the desk, rattling the desk lamp. "Don't get too cocky because I've allowed you into my house. Money was involved. It's always about money. I could give a rat's ass about the house or your girlfriend. What's it to you, anyway?"

Brad didn't like this thug one bit, but he hoped to reach some deep human emotion. "I love her and I want to see her happy."

Audra walked slowly toward Druthers. "This is all my fault. I'm trying to make things right. The deal fell through and everyone walked away, except you."

He narrowed his eyes at her. "What are you prepared to give me in return for walking away?"

"Nothing," Brad replied.

Druthers threw his head back and laughed. "You like to live a dangerous life, Mr. Calverton." He turned serious and steepled his hands under his chin.

"I—" Brad began.

"Shh. Let me think about it."

Brad looked at Audra, who shrugged.

"Meeting is over." Druthers gave them a smile that never quite reached his eyes. "You can tell your ladylove that she can enjoy another sunrise."

Brad didn't take the thinly disguised statement lightly. He moved forward to shake his hand. "Thank you."

Druthers didn't extend his hand. "All in a day's work. I like having the power to grant your smallest wishes. Today I'm feeling very generous."

Brad grabbed Audra's arm and backed out of the room. Scared and ecstatic, he wanted to run to his car. Outside the house, he called Nicole to give her the good news and hopefully ask for a second chance. He was disappointed when she didn't pick up and he had to leave a message.

Audra watched Brad turn off as she drove home. It had been a stressful day and all she wanted to do was soak in a tub with a glass of wine. Maybe one day she could look back at the experience without her nerves being rattled.

Sixteen

Nicole awoke at the annoying blast of her alarm clock. Her guests were going on a day trip to the outlets in Pennsylvania. They were leaving at six o'clock in the morning to catch the bus, and since Gertie didn't arrive until seven, Nicole had to prepare breakfast.

Nicole stirred the oatmeal, yawning occasionally. Thank goodness they only wanted hot cereal and fruit. She had also packed a brown-bag lunch for them to hold them over until they got to their destination.

"Aren't you joining us for breakfast?" Janet asked.

"Nope. I'll just enjoy my coffee in semidarkness."

Janet and Alister laughed. "I'm so sorry that we got you up early," Alister offered.

Nicole waved away his guilt. "Don't worry about me. This shot of caffeine will do the job." She sipped her coffee and smacked her lips with relish.

An hour later she had dropped them off at the meeting spot at the Baptist church in the downtown area. Wide awake now, Nicole looked forward to following through on decisions that she had made overnight. She didn't want to reconsider or delay any action on her part.

Quickly she made up the guests' bed and replaced their toiletries. Then she opted to take care of any outstanding paperwork, glad to see that she didn't have any guests scheduled. The usual anxiety of having an empty calendar would have caused her stomach to bunch. However, since her decision, she was quite calm. She continued working on all the paperwork until her in-box was clean. She stacked her outgoing mail at the end of the desk; she'd take it down to the post office later.

Taking a deep breath, Nicole decided that it was time to start the first of many actions that would have the most impact on her life. She reached for the phone and dialed her ex-boss. "Hi, Lena, it's Nicole."

"Hi there. I hoped that you would return my call. How are you doing?"

"Fine. You said it was important." Nicole didn't mean to sound so rushed, but she crossed her fingers that Lena would say what she secretly wanted to hear.

"Nicole, I need you here. Now before you say no, listen to me. I'm willing to work with any schedule you will need to run your business. But you've got the contacts and the knowledge and no one can replace you. Maybe, even be a consultant." Her boss paused. "Can you at least think about it?"

Nicole pressed her eyes closed, pinching the bridge of her nose. "Okay, Lena, you've got me. I want to plan my schedule and it may not be permanent, but it'll get you through this legislative session."

"Thank you, thank you! So, when can I see you?"

"I've got guests leaving tomorrow. I can come the day after to iron out the details."

After Lena hung up, Nicole held the receiver to her forehead until the taped voice of the operator prompted her to hang up. With one phone call, she had done more than made a decision. She gulped, her throat suddenly feeling very dry.

She went to the kitchen to get a drink of water and to gather up her courage once again. She picked up the receiver and this time dialed the real estate agent who had sold her the property. "Hi, Cecil. It's Nicole Montgomery.

Her real estate agent responded, happy to hear from her.

"Looks like I'll need your services."

"Yes?"

Nicole could hear the smile dying on Cecil's face. "I want to put the B-and-B up for sale."

"You're kidding, right? What happened?"

"I love it, but it's more than I bargained for. I'm really not up to explaining. Could you help me?"

"How soon?"

"As soon as possible."

"If you have time we can talk today. I'll bring over the necessary paperwork, just in case I can't convince you to stay the course."

"See you in an hour?" Nicole hung up and this time, wiped away a tear that had spilled down the side of her cheek. There was too much to do in a short time to indulge in a weeping session. She bit her lip, praying for the fortitude to go through with everything.

One more call to make. She dialed and heard the connection ringing. "Hi, Brad. You called?" Even to her own ears, her voice had a hollow quality.

"Nicole, I hoped that you would call me. We need to talk."

"Not really. I think that I heard and saw enough." Overnight, she'd decided not to meet with him after all.

"I have some good news for you."

"We don't need to meet for that," she shot back. Her irritation was more directed at herself and her body's reaction to the familiar voice. But it was that same voice and its owner who had betrayed her. "I don't even know why I called. Goodbye, Brad."

"Wait a minute," he rushed. "Look, if you don't come to see me before I leave, then I'm coming to you."

She didn't respond; instead she pressed down the button to disconnect the call. Her heart and mind warred. Why couldn't she agree to meet him, to see his face one more time? Her heart yearned for more than an image of his face. It was quite capable of forgiving. But her head got in the way.

She pounded the wall with her fist. Damn! There was no way that she was going to become some weak woman addicted to a no-good man. Her friend Toni was a perfect example of the resulting effect. She shook her head to clear away the wimpy thoughts of love and happiness. She'd close this chapter of her life and reconnect to what she knew. So much for Brad Calverton . . . there were other important details to attend.

The necessary form to place the property on the market sat in front of Nicole. She took the pen from Cecil with hands shaking and signed each document.

"May I ask one more thing?" Cecil asked.

"Sure."

"What about registering the property with the historic society?"

"I can't register it as yet because the formal hearing and approval won't occur for another month or so. I don't have kind of time."

"So, that's it?" Cecil eye's spoke volumes about what he thought of Nicole's decision.

"Look, the room was there before I came along, and the next fortunate owners can have the responsibility."

"What if they have it sealed or level this house?"

Nicole had fought to keep this house out of the hands of the greedy land developers. Now she was willingly handing it over and she felt low.

Cecil placed her hand over Nicole's. "Look, all I'm suggesting is that you put off the decision. It is yours to sell, but another month or so won't hurt anything."

Nicole pulled her hand away and placed it in her lap. She'd made up her mind and there was no turning back. "Do you have the sign?" she asked in an icy tone.

Cecil sighed and nodded. "Are you sure you want to put it up before your guests leave?"

"No. I'll put it in the garage until they leave tomorrow. Well, I think that's about it. I don't mean to sound rude, but I have to get to another appointment." Nicole escorted Cecil to the door.

There was no other appointment, because she definitely wasn't going to see Brad. But after formalizing the destruction of what had become a part of her dream, she wanted to be alone.

Sitting in front of the television with a big bowl of ice cream, Nicole nursed her depressed mood. She'd already gone through a bag of ripple potato chips and half a box of chewy candy pellets. Her guests had called and said that the bus wasn't leaving Pennsylvania until late, enough time to continue her death by junk food.

A knock on her living room window startled her. She froze on the couch, staring at the window. A dark shadow moved across the window toward the door. The loud knocking sprang her from the couch and she backed away. The memory of the man who had threatened her earlier was back. She picked up the phone to call the police.

"Nicole," a familiar voice called. "I can see you. Open the door, it's freezing out here."

Nicole obeyed, although she tried to unlock the door with the bowl of ice cream safely nestled in her arm. She flung open the door and turned to resume her seat. "What do you want, Brad? You scared me half to death." Her heart thumped against her chest.

He surveyed the room, flicking aside the empty potato chip bag. "Why didn't you come to see me?" He found the half-filled box of candy and emptied a few into his hand.

"I wasn't under the impression that it was an order." Nicole hoped he choked on a piece of candy. Then the traitorous side of her thought that giving him an abdominal thrust would be most pleasant. "So, now you're here, what's on your mind?"

"You. I can't seem to stop thinking about you. I only have a few minutes or I'll miss my flight." He sat opposite her and kept his eyes on her. "But, if that's what you want me to do— miss my flight—then I'll stay. You only have to say the words."

Nicole stuck a large helping of ice cream in her mouth, licking the spoon for effect. Maybe if she kept her mouth full, then she wouldn't run the risk of saying something simpering.

"I went to see Druthers today. The man who sent his goon to threaten you." He smiled. "He's agreed to back off."

Nicole melted under his smile. His kissable lips and white toothy smile drew her in and she felt the answering response of her lips curving into a smile.

"I'm taking the credit, but I've got to share it with Audra."

Nicole's spoon clattered to the bowl. "It always comes back to Audra," she said sarcastically. "Should I expect her to come popping up on my doorstep, too?"

He frowned. "It's never been about Audra. I went over to her place today because she knew how to get in touch with this guy."

"I know. I saw you."

"And you didn't say anything?"

"Didn't know if you'd hear me with Audra's face jammed up against your ear."

Brad looked at his watch. "Damn, I need to know right here, right now. Do we have a chance? I want you so badly that I can't think of anything else."

"You'll get over it. Think of it like a virus. It just has to run its course; then you'll be better than ever with antibodies to boot."

Brad stood, looking down at her. "You obviously aren't ready to hear me out. I don't blame you. I'll be back, Nicole."

She could have let it go at that, because who cared if he did or didn't come back? "I won't be here. The property will be on the market tomorrow and with the publicity, I expect that it'll be sold in a matter of weeks."

"What?" his voice thundered. "Why?" He grabbed her up, staring down into her face.

Nicole couldn't deal with the disappointment in his eyes. She pulled away, but couldn't get out of his grip. "I would think that you of all people would be happy. You can have your retreat.

Isn't that why you showed up at my place? Anything else you got was a bonus."

He dropped his hands to his side. "I wish you all the luck in the world, Nicole. One day I hope you find that perfect someone who won't break your heart or make mistakes. While you grow old waiting for someone to meet your high standards, remember this: I love you." Without another word, he walked out of her apartment and out of her life.

Eighteen

Nicole walked into the real estate office, fighting back tears. Failure didn't sit well with her. As she sat in the conference with the buyer's lawyer across from her, she wondered what kind of man wouldn't even have the courtesy of meeting her on the final day. She adjusted her suit jacket. Never mind, in an hour or so, she'd be free to go back to what she knew, away from the country to the political hotbed of side deals and negotiations.

"Before you sign any paperwork, there is one thing that my client requests."

Nicole's head snapped up from the thick pile of papers waiting for her signature. Her eyes narrowed, as she contemplated what game the lawyer or his client had in mind.

"Go ahead," Cecil prompted.

"My client asks that Miss Montgomery visit the property after she has signed the paperwork."

"Why?" Nicole looked at Cecil and then back to the lawyer.

"There's something in the house that he wants you to have."

"Couldn't he have brought it, or have you bring it?" Cecil offered. "I'm not comfortable with this, but it's up to Nicole."

Nicole tapped the table with her nails. She maintained eye contact with the lawyer, looking for a hint of a smile or evidence that an elaborate joke or something sinister was at hand. "Is this the only request?"

The lawyer nodded.

"Fine." She picked up the pen and began signing the paperwork.

"I don't think it's a good idea, Nicole."

"It's okay, Cecil. I will go over there on my way to the airport." She was flying back to her parents' house for a monthlong vacation before heading back to her job. She pulled out her cell phone. "I'll even have this in hand when I go over there."

Cecil blew out an exasperated sigh. "Not good enough. You call me before you get there and keep me on the line until you leave."

"That seems sensible enough," the lawyer stated.

The remaining hour closed with Nicole signing away her dream. Her hand shook as she signed the last page, pausing on the last letter of her name to concentrate on not breaking down in sobs. When she had control, she set down the pen and leaned back. "Here are the keys." She slid them across the table, reluctantly pulling back her hand.

"I'll take this set and you can take the other. Simply leave it in the house."

Nicole got her pocketbook and stood. She wanted to be alone, concealed by the night's darkness to give in to the turmoil of emotions. "Thank you for everything, Cecil." Then she turned to shake the lawyer's hand. Looking into his eyes, she saw pity reflected back at her. "I hope your client is happy."

Nicole drove away from the office and headed out of the small downtown area toward the place she once called home. At nine o'clock on a weeknight, the streets were deserted. As she turned down her street, the occasional street lamp was now nonexistent. Only her headlights guided her down the long, dark road. She'd turned off her radio to keep the quiet, contemplative mood.

She slowed down as she approached the house, her heart aching from the loss. At least she didn't have to go into a dark house, because the porch light and a few inside lights were on. She'd almost forgotten her promise. Pulling into the driveway, she dialed Cecil's number. "Hi, Cecil, I'm outside now."

"You weren't suppose to call me when you were right outside the house."

"I know, I know." Nicole stepped out of the car and closed the door. The sound seemed amplified in the quiet neighborhood.

"What are you doing now?"

"Walking up to the door." She placed the key into the lock and opened the door slowly, at first. "Oh."

"What!"

"Um . . . the lights." Nicole looked around the foyer and then into the living room. Small candles were lit and lined a pathway toward the staircase. Each step had a candle on each side as far as she could see. "So many lights," she whispered.

"What the heck are you saying? I can barely hear you."

Nicole followed the path, her heart thumping painfully. She was scared and intrigued, all at the same time.

"Talk, Nicole, or I'm driving over there right after I call the police."

"No, don't call the police." Her hand dropped to her side. Walking deliberately slowly, she approached the step, staring at an interesting sight. She brought the phone up to her ear. "There are flower petals on each step. Looks like roses to me."

"Nicole," Cecil shouted. "That's it. Do not go up the stairs. Nicole!"

Nicole looked up the stairs, waiting for some explanation to present itself. The flower petals perfumed the air. She stooped and trailed her fingers along the silky parts. Then a soft melody played. Nicole tilted her head, listening. "There's music."

"Nicole?"

"Cecil, I know the song." She hummed the melody as she ascended the staircase. The song made her blush. "It's okay, Cecil. I'm safe."

"Are you sure?"

At the top of the stairs, she continued to follow the candles where they led into the honeymoon suite. She stopped in the doorway and leaned against the door frame. "Cecil, I'll call you later. No need to worry."

"Okay." Cecil still sounded doubtful. "I'll talk to you later."

Nicole took a deep breath, fighting to maintain calm. She couldn't get weak now. "Why, Brad?"

He sat in the armchair directly opposite the door in a silk, forest-green robe. "You were about to throw away something dear to your heart."

She wondered if he was talking about the B&B or him. "Sometimes, the best of matches don't work. Instead of me spinning my wheels to prove otherwise, I decided to move on."

"Giving up was never part of your vocabulary."

Nicole flinched at his accusation, no matter how accurate. "It still isn't. I'm moving on, there's a difference." She walked into the room, looking at the petals on the bed. "So you got what you wanted—my B-and-B. Congratulations."

"I only bought it for one reason."

"Whatever. Well, it's time for me to go. You got me here on a bogus reason and now you're wasting my time."

"I never lied. There is something here for you." He pointed to the bed.

Nicole followed his motion toward the bed and saw a small black box on the pillow. She looked back at him. "Brad, it's better if we go our separate ways. I hope you enjoy the house. It brought me happiness at one time." She could have kicked herself for the tremor in her voice.

"Nicole, don't leave." Brad got up and walked up behind her. He didn't touch her, but Nicole could feel his body heat against hers. "Turn around, please."

His voice stroked her the way she wanted his hands to. "Is the plan to seduce me as a final conquest?"

"Stop being cruel. I need you to give me a second chance.

I screwed up, but not out of malice. I never meant to cause you any pain."

"It's more than your relationship with Audra, Brad. You kept your past from me like a top-secret document. Trust. That's what you couldn't give me."

"Would you have liked me or even respected me after you knew of my childhood and its problems?"

"Yes."

"Really? Do you remember how nervous you were when the boys first got here? That's who I am, Nicole. Those boys keep me grounded because I've spent a good number of years with my back turned on my past. A few weeks ago, I found out that I have a brother—"

"What?"

He nodded. "I'm still in shock. I have to give him this." He walked over to the bureau and picked up a worn sealed envelope. "I've got one, too. It's from my . . . mother." His voice broke.

Nicole slowly walked toward him and touched his shoulder gently. "I've been so selfish," she whispered.

"Listen to me, Nicole. I've got money and it can buy me most anything. I bought this B-and-B for you because you are the woman I want, need, love. I can't exist without you, Nicole." He smiled. "I tried."

Nicole stared at the open robe and hairs curling out at his chest. She bit her lip, ashamed at her thoughts.

"But the one thing that I can't buy is your faith in me." He touched her cheek, tentatively. "I've been looking for you all my life."

Nicole threw her arms around Brad's neck. Hot tears splashed down her cheek and his neck. "I've never been in love before. It hurts. I want things to be so perfect and they're not." Her eyes were temporarily blinded with the tears. "I can't control anything." She hiccuped. "We just need a little time and we'll adjust. This is the best—"

"Oh, shut up." He held her neck and kissed her softly.

"Stop fighting it. You love me and I love you. You've got a job, or at least you had one. I've got a job. Did I say that you loved me?" He kissed the tip of her nose.

Nicole pulled out of his arms and retrieved the little box from the pillow. She flipped up the top and saw a marquis diamond twinkling back at her. Its brilliance was captured by the flickering candlelight.

"Nicole Montgomery, would you marry me, please?"

"What about Audra?"

"Audra and I were never, and never will be, an item."

"And Shaunice?"

"Is history. If it makes you feel better, she moved back to her mother's place in California." Brad sighed. "I can't fight against your fears any longer. I don't know what else to say."

"Will you let me help you look for your brother?"

"Thought you'd never ask."

Nicole bit her lip, still battling with her demons. It would take some getting used to, leaning on someone's shoulder. "I'm used to being on my own, never having to depend on anyone. When you came into my life, you turned it on its head. I wanted you and I always said that, but I know now that I wanted you as long as things went my way." She looked down at the diamond, twinkling at her. "I don't know how to be the weaker sex."

"I don't want you to be. That's not what attracted me. I want a woman who can stand side by side with me, loving me, supporting me, and even telling me when I do something wrong." He took the ring out of the box and slid it onto her left hand, fourth finger. "Don't be afraid, Nicole. Don't turn your back on me." He lifted her chin and kissed her, tasting her lips with quick flicks of his tongue. When she wrapped her arms around him in a deep embrace, he scooped her up by her butt and carried her to the bed.

"Do I get to be Ms. Nicole Montgomery?"

He growled in her ear. "How about Mrs. Nicole Montgomery hyphen Calverton?"

"Even better." Nicole sighed.

Nicole gladly wrapped her arms around his muscular frame. Tears of pure joy welled and she blinked them back to see his handsome, smiling face lower to hers. Surrendering completely, she opened her mouth to welcome his deep kiss, and opened her heart to love and be loved forever.

Dear Readers:

Thank you so much for your support with my debut novel, *Open Your Heart*. Your feedback was reaffirming and appreciated. Sorry, folks, no sequel. I had several requests.

However, *Finders Keepers* is the first of several books about the citizens of Glen Knolls, Maryland. You met Nicole and Brad, visited the bed-and-breakfast, and hung out with girlfriends. Coming up, Brad has to find his brother and Toni must move on with her life and new baby daughter. So, stay tuned.

Please keep the letters coming, I will respond to each of you. If you would like to be on my readers list, please send an e-mail to MichelleMonkou@aol.com or write to: P.O. Box 2904, Laurel, MD 20709. When you have a chance, stop by and sign my guest book at http://www.michellemonkou.com.

Peace,
Michelle Monkou

ABOUT THE AUTHOR

Michelle Monkou sold her first contemporary romance to BET in January 2002. She attributes her success to discipline and respect for the craft and supportive writer networks like Romance Writers of America.

Michelle earned a B.A. in English from the University of Maryland and an M.S. in international business from the U of MD's University College. She works for a leading trade association for the life insurance industry and writes reviews for Crescent Blues e-magazine.

Born in England and raised in Guyana, Michelle attributes her creative source to the cultural diversity she experienced. She currently resides with her family in the Washington, DC, metropolitan area.